FORGETTING

to

REMEMBER

ALSO FROM M.J. ROSE

FORGETTING
to
REMEMBER

M. J. ROSE

Forgetting to Remember
By M.J. Rose

Copyright 2024 M.J. Rose
ISBN: 978-1-957568-94-2

Published by Blue Box Press, an imprint of Evil Eye
Concepts, Incorporated

DEDICATION

To Sarah Branham with love and thanks for your kindness and
care with my words.
And to Ann-Marie Nieves for presenting those words to the
world with so much effort and enthusiasm.

"To make beautiful the unknown, that is the impetus of art."
~ Joel Arthur Rosenthal, JAR

Sudden Light

Dante Gabriel Rossetti (written in 1853 or 1854)

I have been here before,
But when or how I cannot tell;
I know the grass beyond the door,
The sweet keen smell,
The sighing sound, the lights around the shore.
You have been mine before—
How long ago I may not know:
But just when at that swallow's soar
Your neck turned so,
Some veil did fall,—I knew it all of yore.

Jewels should stir something deep inside you, a primal urge for endless knowledge, and a desire to crack open the capsule that is the very structure of the jewel. The annals of history it has witnessed and the individual moments, glances, and fleeting ideas this object has been privy to are insurmountable to comprehend. But with one interaction, you brush up against that well of experience, with breadth and depth, and it all comes rushing to the surface of the present, just for you. ~ Levi Higgs, author, art historian.

$\mathcal{A}$UGUST 1790, $\mathcal{T}$UILERIES PALACE, PARIS, FRANCE

"Sit still, Your Majesty," Élisabeth Vigée Le Brun said. "This is actually more difficult than painting a full-length portrait."

Marie Antoinette laughed but did as her portrait painter asked. She folded her hands and sat as still as she could, imagining the look on her dear Axel's face when he received the miniature portrait of her eye.

She'd asked her jeweler to take some rubies from one of her bracelets, frame the tiny, ivory painting with the luminous gems, back it with gold, and fashion it into a stickpin for her lover to wear on his cravat. Near his heart.

And she'd already planned for Mademoiselle Le Brun to paint Axel's eye when he returned to France so she could have a brooch to pin near her heart, as well.

Of all the men in her life—other than her husband, of course—Marie had known Axel the longest. And of all the men in her life, including her husband, she relied on Axel more than any other. He would save her and her family from the Jacobites. Even though the previous plan had failed, there was a new one being devised. She trusted that he would succeed.

It was fairly boring to be painted, so while she sat as still as she could in her pretty méridienne chamber, the private parlor hidden behind her bedroom, decorated with mirrors and lilac textiles, Marie Antoinette mentally composed the letter she would send to Axel accompanying the gift.

My dearest,
I am alive here, my beloved, for the reason to adore you, and I grieve all the forgotten hours I am forced to spend with other people—every one

of them wasted when I could be with you, in your arms. Every one of them lost, squandered, and never to be regained for us to share.

For all the hours ahead when I cannot be with you, I send you this.

I wish that you will wear this portrait of my eye next to your heart, where our secret love lives. No one will know that it is of me but you. When you return to Paris, I want to have Élisabeth paint one of you, for me, so that I may carry you with me in the same way.

We have given each other so many things over the years—friendship, love, trust, passion—that I have rimmed this portrait in rubies to signify my passion for you and to remind you always that you alone have my heart.

Farewell, the most loved and loving of men. I kiss you with all my heart and await the next time we shall meet.

As soon as Élisabeth called the session to an end, Marie Antoinette took pen, ink, and paper and wrote out the message. Even though the jewel would not be ready for weeks, she didn't want to forget her thoughts. To protect her secret, she placed the letter in an envelope, then melted wax, dripped it on the closure, and pressed her seal into it. The insignia contained her initials and the image of a flying fish, which she'd borrowed from Axel von Fersen's coat of arms.

There were five words inscribed underneath.

Tutto a te mi guida. Everything leads me to thee.

Once the stickpin was finished, she would send her courtier to Sweden to deliver her gift. And then she would wait for Axel's letter of thanks to arrive, hoping that within it would be the encoded information for the new plan that would save her.

CHAPTER 1

London, 1947

It wasn't until the evening I discovered Ashe Lloyd Lewis's grave that I found out I'd been mistaken about the past. I'd always believed it was set in stone—familiar and trustworthy—whereas the future was the mystery, offering only the unknown. But when I visited Highgate Cemetery the night before Halloween, at the end of a most unsettling day, I began a journey that would prove I'd been wrong: the past is as unfathomable as the future.

It is only the present you can trust, and only a bit at that.

The day had started off with a curious invitation to tea from my employer, Mr. Gibbons, the director of the Victoria and Albert Museum. As requested, I arrived at the museum's Green Room at three p.m.

Entering the restaurant is like stepping back in time. Decorated in a beautiful green-blue scheme, designed by William Morris's company, Morris, Marshall, Faulkner & Co., in the 1860s, every inch, floor to ceiling, is covered with organic patterns. The large, stained-glass window at the far end includes painted figures designed by Edward Burne-Jones.

Anywhere the eye landed was a treat, but the room's beauty did little to distract me that afternoon. Typically, Mr. Gibbons invited us to his office when he wanted to discuss something. He didn't take meals with employees.

I was shown to a table to discover that Mr. Gibbons had arrived early and was already seated. He greeted me cordially, and after we'd ordered, complimented me on my most recently curated exhibit.

I thanked him, though I knew it had been a success. My staff and I had taken more than two dozen antique fabrics from our holdings and matched them to clothing and upholstery captured in portraits from the fifteenth century through the nineteenth.

"I was especially pleased to get a lovely note from Lady Alice, the Duchess of Gloucester, praising the show," Mr. Gibbons said, then went on to share some of her comments.

We were halfway through our Earl Grey and salmon sandwiches when the director cleared his throat. I'd been working for Mr. Gibbons for seven years and knew this tell. Before delivering bad news of any sort, he always cleared his throat.

I felt my back go up. Certainly, nothing I had done deserved a reprimand. My job was my life. I prided myself on my devotion to the museum and my department.

My best friend, Sybil Shipley, often told me she wished I gave my relationships half the effort I gave my job. But I was more comfortable with objects than emotions. I could read a vase or a necklace better than a face. I wasn't prideful about my looks or intellect, but I *was* proud of how I ran my department, and I could be stubborn when it came to others' suggestions.

"You know obstinance isn't the only way to get things done," my mentor, Clio Oxley, used to say whenever I dug in. Both my brother and I had taken after my father when it came to willfulness. As an archaeologist, his doggedness and certainty had been the very traits that elevated him above all his peers. That was true of me, as well. My tenacity had gotten me all the good things in my life. It had also cost me, delivering all the heartache I'd endured. I'd had my one chance at love and squandered it. But I was fine. Beauty surrounded me every day while doing a job that filled my soul. I could cope with being alone. Hadn't I proven that by now?

"Mrs. Maycroft." Mr. Gibbons cleared his throat again. "I find myself in the unpleasant position of asking you to take a bit of a demotion."

I was stunned. He had just complimented me.

"A demotion? But why?"

"It's nothing you have done. Nothing at all. No, no, you're one of our most exemplary employees. It's the damn war, still."

I didn't like what I was hearing, but the reference to the war explained it. In the last two years, women all over England and at every company had been asked to take demotions so that returning soldiers could regain their pre-war positions. Mr. Gibbons had reorganized the staff at the museum several times to accommodate re-hires. Except I'd believed my job was secure since I'd inherited it from a woman, not from a man who had gone off to war.

I was Keeper of the Metalworks. Only the second woman to ever hold the post—or any Keeper post at the museum, for that matter. I had the keys to all the vaults that housed items in my department. I was in charge of all exhibitions that included ironwork, jewelry, continental silver, arms and armor, medieval champlevé and late nineteenth-century enamels, brass work, and pewter from the Bronze Age to the present. I was responsible for hiring and firing all research assistants in my department. Since my promotion in 1944, Mr. Gibbons had done nothing but praise me. My show, *Bejeweled: Artists, Artisans, and Models in the 19th Century*, had been such a success I'd been approached to write a book on the subject, which was almost finished.

So now, sitting in one of my favorite rooms in the museum, my tea growing cold, the bread on my sandwich curling, I tried but couldn't make sense of the request.

"I don't understand," I finally admitted. "The person who held my job before me wasn't a man who went off to war. It was Clio, and sadly, she's not coming back."

"No, but Hugh Kenward has returned from the front and is returning to the museum."

I felt sickened at hearing his name.

"If you would agree to go back to the job you held under Mrs. Oxley as head research assistant to the Keeper, I will agree to keep your salary at its current level."

"Which would allow you to move Mr. Kenward into the Keeper's position, a job he didn't have before the war." If I was being impertinent, I didn't care. Of everyone, I couldn't tolerate the idea of stepping down for Hugh Kenward.

Mr. Gibbons took a sip of tea instead of responding.

"And here I thought you were happy with my work," I said, unwilling to let the matter go.

"Of course, I am. You stepped into Mrs. Oxley's shoes with great success. She would be so proud. The problem is that Mr. Kenward, a war hero, cannot be asked to work *for* you, Mrs. Maycroft. You know that. And with so many men having already returned, and so many reorganizations to date, I am at a loss for how else to solve this new dilemma."

I pushed my cup and saucer away, first one inch and then another.

"Even though you well know it's not fair to ask me to take a demotion?"

The director frowned. "The war wasn't fair, Mrs. Maycroft. Will you agree to at least think about it and see if there isn't some way you can accommodate this change? We really don't want to lose you..." He paused. "Either of you."

So, I was not only being asked to step down but also

being told that *any* job at the V&A was in jeopardy if I refused. But how could I work for Hugh Kenward?

It was bad enough he was returning to the museum at all and I'd have to work alongside him, but to answer to him?

I debated bringing up my past history with the man. I worried that even though the director valued me, reminding him of the long-ago problem wouldn't help me now. If questioned, Hugh would certainly defend himself and say I had encouraged *him*. And in situations like these, wasn't the man always believed? Especially when he had fought for his country and won medals for valor?

Hugh Kenward was charming and well educated, but so were many others. What made Hugh that much more important, and the reason he was Mr. Gibbon's favorite, was his relationship to the throne. As a third cousin to the king, with a duke and duchess as parents, we mere mortals couldn't compete. Hugh had been in the process of being groomed for a top position at the museum when England entered the war, and he went off to fight. From the gist of this conversation, it seemed that grooming would continue.

But the fact was, for all of Mr. Gibbons' bravado and all of Hugh's connections to the Crown, I had a few things going for me, as well. My father had recently been knighted for his war efforts, and it wouldn't do to let me go either.

Mr. Gibbons was in a tough spot, but I would not make it easy for him. I'd worked too hard for my position.

"Thinking about it won't change my mind. I wouldn't be able to do my job to the best of my abilities," I told the director, "working for someone who is neither senior to me nor has as much experience as I do. I was here years before Mr. Kenward arrived, and I remained throughout the duration of the war. And you know as well as anyone what I did to safeguard the museum's treasures and what risks I took. As much as many soldiers."

Like many other families who had homes far from

London, safe from the bombings, my father and I, along with my mother's best childhood friend, Lady Barbara Silversmith, had taken in many national treasures and hidden them at our family homes in ancient Forest of Dean—some from the Imperial War Museum, and others from the V&A.

I could hear my heart beating loudly in my chest as I hoped Mr. Gibbons wouldn't lose his famous temper and fire me on the spot for insubordination.

He looked down at the tablecloth and slowly smoothed out a wrinkle with a forefinger. After remaining silent for another few seconds, he finally spoke, slowly and carefully, as if holding back his rage.

"Your refusal will make things quite difficult," he said. "We all are thankful for your war efforts, and know full well how valuable you are to the museum. At the same time, our duty is to restore every man to a position commensurate with his stature. So many—thankfully—have returned. I simply don't have another position to shuffle. However, I don't want to lose one of my most valued members of staff, Mrs. Maycroft. If you are adamant, the best I can do is think on this and see if there is another solution," he said. "And I'm very much looking forward to reading your new chapter on May Morris's jewelry. I have it on my desk upstairs and should be getting to it this afternoon."

With that, he brought the conversation back to neutral territory and the beginning of the end of the uncomfortable meeting.

CHAPTER 2

My goal to one day be employed at the V&A took root when I was thirteen and first met Clio Oxley.

As a child, I had been inexplicably drawn to Pre-Raphaelite paintings. Whenever I visited the V&A, regardless of what other exhibit we'd come for, I always dragged my father or one of my grandmothers to see them.

In seventh form, we were assigned to pick any object of any kind in the V&A that was more than fifty years old and write a paper on it. I had chosen my favorite painting—*La Belle Dame sans Merci* by Ashe Lloyd Lewis.

The work is based on the 1819 John Keats poem about an enchantress who seduces a knight with her beauty and song, bringing him to his ruin and condemning him to wander forever.

In the composition, their mutual desire binds them. The lady, lush and lovely, kneels at her knight's feet. Her head is slightly turned away from the viewer, but we can see her parted lips, the flush of want on her cheeks. The way she's wrapped her long red tresses around his arm, binding him to her. The knight is turned toward us. His expression full of longing for the beautiful wood nymph. It was that which mesmerized me. I wanted to step into the painting, to tell him not to give in to her but hold back and protect his heart—for me.

I had a young girl's crush on that knight in armor. A man I would never know but whose passion imprinted on me. His yearning meant something to me, and the painting became a kind of testament to what I believed love looked like.

His full medieval armor is decorated with golden symbols, and I studied all the bejeweled designs, delighting in all the meanings I could read into the artist's choices.

There's even more jewelry in the painting. La Belle Dame has a bracelet of ruby hearts on her left wrist, suggesting her innocence. As do the white daisies in the grass beneath her. Some critics claim the two symbols are there to trick the knight into believing she is pure. I chose to believe that Lewis didn't see her as a femme fatale to be afraid of. It was a time when women were becoming more assertive. To me, it was a celebration of the woman's power. As opposed to other illustrations of the poem suggesting the knight was to be pitied for his fate, I didn't believe he would regret his adoration or that they were destined to be separated for eternity. There was hope in the painting, too, perhaps not to be experienced in this encounter but in a later one.

Upon choosing *La Belle Dame* for my assignment, I found I needed more information about the painting than I could research in our local library. I applied and received permission to work in the revered V&A's National Art Library, which was not ordinarily open to students my age.

I visited the library several times to research my opus. One afternoon, as I took notes, a woman stopped by. She said she'd noticed me there before and saw from the books on my table that I was studying Ashe Lloyd Lewis. Could she offer any help? Her name was Clio Oxley, she worked at the museum, and was a distant relation of the artist.

I knew he had died in a fire at his studio in January of

1868—*La Belle Dame* was one of just a few of his paintings to survive. Sitting on a bench outside the library's entrance, Clio told me the blaze had been set by a jealous husband, who had commissioned Lewis to paint his wife's portrait. She recounted stories about the artist that weren't in any of the history books, information I never would have been able to find on my own, which I included in my paper.

When I received an *A*, my grandmother Imogine suggested that I write a thank you note to Mrs. Oxley. In return, I received an invitation to attend an exhibit she had curated and to take tea with her. During our chat, it transpired that she was looking for a summer intern and offered me the job. A chance to work at the Victoria and Albert—to be surrounded by art and antiquities, to visit *my* painting whenever I wanted—was a godsend. I was supposed to be spending the summer with my father at a dig in Egypt, but he had contracted malaria, which had delayed the expedition until the fall. I was to stay at home.

I had been bereft. Like my father, my passion lay in lost history and found objects. One of our favorite pastimes was going mudlarking in the Thames. Ordinary objects, a shard of pottery, a five-hundred-year-old button, a Roman glass bottle, would occupy my imagination for days. As I cleaned, cataloged, and studied each piece we found, I imagined who had owned it, what they were like, and how the treasure had wound up in the river buried under decades of mud.

That summer, Clio took me under her wing. Like my father, she was innately curious, fascinated by history, and meticulous in how she cared for its remains. My father had always turned discovery into a game, and so did Clio. She snapped me out of my melancholy about being in London instead of Alexandria. And after that summer, I spent alternating holidays either in Egypt with my father or working with Clio. Eventually, I surprised myself—and him—when I decided that I preferred the dusty halls of the V&A to the sandy deserts of Egypt. Upon graduating from university, Clio hired me to be one of her research assistants in the Metalworks Department and shepherded my career for the next ten years.

She had begun working at the museum during World War I when many women took on the jobs of men who had gone to the front. From there, she'd worked her way up to be the first woman to hold the position of *Keeper* of a department.

Clio often joked that she was an example of what her generation called *superfluous women*. Women born at the end of the nineteenth century were expected to marry and raise a family. But when the Great War came, so many men were called to fight that marriages were delayed, and women had to take on the jobs left vacant. The running of the country depended on those women. By the time the war ended, three quarters of a million British men had been killed, and hundreds of thousands more were maimed, some physically, others mentally. There weren't enough husbands to go around. Anyone left without a ring on her finger was at that point considered *superfluous*.

Growing up, I'd never thought my generation would follow so closely in their footsteps, but we have. Our own World War saw to that, and one day, many of us will surely be referred to as *superfluous*, as well. Very possibly, I'd be one of them. Unmarried, childless, and perhaps soon to be jobless. One could hardly get more superfluous than that. What's more, given the number of men flooding the job market, my chances of obtaining a similar position in another museum were practically nonexistent.

What would I do? Without my stature as a V&A Keeper, I doubted I'd have the credentials or access to research and write another book. I'd have no choice but to retire to Woodfern, keep the victory garden growing, raise chickens, and tend the sheep.

How exciting, I thought bitterly.

"Silly girl," I heard my grandmother Ruth say. "Thinking about your job again. You should be having babies, not rooting around with rusty suits of armor."

My father's mother, who'd lived next door to us while we were growing up and, along with my maternal grandmother, Imogine, was very much a fixture in my life after my mother died, had frowned upon most of my decisions. She didn't understand my ambition, even though it mimicked her son's. No matter how much I explained why I loved my job in one of Britain's finest museums, she tut-tutted that I was unmarried with no prospects and asked how long I expected her to wait for a great-grandchild. Unspoken was the family tragedy that had put all the burden on me. My brother had been killed at the very start of the war. If there was to be any progeny, it was up to me to have them.

When my father heard her go on like that, he'd put his arm around my shoulders and tell me not to mind his mum. While I knew he would have preferred I'd become an archaeologist like him, working for the V&A was a close second. He was proud of my career, which I probably would not have had if not for Clio Oxley.

My progress under her in Metalworks had been steady. By the time I was thirty, I was her head research assistant and considered the museum's rising star—or at least until the spring of 1938, when they hired Hugh Kenward.

The rumor mill made it known that the director was grooming the presumed Cambridge upstart for a top position, which made me both jealous and angry. He had the proper credentials, having read history at university, but then he turned to acting of all things and spent five years in the theater. I'd spent those same years working my way up at the museum. But despite any ability or experience I might have, the system would only allow a woman to rise as far as Keeper.

So, I admit, I didn't just ignore Hugh when he joined the staff; I was downright unfriendly, ignoring his efforts to win me over with this boyish charm. Despite my attitude—not to mention the dusty clothes and simple hairstyle—he had sought me out.

"You could be a beauty if you just put some effort into it," my grandmother Ruth would say whenever she gave me one of her *improvement gifts*, as I thought of them. Eyeliner, rouge, lipstick…she never tired of buying me new cosmetics and feminine, frilly, brightly colored outfits from the finest shops on Bond Street. And she never took the hint when I eschewed the makeup and clothes and continued to favor white blouses and dark trousers or simple skirt suits in neutrals. Such was the wardrobe both my mother and grandmother, Imogine, had worn, having been professional women like me.

Grandmother Ruth would tear out magazine photos of hairstyles she thought would flatter my face, but I kept my hair in a chignon to keep it out of the way. And when I was promoted to head research assistant under Clio, she gave me a bottle of perfume from the House of L'Etoile.

"The scent of dust mites isn't going to attract the kind of men you need to meet," she'd said.

Hugh Kenward didn't seem to need an alluring scent to attract him. And silly fool that I was, I didn't question why a man of his background, charm, and film-star looks would find me attractive.

His first overture was to gift me with a novel, *Winged Pharaoh*, by Joan Grant. He'd said he just finished it and thought I'd enjoy it based on an essay I had written and published in the V&A catalog. Grant had attributed the source of her story to her *Far Memory* extrasensory abilities, particularly the ability to remember her own past lives.

I was astonished at the time that Hugh would have any sense of what I might like. I'd curated a show about Pre-Raphaelite metalworks that included an engraving plate of *St. Agnes of Intercession,* done by Dante Gabriel Rossetti, to illustrate his short story of the same name that also dealt with past lives. Reincarnation was a subject that had always fascinated me, ever since I was little and my father told me stories based on ancient Egyptian beliefs.

About a week after the gift, Hugh invited me out for a drink to talk about the book. He knew a lot about my father's work and admitted he had originally wanted to be an archaeologist.

"My father arranged for me to go on a dig when I was fourteen in Sutton Hoo, but it turned out I didn't find the dirt and muck as appealing as reading about it. I seem to be very good at romanticizing reality. I did that in the theater, as well, but I'd much rather hear about your interests in reincarnation. That subject certainly lends itself to romanticizing, doesn't it?"

Hugh had a curious mind and was quite open to mystical ideas. I usually kept my interest in the arcane to myself since so many people were put off by it, but I found myself opening up to Hugh.

Finding we had much in common was a surprise, and next came invitations to plays and concerts. What I'd taken for a friendship turned romantic when he took me on walks in Hyde Park, followed by dinners in the most interesting restaurants rich with history he loved to discuss. One was Agatha Christie's favorite, Kettner's Townhouse, originally opened in 1867. The mystery writer was at a corner table one night when we were there, and when I was too embarrassed to ask her for an autograph, Hugh gallantly did it for me.

It wasn't as if I'd never had a suitor. Samuel Parker and I had been a couple for years at that point. A friend of my brother's, I'd known Samuel since I was fifteen and he started coming round the house. After graduating from Cambridge, he'd entered the Royal Navy and was away for long stretches of time. But since I was serious about my own studies and then so ambitious about my job, the separations didn't trouble me, and I never went out of my way to date anyone other than him.

That changed with Hugh Kenward.

One night, after dinner and a film, a lively musical called *We're Going to be Rich,* he walked me home as usual, but when we reached my building, before I could thank him for the evening, he reached out and took my hand, touching me for the first time.

"You know you're awfully hard to resist, Jeannine," he said as his eyes locked on mine. "Must I keep trying to?"

Before I could determine how to respond, he leaned in. He was only the second man whose lips I'd ever felt on mine, and his kiss was nothing like the gentle ones I'd known before. Hugh's was passionate, determined. And I melted.

After a few moments, he released me and stood back a bit, looking at me with twinkling eyes.

"You're different than the women I've known, either while at school or those my parents have tried to match me with. I like your dusty woolen skirts and…"—he fingered one of my curls—"and these naughty, fiery locks that insist on coming out of your hair clasp. I like your secrets, Jeannine. And I have a feeling I've only begun to learn them. Will you tell me the rest?"

I was breathless. From the kiss. From the admission.

I shook my head. "No, what's the fun in just telling you? You'll have to discover them for yourself."

"Ah, testing to see if I still have a bit of that desire to be an archaeologist in me?"

"I might be."

"Well, let's see what I can learn from doing this…"

He put his hands in my hair and pulled my face to his, kissing me again. And I slipped into the embrace, getting lost in the passion.

When the kiss ended, Hugh whispered, "'Hear my soul speak. The very instant that I saw you, did my heart fly to your service.'"

He was quoting Shakespeare to me, and I was swooning.

While Samuel and I weren't engaged, it had always seemed a forgone conclusion that we would eventually marry. Certainly, until that spring, I had always believed I loved Samuel, but my reaction to Hugh's attention gave me more than serious pause.

How could I respond to Hugh in that way if I truly loved Samuel?

After those first kisses, our encounters grew more exciting. At the museum, Hugh and I kept up the pretense of simply being coworkers, but we enjoyed a burgeoning attraction on our dates. When I wasn't with him, I felt guilty for betraying Samuel. When I was with him, I couldn't resist.

Looking back, I don't believe it was love, but it was exhilarating to be wooed by someone so charismatic and charming.

I didn't discuss my predicament with anyone and assumed no one was aware of our relationship.

A month later, we went to a West End revival of Oscar Wilde's *The Importance of Being Ernest.* Hugh was as affectionate as usual that evening and took my hand several times during the first act, bringing it to his lips. Once, he leaned over and kissed me full-on.

Enjoying it, I didn't think twice about the passionate embrace.

But someone else did. Mr. Gibbons had been at the same show, in a box right above where we sat. It turned out it belonged to Hugh's parents, who had invited the museum director. Not only did Hugh's mother and father see us kissing, but so did Mr. Gibbons and his wife.

The museum has a strict non-fraternization policy, and Mr. Gibbons went to Clio the next morning to discuss the infraction. He told her she needed to let me go. I was to be fired immediately. But Clio fought back. As I later learned, she had been suspicious of Hugh's attention to me and told Mr.

Gibbons she believed I'd been set up.

"I think he sees her as his only competition and planned all along to put her in exactly this position. He must have known you would be at the theater and sitting beside the duke and duchess, no less."

"Regardless of his motives, she broke the rules. She agreed to see him," Mr. Gibbons countered.

"If you are going to fire her, you must also fire him for pursuing her."

Clio later told me that Mr. Gibbons harrumphed and stammered. It had never occurred to him that Clio would call him on the double standard and let him know she was aware that he'd been willing to overlook his protégé's infringement but not mine.

Chagrined, Mr. Gibbons agreed to give me a second chance, which I appreciated, but I was mortified by the thought that Hugh's affection had been a ruse all along. I felt like a fool. I was grateful to Clio for standing up for me, but I didn't want to believe her.

She didn't argue her point. Clio never worried about whether or not people agreed with her. She said her piece and moved on. Whether Hugh's attentions were on the up and up, Clio said he and I had to stop seeing each other if I wanted to secure my position at the museum. She also told me that Mr. Gibbons had told Hugh the same thing, so I was surprised when Hugh stopped by my office at the end of the day and asked if I'd have a drink with him to talk things over.

"We can't," I said. He was standing close enough to my desk that I could pick out his scent. Smelling it sent little jolts of electricity through me.

"Please leave me alone, Hugh."

"We need to talk. It will all be aboveboard, I swear to you. But we can't simply never speak to each other again."

"We most definitely can."

He was looking at me so intently I felt his gaze as I would

an embrace. I looked away.

"Jeannine, please. Just one drink. I want to talk to you."

Reluctantly, I agreed. If I had to give him up, I wanted to at least know if what we'd had was real and not what Clio had suggested. I couldn't bear the idea that I'd been such an idiot.

As we walked to the Goat Tavern, one of our favorite pubs, we didn't talk. We certainly didn't touch, at least not on purpose. Hugh's arms brushed mine once, and I felt my body react. *Traitor*, I told myself. *He's poison to you now.* I alternated between heartbreak and fury.

Finally seated across the table from him, sipping my gin and tonic, I tried to suss out the truth behind his too-blue eyes.

"I wish I'd never taken you to the damned theater," he said. "The very last thing I want to do now is stop seeing you."

"And why is that?" I asked.

I was surprised that the seed of doubt Clio had planted in me had taken root so fast. How had I ever believed I was attractive and clever enough for him? He'd gone to Cambridge and was a cousin to the king. And his looks! He was so handsome with a bit of Cary Grant's impishness. The wind had tousled his blond curls the same way I used to do while kissing him.

Of course, he had set me up. Why hadn't I realized it earlier? Now, it would take all my strength and determination to turn liking him so much into hating him. If only I could maneuver the conversation so he would admit what he'd done, then I could move on and be done with him.

He cocked his head and gave me a curious look. "And why is that? Why don't I want to stop seeing you? Because of how much I enjoy your company, of course," he said as if I'd asked him the most ludicrous question. He took a sip of his Guinness. "Don't you feel the same way?" he asked.

"It doesn't really matter now, does it? We've been found

out and scolded, and we both care too much about our jobs to risk them for something as frivolous as what we have."

Even I was surprised at how cold my voice sounded.

"Frivolous? I didn't think it was frivolous. And I didn't think you'd be so bitter about it," Hugh said.

"What *did* you think? That I'd quit my job so we could go on as we were? Me working somewhere else, you rising to the very top of the ladder at the V&A?"

I hated the sarcasm I heard lacing my words, but I was so angry. If Hugh had set me up, I had to know. And then I'd get him back for it.

He frowned. "No, Jeannine. I never imagined you'd quit. You're one of the museum's stars. I imagine I hoped you'd agree to keep seeing me, and that we'd just be more careful."

"So you can really finish me off at the V&A?"

"What on earth are you talking about?" He looked truly hurt. I wished I had the ability to see into his soul just then and know what he was really thinking. Did he mean what he'd said about his feelings? The pragmatist in me knew it didn't matter. One way or another, for one reason or another, this man had charmed and seduced me into nearly losing my job and betraying Samuel. I couldn't even contemplate what Hugh was suggesting. Go on seeing each other? Even sitting there with him was wrong. No, I didn't need to find out what his game had been, I just needed to get away from him. And stay away. I would not be some weak woman who risked it all for a man.

I took a long sip of my drink and stood. "Please, stay away from me, Hugh. Unless it is strictly business and other people are around, don't even speak to me. I've worked much too hard to chance my reputation on you."

I'd said the word *you* as if it were the word *offal.*

Hugh looked stunned.

I left before I could hear his response.

In the end, the fiasco had not only hardened me and

made me suspicious, it had also tarnished my relationship with Samuel. Knowing how Hugh had made me feel, and how I'd responded to him, I felt guilty when with Samuel.

As for Hugh, he did as I asked and never approached me again. We only spoke to each other when necessary. I was always on guard with him. Had I been a fool? Or had the attraction been as real for him as it had been for me?

More than once, I thought about quitting the V&A to get away from my questions and doubts.

"If he was using you, that's exactly what he'd want," Clio had said when I broached the idea. "If he wasn't, then there's no reason to go." She did everything she could to build my confidence, and encouraged me to dig in my heels. "It might feel like you're living a nightmare now, but that will end. Time heals all, Jeannine, it really does."

But before time could heal me, a new nightmare replaced the old one. England entered the war. Like Samuel and my brother, Hugh joined the Royal Air Force.

And Samuel asked if we could marry prior to him going off to fight. I said yes. We had a quiet ceremony in the vicar's office. I married him despite my guilt over Hugh—or maybe because of it. I hoped it wouldn't be a barrier between us, but I never had a chance to find out.

So many men did not come home. Samuel didn't. My brother didn't. Millions more didn't. But, of course, Hugh did. He was one of the four-point-three million service men who, starting in 1945, slowly began returning to civilian life through the government's demobilization plan. And he had returned a highly decorated hero.

CHAPTER 3

Just an hour after our tea, Mr. Gibbons' secretary called and asked me to come to his office. Upon entering, I was shocked to see Hugh Kenward already there. He hadn't formally come back to work yet, and it was the first time I'd seen him in more than seven years. He'd aged, but more than that, the war had changed him. No one had survived unscathed, but there was a haunted look in his eyes, and gray in his blond curls. Both of which made him—disturbingly—even more good-looking, but not in the way I remembered. The electricity that used to surround him was gone. I didn't feel the pull. Clio was right. Time had smoothed over the edges of my feelings.

"Thank you for coming, Mrs. Maycroft," Mr. Gibbons said.

"Good to see you, Jeannine." Hugh stood and extended his hand.

I took it. I didn't recognize the calluses on his palms.

"Congratulations on your war record," I responded. I could, after all, admire the work he'd done without liking him.

Hugh dipped his head in thanks and smiled warmly. "And yours. I heard all about how you protected the museum's valuables. Quite heroic." I couldn't detect any rancor in his voice; his words seemed heartfelt.

I hadn't expected that. Or perhaps he was just showing off in front of Mr. Gibbons. I nodded in thanks as he had.

"Have a seat," the director said to me, pointing to the empty chair.

The director's office had been decorated in the early 1930s by a famous architect, M.N. Peale, and was kept in pristine condition. The walls were a mural of swamp cypress plywood panels in an Art Deco design. The chairs and desk were made of the same dark apricot-colored wood and echoed the geometric design, as did the wall sconces and lamps. The drapes and upholstery were a deeper version of the wood's color. I focused on the patterns to keep myself calm.

I took the chair next to Hugh, both of us across the desk from Mr. Gibbons. I tried to ignore the man beside me, but it was impossible. Hugh was wearing that same damn cologne I remembered. It had always lingered in a room after he left. Now, it was a bittersweet reminder of the time we'd been lovers.

"I'm in an impossible situation here. Hugh, you deserve a Keeper post, but there isn't one open, and I've already move around everyone possible. Mrs. Maycroft, you've earned your post, and it's not fair to ask you to leave, but I have no other option. So, I'm going to give you both the same assignment," Mr. Gibbons said. "The decision of who becomes Keeper will be based on how you each handle it. The other will be invited to stay on as the head research assistant with a promise of a promotion as soon as a spot becomes available."

Hugh made a sound—a cross between a harrumph and a cough. I assumed he had been ready to object and then thought better of it.

Mr. Gibbons waited for a moment and then looked at me. When I didn't comment, he continued.

"The assignment is to curate one half of our Valentine's Day exhibit. You'll each have one of the two galleries to fill and a catalog to create. The gallery that gets the most visitors, the catalog that sells the most copies, the comments in the victor's log, along with the critics' reviews of the two shows will determine who becomes Keeper. And again, as reassurance, the runner-up will be given the job one rung down and a promise for a promotion as soon as possible."

As I walked back to my office, I decided I would quit. Like so many of us after the war, I was worn down. I shouldn't have to prove myself again. I'd been doing that for long enough.

I think I would have resigned the next day had it not been for what happened that evening.

I didn't wait for the workday to officially end. At four thirty, I took the train to Highgate Cemetery. I needed to talk to Clio about the situation at the museum.

I had always found cemeteries places of solace since Grandmother Imogine, my mum's mum, used to take me with her all the time to tend to my grandfather's grave in Highgate. We'd sit on the bench inside the mausoleum with the lovely cobalt, emerald, and violet colors from the stained glass shining down on us, and she'd tell me stories about their love affair. She was an herbalist, like her mother, and he was a botanist. They met at the Chelsea Psychic Garden where she went to study her craft, and he had been working for the head of the gardens. My grandfather used the language of flowers to woo her, making bouquets based on the meaning of the flora. When we visited his grave, she always left a bouquet for him with a special message. She taught me the meanings of all the flowers.

I have never forgotten the last time we visited. She'd brought yellow marguerite daisies—a bouquet I'd never seen before. She died a week later. Months afterward, I discovered the meaning of those particular flowers: *I am coming soon.*

My love of Highgate Cemetery came from Clio. When I began working for her, I admired the framed rubbings hanging in her office. I learned she was a renowned practitioner of the ancient art. I was fascinated and asked if she could teach me, which she did, and it became a shared activity for us.

The process of capturing an image of an engraving on textured paper was soothing in the act and exciting in the result. Depending on the paper and whether you used colored crayons, chalk, or graphite, the resulting visuals were quite different from what appeared on the stone.

Just before the start of the war, a publisher had commissioned Clio to write a book about the art of rubbings, which would include over two dozen examples of her work. I assisted in her efforts. We spent at least two Saturdays a month at Highgate for four years. It was a rare oasis of calm amidst chaos. Clio was killed before she could finish the book, and her publisher asked if I could step in. Honored, I agreed. Even after the book was completed, I continued to visit Highgate whenever I was troubled. Always to visit with Clio, and often to find a new stone to capture on paper.

Never had I needed her counsel more than that October evening. My precious job was being threatened by a man Clio had mistrusted.

The fog rolled in as I walked toward my destination—the Oxley plot in the West Cemetery. As the sudden dampness descended, I shivered and tightened the belt on my trench coat. Carefully, I navigated the sinuous paths overgrown with hemlocks. Formidable even on a bright day, they were treacherous in the damp evening.

Reaching the winding wooded hill, its step incline slippery with wet fall leaves, I took more care. The forest seemed especially disturbing tonight. I thought about turning around, but I was more than halfway there, and so I carried on. That was what I'd learned to do, what we'd all learned to do since the war. Take one step and then another. Keep moving forward, even when you barely have the stamina to move.

When I finally glimpsed Angelos through the dense

foliage, I was relieved that I'd found my way yet again—because it's far too easy to get lost in this part of Highgate. As always, she watched my approach with her dark eyes, staring with consternation it seemed, as if I were trespassing on her domain.

Even though I'd visited many times, my first sighting of the stone angel always caught me off guard. Her glass eyes seemed so real, giving one the sense that a living woman was trapped inside the lifeless one. Someone who, I believed, was jealous of my ability to come and go from this place. Who had secrets she'd resolved to keep to herself. I'd named her Angelos after the angel who presided over the realm of the dead in Greek mythology.

I knew it had to be my imagination, but that evening, I felt as if her glass eyes followed me as I laid the bunch of violets I'd bought at the entrance to the cemetery on Clio's stone.

Still feeling the angel's eyes on me, I gave my hostess my full attention. Oak boughs, heavy with their autumnal leaves, formed a canopy above her, sheltering her, protecting her. Fog blurred the edges of her realistically carved wings and softened her face.

Clio often said she found the angel calming, whereas I found it Delphic. For me, she transcended art and became mystery. How had her carver managed to bring so much life to hard stone?

It wasn't the passionate intensity of her midnight-blue eyes alone but the combination of her enigmatic expression and the kinetic energy implied in the positioning of her wings. They seemed ready to lift her aloft. There was also the powerful grip of her elegant fingers on the branch of lilies she held. Every part of her suggested she was impatient with us, frustrated that we never guessed what she had to share.

The statue's torso was covered with a tangle of verdant ivy. When the wind blew and made the leaves tremble, it seemed as if the angel was taking a deep breath.

For a wild moment, I wondered if she would finally speak and tell me her secret this evening. My gaze wandered to the enigmatic carvings on the base of her plinth. This part of the sculpture had been hidden by a holly bush for years. Clio had never been aware of the inscription until the shrub at the statue's feet died, and she had it removed. Only then did we discover the complex flower and leaf scroll with letters, numbers, and odd symbols worked into the swaths and swirls.

We had taken rubbings of them and had been trying to decipher the curious message when fate intervened, and Clio and two thousand seven hundred other civilians were killed during the Nazis' last set of London bombings in September of 1944. I was thirty-four and suddenly given her position, Keeper of the Metalworks, at the V&A. A bittersweet promotion at best.

I had the rubbings in my office and sometimes pulled them out, poring over them and hoping to find a key to understanding their message. Would they reveal who had carved the stone angel? Tell us who was buried beneath the three broken and no-longer-readable tombstones by the large yew tree in the north corner of the plot?

In mythology, the yew is rich in lore. Associated with Hecate, the Greek goddess of death, witchcraft, and necromancy, the tree supposedly purified the dead upon their arrival in the underworld. Believing it brought eternal life and kept devils away, mourners put yew branches in loved ones' coffins.

Our most significant clue to the plot's enigmas was a plaque that Clio and I had discovered at the foot of the wrought iron gate, previously hidden by more of the invasive ivy that obscured so much of the family burial ground.

According to the inscription, the angel had been installed in 1863 by none other than Ashe Lloyd Lewis, Clio's relative, and the artist who had brought us together.

Hearing rustling, I turned. It was now nearly six o'clock, and Highgate was officially closed to the public. Which meant I'd be told in no uncertain terms to leave if I were discovered. I couldn't blame the management for being strict about trespassing after hours. There were many stories about what transpired at night inside the cemetery's gates—legends of ghosts and macabre tales of witches carrying out grisly ceremonies, as well as the more mundane but factual reports of dangerous and undeterred grave robbers.

In this case, though, the rustling in the north corner proved to be a small, inquisitive fox, standing quite still and staring up at me.

"Hello," I whispered, happy to see my old friend.

I hadn't seen the creature in several visits.

As I sat on the cold marble bench, the fox nearby, I tried to connect with Clio's spirit. As someone so fascinated with history, it should come as no surprise that I was a bit obsessed with the idea of communicating with the dead. And given my family history, I felt that I should be able to accomplish the feat. After all, I was a Daughter of La Lune, a descendant of a sixteenth-century witch, and one of a long line of women who had strange, wonderous, and according to some, frightening abilities.

Except, as far as anyone knew, I was the first Daughter who possessed no magick. That lack made all the women in our family treat me differently. It had made me ashamed as well as ambitious and competitive. Ironically, it was the latter two attributes that had helped me achieve success in my chosen career and ultimately landed me in the troubled state I found myself in that evening in Highgate.

CHAPTER 4

Yes, women in my family could commune with the dead, but I was not one of them. And even though I had never had a glimmer of connection with Clio's spirit in the three years since her death, I couldn't give up. I had been turning to her for advice since I was thirteen years old. I yearned for her wise counsel. But after a frustrating half hour trying but failing to receive any messages from beyond the grave, it was time to leave Highgate and return to my flat.

Yet as the air grew colder and the fog thicker, I remained. I was distressed. I was worried about my job. I missed Clio.

And even though he'd now been gone six years, I missed my brother, Percy, who had been aboard the Prince of Wales battleship when a Japanese torpedo bomber targeted it off the East coast of Malaya. On December 10, 1941, it sank, and Percy was lost at sea, along with three hundred and forty-seven other sailors—one of them being his best friend and the man I'd married, Samuel Maycroft. My friend, whom I'd wed before he shipped out to war out of...what? Caring? Kindness? Hope? Guilt? Love, certainly, but that of a dear friend, not the passionate kind.

Although the Prince of Wales was the most advanced

ship of its day, the heat and humidity in the Malayan waters had disabled the anti-aircraft fire control radars and wrecked the ammunition used in her anti-tank guns.

It was a tragedy for all of us—my grandmothers, my father, and me. Of all of us, I think my father suffered the most.

Percy, who was four years older than I, had followed in my father's footsteps and worked alongside him day after day in Egypt until the war broke out. I was in Oxford studying history, absorbed by my work. As much as I missed my brother, his living so far away when he volunteered to serve didn't affect my daily routine the way it did my father. But on that October evening, with both Percy and Clio gone, Samuel gone, my father in Egypt, my grandparents gone, and my mother gone so long ago, the sadness seemed lodged in my chest like a pill that would not dissolve.

I stood and walked to the three-meter-high granite pyramid in the left corner of the plot. Reaching out, I put my hand on its apex. This was Clio's marker. Little did I know the day she first brought me here to do a rubbing that we'd stumble on a seemingly unsolvable mystery. Nor did I imagine I'd be here grieving her so soon.

I was not alone in my misery. London was filled with people who pined for loved ones. We all shared a collective grief and ached for the world we had known before the war. We longed for a time when our daily existence was not scarred by the knowledge of what evil rested just beneath the surface at every turn. But knowing I was not alone in my sadness didn't help alleviate it. And now, Hugh had come back to the museum, and we were in competition for my job—the only familiar and stable thing in my life. I felt all the losses even more.

I sighed, and as if called, the fox crept over. She sat at my feet for a few moments, looked up at me, and then ran to the opposite corner of the plot under the shade of the yew. She sat in front of what looked like some of the tree's aboveground roots overgrown with ivy, the edges of the green leaves just starting to turn crimson. The fox faced me, holding my stare. It was a most peculiar experience to be so boldly observed by the animal. Almost as if she was trying to tell me something.

Clio had once joked that the fox was my familiar, claiming the animal never visited unless I was here.

"She even looks like you, Jeannine." I could almost hear Clio's voice in the wind. "Your fiery red hair is the same shade as the animal's fur. And your pointed nose and chin bear a true resemblance to the fox's little face. Or hers to yours."

Now, I stood motionless, mesmerized by the fox's gaze and how she seemed to be guarding her corner until, as suddenly as she had appeared, she darted off, disappearing into the shrubbery.

I walked over to where the animal had situated herself. Had she been protecting something? I pulled away a bit of the ivy and then a bit more. Even though I visited Clio here monthly, I'd never noticed this oddly shaped clump of ivy. Neither had Clio when we'd come together. Despite the hour, I set to removing some of the mess.

In less than ten minutes, I'd unearthed a flat marble stone embedded in the earth with some tree roots growing over its borders. I tugged and yanked at the root vine's tendrils until I could read the incised inscription.

Ashe Lloyd Lewis. 1828-1868
"Eternity was in our lips and eyes." William Shakespeare

Chills ran up my arms and down my back as I reread the words. I had the sense that something deep in my psyche had just shifted. I knew there was a monumental importance to this find. Kneeling, I put both my hands on the stone and felt a great wave of longing as if missing the man—someone I didn't even know. As if I had been deeply connected to him, and now my heart was breaking from the loss.

Except none of that made sense.

I stared at the plaque. I read his name, the dates, and the quote again. Then I brushed away the dirt covering the lower quarter of the stone, revealing a carved eye with a single tear escaping its corner. The chiseled pattern framing the eye created a familiar image, but I couldn't place it.

Was it something I had seen in the museum? I couldn't recall.

I wished I'd brought paper and crayons so I could take a rubbing and study the markings at home. I'd have to come back. I had so many questions. Would any of them ever be answered?

The first was why Clio had never told me Lewis's grave was here. She knew how much I admired him and was obsessed with his painting. Even if she'd forgotten, certainly she would have been reminded when we found the plaque stating the angel sculpture had been placed here by him. Unless she hadn't known about this grave. Was that possible? The Lewis marker was in the ground and in the farthest corner of her family plot, obscured by overgrown roots and vines.

I'd never know why Clio hadn't told me, but she had, in her way, led me here. And now I had another gravestone to pay my respects to.

I brushed off what was left of the debris and whispered to the marker that I'd be back and bring violets for him, too. Next time.

I thought I heard a whisper of thanks, but of course it couldn't have been—it was just the wind and my overstimulated mind.

By then, it had grown dark. As beautiful as the Victorian cemetery could be during daylight hours, it was threatening at night. As I made my way out of the plot, I found obstacles at every turn. The upturned rocks on the unpaved paths seemed all put there to trip me. Tree roots that had broken through the ground were treacherous. Fallen branches were hazards. As I navigated them all, I tried to detect the landmarks that marked my route to the plot, but the shadows obscured them. I was frightened I'd take a wrong turn and get lost. Eventually, I found my way. I only hoped I'd be as successful navigating what awaited me at the museum.

CHAPTER 5

A yellowed notice, curling at the edges, was stamped with a single word: *Restricted*. A brass padlock affixed to the doorknob ensured no entry was possible. From the color and condition of the paper and the dust on the lock, I guessed they'd been in place for at least fifty years.

I reached out, put the key in the lock, and then hesitated. Certainly, the warnings didn't apply to me since I was the Victoria and Albert Museum's Keeper of the Metalworks and the person with the key.

Did they?

I took a deep breath. The air held a scent that seemed to promise hidden bounty. The museum's underground crypts housed thousands of treasures there wasn't enough exhibition space for in the main galleries. Whenever I ventured down to the tunnels in search of an objet d'art for a show I was putting on, I felt I was walking on hallowed ground. In my mind, I always heard Gregorian chants somewhere in the distance and felt connected to the mysteries of the past from whence these items came.

Since childhood, I had felt as much at home in museums as anywhere else. On our travels, my father always took me to these cathedrals to history. And when he was on digs and left me at home with my governess and one of my grandmothers, visiting a museum my father had taken me to helped me miss him less. The art we'd seen together kept me company. And no institution felt more like home than the V&A.

That morning, I remembered Clio once telling me that in 1929, she had put on a show devoted to love objects. There was no accompanying brochure, but I found her notes on the exhibition and was intrigued by several items she'd described. I thought I might try to follow in her footsteps and add a twist or turn of my own for the Valentine's Day exhibit.

After a restless night of sleep, I knew there was no question. I wouldn't quit my job. Of course, I would take up Mr. Gibbons' challenge and fight for my position. Clio had always told me that some people succeeded because they were destined to, but most succeeded because they were determined to. I reminded myself that I had the determination necessary to succeed.

Returning to Clio's notes, I took stock of what I'd already found and what was still left to discover. I'd already collected the Victorian greeting cards she'd mentioned. They were sentimental, sweet, lavishly illustrated, and perfect to showcase.

I'd found a group of engagement and wedding rings with wonderful inscriptions and designs, as well. And I'd uncovered a collection of heart jewelry, much of it from the Victorian era.

At the bottom of the last page of notes about the show was a cryptic notation—*Section C, Room 516. Speak to D about the history of this collection—and if we still need to keep it secret.*

That scribble had brought me to this out-of-the-way corner of the vast underground and a storage room that was barred to all—except the keeper of the key.

Having worked in the museum for my entire career, certain nooks and crannies felt as if they were my personal hiding places. This was especially true of the basement rooms in section C—the *dungeon* as some of my coworkers called it—where the smaller items in my department were stored. I didn't think any room had escaped my notice, but I was wrong. Number 516 was at the end of a shadowy tunnel, around a corner, and isolated in an alcove that had, until now, eluded me.

I was excited as I searched my key ring for one that fit the padlock. Would I find a forgotten cache of jewels behind the door? I had a special affinity for jewels. As a scholar, I knew that each piece in the V&A had a precious history behind it, and I deeply appreciated the effort that went into creating them. One of my cousins, Opaline Duplessi, was a well-known French jeweler, and I had learned a lot about jewelry design and manufacturing, as well as the romance behind the accessories men and women had adorned their bodies with since the beginning of time.

When I was a girl, Opaline had schooled me in the secret language of stones and their properties and even taught me how to cleanse antique jewelry of its aura if there was malevolent energy attached to it. While quite esoteric-sounding, it was a simple chemical—not magickal—process. The act of cleansing can be important because objects take on their owner's vitality, and whether you are buying an antique piece or working with one, you don't want to be affected by someone else's negative energy.

All you had to do was place the piece of jewelry in a carved crystal bowl made of selenite, along with a bouquet of a specific kind of sandalwood, sage, and lavender from a certain grower in Provence, and a few drops of eucalyptus oil. Let the piece sit for forty-eight hours near an open window, and it's done.

Anyone can use this particular cleansing method, but few know where to get the exact herbs or have the formula for the right amounts. Cleansing a piece sometimes almost made me feel as if I was really a member of the La Lune side of the family and that I did have a gift, after all.

Whenever I allowed myself to dwell on my lack of magickal talents, I tried to turn the negative into a positive—one of Grandmother Imogine's oft-repeated mantras. I would remind myself of the benefits of being ordinary. I knew how many women in our family had been considered odd by their peers, seen as outcasts or worse, labeled *disturbed* or *touched*. In certain eras, they'd been in mortal danger. Opaline also wondered if, since I had no gifts, I was also immune to the La Lune curse: to only have one true love in your lifetime.

Oddly, though, we didn't know. I had never loved a man the way I imagined I would. How my mother had loved my father, and Grandmother Imogine had loved my grandfather. The way books and movies portrayed romantic love.

I'd had crushes. A terrible one on Hugh Kenward. I'd loved Samuel, but it had been a deep and abiding comradeship, which I supposed came from knowing each other from such a young age. My mourning for him was tied to my mourning for my brother, Clio, and so many other things. That day, as I stood in the basement of the V&A at the door to room 516, I was but one of millions as close to trauma as I was to recovery.

I turned the key, and the padlock sprang open. I removed it and broke the seal on the doorjamb. Hardened red wax crumbled and fell to the floor. I put my hand on the doorknob. Was this an act of transgression? Why was the door sealed in the first place? Why the warning? There were valuable items in storage, well protected throughout the dungeon, but I'd never seen anything this arcane before.

I stepped over the threshold into a room barely larger than a closet—just enough space for one chair and five storage shelves on the facing wall. In the light of my torch, I saw a large, black jewelry tray on each shelf. I pulled one forward and peered down at the glittering array of treasures.

There were six brooches, each a frame of precious gems surrounding a miniature painted portrait of an eye looking up at me. The next tray contained rings featuring eyes, also framed with stones.

All together, the shelves held five trays containing forty-two rings, stickpins, pendants, and brooches, each and every one featuring either a male or a female eye. As I examined one particular brooch, I realized I had seen several of these before. A long time ago, when I first started working for Clio as her research assistant. I'd walked into her office and found half a dozen of these mysterious objects laid out in an open black leather case.

When I'd asked what they were—having never seen anything quite like them—Clio had launched into the history of the objects, which she nicknamed *lovers' eyes*, even though the correct name for them was simply *eye portraits*.

Clio told me the eye was one of the most universal symbols. From ancient Egypt to ancient Greece, the eye had been used to depict gods, goddesses, and to ward off evil. She told me that many Italian churches had the Eye of Providence—the all-seeing eye of God—looking down from the cupola. The Masons had adopted the symbol. In France, it signified watchfulness and appeared on the state police's buckles and belts. During the revolution of 1789, members of the Revolutionary Party used it to signal their allegiances to initiates.

"There is even a mention of a lover's eye portrait of Marie Antoinette in a letter written by Élisabeth Vigée Le Brun, the only woman who ever achieved the rank of painter to the Crown. In the six years she worked for the court, she painted at least thirty portraits of Marie Antoinette. One of them mysteriously disappeared—unsurprising given its size and history. It was a miniature portrait of the queen's eye, which Marie Antoinette had made into a stickpin encircled with rubies to give to Count Hans Axel von Fersen of

Sweden. They had met as teenagers at a masquerade ball, when she was still Dauphine of France. He was a constant guest at Versailles, and it is said they became lovers in 1783.

"My predecessor told me a donor gifted that brooch to the museum in the late 1860s, along with the letter from the queen to the count when she gave him the portrait, but that it has been lost."

"Do you think we still have it?" I was instantly intrigued.

"I don't know. I've spent hours searching for it over the years but haven't come across it. We do have quite a few other examples besides the queen's lost eye. Bejeweled eye miniatures became a fad at the end of the eighteenth century after Prince George of Wales gave a portrait of his eye to an unsuitable marriage partner he was wooing. Refusing to give up Maria Fitzherbert, he sent her a love letter and a portrait of his eye encrusted with diamonds. He referred to the brooch as *your lover's eye*. That's where I got the term I use for them."

"What happened to the prince and Maria?"

"Eventually, he secretly married her. He even had the same artist create a locket containing a portrait of her eye, which he wore around his neck. Of course, once the romantic story got out, painters were hired to create similar pieces by those with the funds. Since the eye was recognizable only to the recipient, the lover's identity remained a secret, and the pieces became clandestine love tokens."

Enchanted by the romantic notion, I bent over to examine the jewels. I was drawn to a particular brooch of a man's eye, the iris a twilight shade of blue. The painting was framed by opals, shimmering with green, blue, and lavender flashes.

The eye seemed to be looking at me with an intimacy and intensity that made me feel as if he were flesh and blood, standing right before me.

I reached for the brooch, but Clio put her hand out to stop me.

"Jeannine, no. They are all very fragile. Most of them need repairs. Honestly, you know better than to just pick something up. All these will need to be taken to the workshop and restored at some point. So many of them have loose stones and wobbly backs. All we need is to drop a diamond and be unable to find it."

Of course, I knew the protocol—like everyone at the museum. Every item was precious, valuable, and potentially fragile or unstable. It was unlike me to just reach out like that. I hadn't only learned to respect objects at work. I'd been surrounded by ancient art in our home since I was a small child and was well versed in the rules. I'd never before been so careless. It surprised me. And from Clio's tone of voice, I'd surprised her, too.

"I am sorry," I said. "I don't know what I was thinking. Or *not* thinking."

"No harm done."

"Are you putting these into an exhibit?"

"I thought about it, but no. Maybe if I had the Marie Antoinette eye, perhaps, but we don't have enough information about any of these to make a compelling story out of them."

"Is that the only reason you're not using them?" I knew from the way she had pursed her lips that she was holding something back.

"Well, it's a bit silly of me, but there is a superstition about them. It's connected to all the ancient lore about evil eyes. Not to mention that the one you were lunging for is framed with opals, which are bad luck."

"I wasn't lunging. And besides, you don't believe all that...what do you call it? Mumbo jumbo."

"I don't usually, but something about these...it's so strange. Just a feeling I can't put my finger on. Isn't that odd?"

"Yes, for you, especially. Maybe it's the superstition. What is it, exactly?"

As the descendant of a witch, I'd always found myths, superstitions, and archaic folklore fascinating. I had a notebook filled with bizarre beliefs, stories, and spells I found written in ancient tomes while on adventures with my father. I kept a running list of questions about them all for Grandmother Imogine. I also had a malachite box filled with amulets and talismans purported to ward off evil and bad luck. Much to Clio's chagrin, I wore one every day. I had on one of my favorites that day, an ancient Egyptian feldspar bead from the Middle Kingdom, approximately 2040 to 1783 BCE. It was the first artifact I'd found on my first dig when I was sixteen. Because of its semitransparent green color, Egyptians considered feldspar precious. It signified rebirth and growth.

"Please, tell me?" I asked.

Clio, who knew all the esoteric and arcane legends about the objects in her care, launched into the brooch's history.

"It has to do with the legend of the evil eye, which goes back thousands of years. It's first written mention comes from Ancient Greece. In his romance, Aethiopica, Heliodorus of Emesa wrote, 'When anyone looks at what is excellent with an envious eye, he fills the surrounding atmosphere with a pernicious quality, and transmits his own envenomed exhalations into whatever is nearest to him.' Many cultures have their own versions. In Irish lore, men could bewitch horses with a single glance. In both the Bible and the Quran, it's written that the eye can release energy rays strong enough to kill animals and children. Those with blue eyes are said to have more potent powers."

I looked down at the opal-framed blue eye that seemed to be staring up at me, communicating with me. The emotion it aroused in me was not fear or evil but a yearning, a longing for something I felt I'd lost.

"And this one that you stopped me from touching? What is the superstition connected to opals?"

"In Europe, in the eleventh century," she said, "people

believed opals could render a person invisible, which linked the stone to criminal activity. Sir Walter Scott used the opals in his novel *Anne of Geierstein* and kept the idea alive. Normally, I wouldn't even think of it, but...well, as I said, there's something about these pieces...." She didn't finish her thought as she closed the case, and I lost sight of the man's blue eye that had so bewitched me.

In the ensuing fifteen years, I'd never seen a miniature eye portrait again or ever thought about them. But here they were, all looking up at me. Carefully painted eyes with loving, solemn, plaintive, or sad expressions, their gem-encrusted frames gleaming in the glow from my torch.

I searched for the brooch I'd been so taken with long ago—a man's blue eye in an opal frame—and all these years later, once again felt him reaching out and sharing his soul with me. I studied it. Was the sense of familiarity I felt simply because I'd seen it before? But hadn't I felt the same way the first time I'd seen it? A shiver ran down my back, and I had the same sense I'd had in the cemetery: that I was treading on something beyond my knowing.

I shook it off. I had work to do. Serious and critical work. I had to save my career.

I studied the other eye miniatures. There was a feminine pale gray eye with a teardrop escaping down her cheek. The artist had captured her sad story in the single tear that glistened as if it were real. I wanted to reach out and wipe it away but imagined if I did, the woman to whom it belonged might chastise me and tell me that we needed to bear witness to loss. That the depth of our grief was the depth of our love. It was a phrase I told myself over and over.

In the last tray was a note on lined paper, in Clio's handwriting.

There is little documentation on the artists who created these marvelous works of art, but I suspect that some of the more famous portrait painters of the various time periods were called upon to execute them. (See list.) We need to do more research to match styles with portrait painters of the day. Also research the archives of British jewelers for records of the framing and mounting. It's quite possible the painters were the ones to commission the frames from prominent jewelers. (See list.)

I examined all the trays, lifting them out and looking for Clio's lists. They would be invaluable in saving me time, but they weren't to be found. I'd have to go into the department files and see if I could locate them there.

I knew instantly that I would use this treasure trove of lovers' eyes to tell my Valentine's Day tale. Fourteen pieces for February fourteenth. I'd include some of the other items I'd gathered, but these would be the main focus.

I spent the rest of my time in the room choosing two dozen eyes that had the potential to be in the show and then set to sketching each one so I'd have a record of it. I had decisions to make about the final fourteen to use and would study my drawings and notes over the next few days.

At ten forty a.m., I put the miniatures away, relocked the room, and headed back to my office. I had an eleven o'clock appointment.

CHAPTER 6

I took the longer route to my office through the painting galleries. Even though I'd worked at the museum my whole adult life, I never tired of looking at its art. These were the only things still completely reliable in a world that was often hard to recognize since the war. People I loved were gone. Buildings I'd grown up walking past had been reduced to rubble. Inhuman atrocities had been carried out for years. But the objects and art in the V&A and other museums were still and forever trustworthy.

I was back just in time for my eleven o'clock appointment.

Mrs. Whitfield was a lovely woman, about thirty or so with soft, chestnut hair that framed her oval face, golden-brown eyes, and a charming bow-shaped mouth. She wore a dark green dress, cinched tightly at the waist, a green felt hat with brown feathers, and fawn-colored kid gloves. She carried a brown leather handbag and had a brown coat draped over her arm.

"It's so nice to meet you, Mrs. Whitfield," I said, getting up and offering my hand. Once she was seated and had declined my offer of tea, she opened her pocketbook and pulled out a velvet pouch.

"This is what I wanted to show you."

As the Keeper of the Metalworks for the museum, I often looked at pieces people were considering donating or had found and wanted to know more about. I especially loved my job when those pieces were jewelry, and I was excited to see what my visitor was holding.

Mrs. Whitfield explained that she had done a garden clean-up at the end of the summer and came across a piece of jewelry while digging out a dead tree trunk.

"My brother and I have a jewelry shop in Chelsea, and I was going to add this to our antique section, but given the history of people who lived in our house, I thought I might bring it in first and make certain it's not something more valuable."

"Who lived in your house?" I asked.

"Dante Gabriel Rossetti, from 1862 until his death twenty years later."

"You live at 16 Cheyne Walk?" I was surprised. I knew Ashe Lloyd Lewis had lived in that house when he was Rossetti's assistant. *What an odd coincidence*, I thought.

And then I could almost hear Grandmother Imogine reprimanding me. "There are *no* coincidences, lamb. When one presents itself, examine it upside down and inside out, and you will eventually find an important connection to your life and its importance. A coincidence is simply a message hiding behind an accident."

"I'm so grateful that you thought to bring it here first," I told her, feeling a thrill as I watched her withdraw a bracelet and place it on the pouch.

I couldn't help but gasp. "I know this bracelet well from Rossetti's paintings. How extraordinary that you found it," I said. "May I examine it?"

"Of course."

I pulled on a pair of white cotton gloves and lifted my

loupe from its grosgrain ribbon that hung around my neck. It had been a gift from Clio.

I examined the thin gold bangle, which had what is known as a large *witch's heart* charm dangling from it. Rather than an evenly designed heart, the tail of a witch's heart—a symbol that dated back to the fifteenth century—twists to one side, usually the right.

Not only did I know about these medallions from my studies, but I also had one that belonged to one of my ancestors. A second coincidence that the bracelet related so specifically to my family heritage.

I'm paying attention, I thought, addressing my grandmother in my mind. She had taught me everything I knew about the witches in our family, their legends and lore. She'd always told me that I should pay extra attention when faced with multiple coincidences since they were extra-meaningful signs. "Magick and mystery are all around us," she'd said. "Our job as Daughters of La Lune is to honor the mystical universe. Open yourself to it whenever it presents itself, Jeannine dear. You'll be rewarded, I promise."

To which my other grandmother would have shook her head and murmured, "Nonsense," but hers was the voice I pushed out of my head.

"This is a very rare find, Mrs. Whitfield. It is featured in a painting by Rossetti called *A Vision of Fiammetta.* It will take a bit of time, but if you are interested, I could authenticate it for you."

"This is quite amazing," she said, seeming a little stunned.

"It is, indeed. Rossetti typically chose jewelry to complement the colors of the sitter's clothing, the setting's rugs, curtains, or other elements on the canvas. It was well known that he had a collection of mostly costume brooches, necklaces, belts, bracelets, and other items in his studio. We actually have several of them in the museum. It's very exciting you've found a new one."

"I suppose I'm going to have to start digging up the whole garden now."

We both laughed at that.

"Well, if you do, I'd be happy to help identify anything you may find. It's sure to have serious historical significance in the art world."

"I think I'll take you up on that offer and the one to authenticate the bracelet for me."

"Will you be selling it? If so, the museum might be interested in purchasing it to add to our collection of other jewelry featured in Rossetti's paintings. Most of what we have was donated to the V&A by one of his circle—Jane Morris's daughter. We have several pieces from other Pre-Raphaelite artists, as well. And we're always on the lookout for more if they are this important."

"I didn't know that. I've spent quite a bit of time here and have never seen that collection."

"It hasn't been on permanent display for a while." I explained that only a small percentage of our holdings were shown at any given time. "But I'm planning a show next summer that will include them. If it turns out you aren't willing to sell us this bracelet, perhaps you would loan it to us?"

"We can discuss that after you authenticate it. And will you be able to give us an idea of its value?" she asked.

"A rough estimate, yes. If you'd fill out this paperwork, I'll be able to get started. The process takes about six to eight weeks."

After she left, I remained at my desk and examined the bracelet again. I'd placed it on the black velvet tray I used to transport pieces from one department to another. It was worn and rubbed in places. I could have used any of the dozens of newer trays in the department, but this was Clio's and had sentimental value to me.

I thought about how much she would have enjoyed

examining the bracelet with me and suddenly felt lonely—a kind of loneliness I had experienced my whole life. When I was a child, I'd thought I was missing my mother, who had died when I was only three years old. I had almost no memories of her. Or perhaps I was lonely for my father when he was away on a dig. But when I realized I felt it even when I was with him sometimes, I understood that my feeling wasn't for the loss of any one person I knew. It was instead for something that would relieve my singularity. No matter who was in my life or how much I cared about them, I always had the sense that I was ultimately alone in a way that would never change. As a Daughter of La Lune, I knew I was different even if I didn't have any magickal abilities. But this was something else. As if I had broken a bone that hadn't healed right and would forever be a reminder of the accident.

When I was young, I invented a companion, an imaginary friend, who I whispered to in the dark and who, I had been certain, whispered back and told me that I'd find a person to wipe away the loneliness one day, the same way my grandmother wiped away my tears.

I named him Seti, after a character in one of the many wonderful bedtime stories my father used to tell me. It was based on a tale he had discovered on the walls of an Egyptian nobleman's tomb.

The drawings told of Seti's love for a woman named Nenet. His parents had not approved of the marriage, as she was rumored to be a sorcerer. But he wouldn't relent. Eventually, they gave him a series of arduous tasks to complete. If he could accomplish them, his parents would agree to the union. The undertaking was impossible for any man, but Nenet used her powers to help him, and Seti succeeded at each one. He spent his long life protecting her from those who wanted to do her harm because of her magick. And she, in turn, protected him from those who tried to steal his lands. They died within days of each other and were buried together, side by side.

As an adult, I'd outgrown my imaginary friend. Still, when I felt that long-ago longing to find someone to soothe my feeling of being out of step, I thought of Seti, and for a moment, missed the comfort and companionship he'd afforded me.

I opened the clasp and slipped the bracelet onto my wrist. I looked down at it and experienced a vivid déjà vu of having seen it on my arm before.

My imagination was acting up. No surprise there. Objects held memories and energy. I had been mesmerized when I visited my cousin Opaline and watched her perform her gift of learning those memories and tapping into that energy by working with a client's family heirloom or a piece of their clothing. I'd longed for a gift like hers, and those were the times I'd felt the most frustrated about being the only Daughter of La Lune without a talent. Usually, one discovered their ability with the onset of their menses. And they were all quite different.

Opaline could speak the secret language of the stones. She had apprenticed to a jeweler who worked with Fabergé and ran her own shop in the Palais-Royal in Paris. She was able to reconstruct people's personal treasures into amulets and, in the process, learn their memories up to and including their deaths and journeys to the afterlife.

Her younger sister, Delphine, who lived in the South of France, was an artist whose paintings foretold the future.

Their youngest sister, Jadine, also lived in Paris and was a well known psychoanalyst who studied with Jung. She read the tears people shed in an effort to help them heal their sorrows.

My grandmother Imogine communed with plants and flowers and could make potions to heal the sick and soothe the soul.

My mother had been a watercolor artist who heard the voices of those who came before us. They told her their stories and secrets as she painted in the tombs where they were laid to rest.

The list of my family members and their talents went on and on. And as far as any of us knew, each female child had been born with a special talent that defied logic. At about thirteen years of age, each was given a spell by the current matriarch to aid in their endeavors. It was said the spells came to the matriarch in dreams, and even she didn't always understand what they meant.

My grandmother, Imogine, had given me mine when I was fourteen. But no matter how many times I recited it, nothing occurred. I had abandoned all hope of it ever becoming meaningful years ago.

All the spells followed the same form and cadence.

One was: *Make of the blood, a stone. Make of a stone, a powder. Make of a powder, life everlasting.*

Another was: *Make of the blood, heat. Make of the heat, a fire. Make of the fire, life everlasting.*

A third was: *Make of the blood, a sight. Make of the sight, a symbol. Make of the symbol, life everlasting.*

Mine was: *Make of the blood, a journey. Make of the journey, a passion. Make of the passion, life everlasting.*

I had always thought it an ironic spell. Other than my passion for the history of objects, I'd never felt any kind of passion like those I'd read about in the wonderful novels of Colette, D.H. Lawrence, Margaret Mitchell and Daphne du Maurier.

I was thinking about that spell and still holding the witch's heart when I felt it warm beneath my fingers as if the gold had absorbed heat from my thoughts. Or, more realistically—because it was wiser to think that way—from the afternoon sun coming through the window.

CHAPTER 7

That afternoon, I walked downstairs to meet my friend Sybil for tea. She'd purchased her husband a pair of antique cuff links for their upcoming wedding anniversary and wanted my opinion as to whether or not they needed an energy cleanse.

When I walked into The Green Room, I saw Sybil right away—it seemed everyone I met arrived before I did lately. As I headed toward her table, she saw me and waved. Sybil was a few years older than me and married with twin boys who were in year eleven at school. She was also in charge of a luxury leather and paper goods company, which had been in her husband's family for generations.

"I got here early and had to order. I'm famished," Sybil said, pointing to her tea and scones. "I never had time for lunch today."

When the waitress came over, I ordered the same.

"I didn't either. I was totally caught up in searching out items for the Valentine's show."

"How are things proceeding with the competition?" she asked. I'd called to tell her after going to the cemetery.

"I think I've come up with a highly unusual concept," I whispered and then looked around to make sure no one was nearby who might report back to Hugh.

I explained about the cache of miniature eye-portrait jewelry I'd rediscovered and my idea to use them as lynchpins to tell stories about famous British romances—some true, others pulled from movies and novels.

"I'll feature fourteen brooches, along with Victorian greeting cards and other items lovers exchange. As you walk through the gallery, the items and excerpts from the books and scripts will take you through fourteen love stories."

"I think that's genius," she said, raising her cup to toast me.

"I don't know about genius. I just hope the public likes it better than whatever Hugh is planning. I can't lose this; being Keeper is so much more than my job."

Sybil put her hand on mine. "I know. Which is why I am forever telling you that it's not healthy for you to be so immersed in your work to the exclusion of everything else. You should be going out, giving yourself a chance to meet someone and fall in love, start a family."

I waved away her words. "I haven't *stopped* going out. I'd be happy to meet someone."

"Maybe you haven't stopped, but neither have you made a real effort, and you know it."

She was right. The truth was, I wasn't interested in opening myself up to any more pain after the losses I'd endured since the war had begun. Before I could respond, a group of three men arrived, their laughter causing both Sybil and me to look over at the door.

"That's Hugh," I whispered to Sybil. "But don't look. Or if you do, be discreet." She'd never met Hugh but had read about him in gossip columns, and I'd told her everything about our past and conflicted present.

"Have I ever been anything but discreet?" she joked as she managed to shift just enough to look without being obvious.

"Which one is he?" she asked.

"The one in the middle. Blond hair, high cheekbones."

"The one who is entirely too handsome and quite sure of himself?"

"That's him."

"You will not lose your position to him," she said. "I won't have it."

I laughed. "And just what are you going to do about it?"

"I'm not sure yet. But we're going to make sure you win this contest."

I sat back and smiled. If anyone could help me, it was her.

"Remind me how the competition will be judged," she prodded. "Attendance?"

"By the public's attendance, yes, but also their comments, critics' reviews, and catalog sales."

"Perfect. That's something we can do something about."

"How?"

Before she could answer, Hugh approached the table.

"Mrs. Maycroft," he said, "I trust you are enjoying your tea?"

"Quite," I said.

"And your guest?" he said, extending his arm before I thought to introduce them. "Hugh Kenward," he said.

"Sybil Shipley." She shook his hand.

"A pleasure. Any relation to Manfred Shipley?" he asked.

"Yes, my husband."

"I had the pleasure of meeting him during the war. We were all relieved that he recovered so well."

"Thank you." Manfred had been badly wounded in the leg. For a while, doctors worried they wouldn't be able to save the limb, but he'd pulled through and had been left with only a slight limp. "His squash days are over, but he can still ride. He's very grateful to his men for getting him to the surgeons so quickly. He was told that made all the difference." She shuddered.

"And we were all quite relieved when we heard the news. Good man. Give him my regards and tell him I'll call on him soon, if I may."

"Of course," Sybil said meekly—quite unusual for her.

"Well, don't let me keep you any longer from your tea." Hugh nodded formally to Sybil and then looked my way. "I'll see you upstairs, Jeannine? At the meeting?"

"Meeting?"

"Ah, yes. We just got the call from Mr. Gibbons' secretary. We are to meet in his office at four p.m."

"Is something wrong?" I asked.

"Isn't something always wrong when it comes to Gibbons?" He smiled.

As soon as he was out of earshot, Sybil leaned forward. "He's quite charming."

I didn't respond.

"And has a lovely speaking voice."

"He studied theater," I said in an underwhelmed tone.

She sniffed the air.

"And wears an intriguing scent, doesn't he?"

"Enough, Sybil, okay? He's all those things, but I am not interested. He tried to get me fired once and is probably planning to try again right now."

"Then we'll do him in." She laughed. "No one is going to get the best of my best friend."

"There are people we meet," my grandmother Imogine had told me, "who stay in our lives despite our wish to be rid of them. Even when we go out of our way to distance ourselves, they stay in our orbit. When this happens, it's incumbent on us to understand that their karma and ours are bound. Yes, be vigilant, lamb, but also be open to learning the reasons we are in each other's lives."

The concept of karma, I'd read, had been traced to the year 1500 BCE where a description appeared in the ancient Hindu text the *Rigveda* and was explored further about seven hundred years later in the *Upanishads.* The concept of our actions in one life having repercussions in our next brings moral and ethical dimensions to the concept of how we should conduct ourselves throughout our lives.

From what my grandmother had explained, it's difficult to determine why we have a karmic bond with someone else. Did Hugh and I have one? From the research assistant rumor mill, I'd heard he'd been engaged during the war but had broken it off shortly after returning home.

I refocused on what Sybil was telling me about the anniversary dinner party scheduled for Saturday. I was to come to her townhouse this evening to help set up the flower arrangements. Grandmother Imogine had taught me the art, and it was something I loved to do. It was probably the only interest of mine that Grandmother Ruth had approved of.

"Who have you seated me next to this time?" I asked with some trepidation. She was so intent on finding me a beau, she invited a potential suitor to every one of her fetes.

"Manfred on your left and Thomas Randall on your right," she said.

I was surprised since he was married. "His wife won't like that. She always gets upset when he wants to talk to me about his newest paintings."

"That won't be a problem any longer. He divorced since you last saw him."

"You need to stop, Sybil." I moaned.

"This isn't me matchmaking," she said. "He's in London the whole week, shopping for paintings to add to his collection. I sat you next to him because he'll want to talk to you about what he's thinking of buying no matter where I sit you. At least this way, he won't be talking over someone's head."

There was logic to what she said, but I still wasn't convinced her motives were totally innocent.

"How long has he been divorced?"

"It's been a year."

"Really, a year?"

"Well, ten months. But I promise I am not pushing you two together. You know how passionate he is about collecting. He'd never talk to me again if I sat you at the other end of the table."

"I want to believe you, but you don't have the best track record."

Expertly changing the subject, Sybil opened her pocketbook and brought out the cuff links—the reason for her request to meet.

I pulled up my loupe and examined the vibrant lapis lazuli bars set in gold. "The hallmarks suggest they are at least fifty years old or older, but they're pristine. Rarely worn. I don't think they need any kind of energy cleansing whatsoever."

"Would you do it, though? Just to be sure? And bring them with you tonight if you can, or to the party if you must?"

"Of course." My friend was extremely superstitious. She never brought any antiques into her home without having me treat them. It was how we'd first met. She'd heard about me through a mutual friend and had come to the museum to ask me to cleanse some jewelry she'd inherited from a nasty aunt.

"And then we can devise our revenge on Mr. Perfect over there," Sybil said, rubbing her hands together. "Unless the Halloween revelers get to him first." She let out a frightfully accurate witch's cackle.

Her silliness made me laugh out loud, which I hadn't done in days. I lightly slapped her on the wrist with my napkin. "You're too much."

Returning to my office after tea, I sat at my desk to gather my notebook and pen for the meeting Mr. Gibbons had called. I felt an immediate chill in the air. Turning, I saw my window was open a crack. As I shut it, I realized I didn't recall having opened it.

Gathering my things, I remembered my pen was empty. Before leaving for tea with Sybil, I'd been editing a report one of my RAs had written on the state of a pair of gates in our collection, and my pen had run out of ink. I needed to fill it before I left. I reached for my ink bottle, always to the right of my lamp, but it wasn't there. It was on the opposite side of the mail tray. That was odd.

We had a cleaning service, but they never came during the day, and besides, they were very careful about moving things to different spots when they dusted. I examined the rest of my desktop. Was anything else out of place?

Yes.

A crystal vase that had been Clio's, which I usually kept filled with flowers, was also in the wrong spot. And my notebook was open. I was never careless when it came to my jottings in the leather-bound journal.

I filled my pen, gathered my things, and left my office. On my way to the meeting I passed my team of RAs, Alice and Andrew—who I suspected were dating despite the museum's no fraternization policy—and Jacob, and asked if any of them had seen anyone go into my office while I'd been downstairs.

None of them had.

"Have you all been here the whole time I was gone?" I asked.

Andrew had been in the library for most of the hour. Alice said she'd been at her desk except for when she went to the mailroom to drop off a package. Jacob had been out running a personal errand.

As I walked to Mr. Gibbons' office, I weighed the possibility that I'd forgotten to close the notebook and had left the window open versus someone coming into my office to drop something off, then thought better of it and…what?

Opened my window? Looked through my things? What reason would anyone have for searching in my papers? I hardly handled anything secretive.

Unless, of course, it was Hugh looking for information about what I planned to do with my half of the Valentine exhibit.

If he had, he might have opened the window to make sure he didn't leave his distinctive scent behind.

Well, if he *was* nosing about, it would have been for naught. My notes about the exhibit were safely locked away in my drawer. Heeding Clio's long-ago suspicions, I wasn't taking any chances of Hugh trying to learn what I was planning.

The war may have changed him on the surface, but I still couldn't tell how much deeper it had truly affected him—if it had at all. Had it given him morals? A heart?

CHAPTER 8

The meeting with the director had been about an upcoming surprise visit from the French president's wife, Michelle Auriol. Most of us would need to spend time over the weekend making plans for the excursions through each of our departments, which would take place Monday afternoon. Hugh was asked to escort her around since, among his many other accomplishments, he spoke French. *As do I*, I thought, but decided not to dwell on the snub, reminding myself that he was related to the Crown, which probably made him a better guide in Mr. Gibbons' mind.

Due to all the activity, I wouldn't be able to return to the vaults until Tuesday, and I'd planned on working there on Monday. It was time to choose which eye miniatures might be included in the exhibition's fourteen. If any of them had to be repaired, I would need to see to that so we could make the deadline for photographing and writing the accompanying catalog text—something I couldn't delegate. The Keeper always wrote the copy. The printer's cutoff date was December 5th. I had four weeks, and then there was Sybil's party over the weekend, and I would need to cleanse her husband's cuff links before then. Time and secrecy were of the essence. I would simply need to go to the vault today and stay well past museum hours tonight.

As I traversed the hallways, I stopped to listen for footsteps, ensuring no one was following me. I'd been on edge since discovering my open window and disturbed desk. I didn't want to believe that Hugh would stoop so low to learn what I was including in the show, but I just didn't know.

As I reached the tunnel, I thought I heard footsteps. Uncertain, I backtracked, saw nothing, and proceeded. Hugh was still on my mind. As ambitious as he was, imagining him being that desperate or reckless was difficult.

Finally, I reached the vault. I forced myself to stop thinking about Hugh. I needed to get on with the matter at hand. After all, it would be too late for Hugh to subvert my efforts once I sent my catalog copy and photographs to the printer.

Reaching room 516 in the dusty north corner of the basement, I opened the padlock, quickly slipped inside, and shut the door behind me. I pulled out the trays of portraits, then unfolded the architectural plan I'd brought. My first task was to sketch out how I wanted my exhibition room laid out.

I'd indicated four glass cases against each of the gallery's three walls, where I would display the lovers' eyes. And I had over three dozen to choose from.

I went through the pieces carefully. Each was fascinating. Once upon a time, someone had commissioned that particular portrait to commemorate a love found or lost. We'd never know who each of these people were or who had wanted to hold their memory so close and tightly. We only knew each had been beloved. Time had, as it does all too often, erased the particulars. All we had left were these beautiful clues.

Which was exactly the point of many of the portraits. They were not identifiable. Lovers could exchange them and keep their identities unknown. The secret passions hidden in these intimate mementos were only recognizable to those for whom they were intended. It stirred my imagination as much now as it had the first time I'd seen the collection in Clio's office.

Every eye was exquisite in its own way, and it was difficult to make my choices, but after a half hour, I'd narrowed the dozens down to eighteen possibilities.

Now, I needed to ascertain which were in good condition, which needed restoration, or which were too fragile to include.

The overhead light in the cubbyhole was dim, but I'd brought a torch. Turning it on, I pointed it at the first pin, put my loupe up to my eye, and went stone by stone, checking for loose prongs and the quality of each gem.

Opening my notebook, I uncapped my pen, did a quick sketch, and next to it, wrote notes about the condition, what—if any—restoration it needed, and then gave it a grade. I wanted only *A*+ and *A* pieces in the exhibit if I could manage it.

As I wrote, the nib flowed across the paper, making a light scratching noise. It was a sound I had always loved, unique to my pen and the kind of notebooks I used. My father gave me my first Smythson diary when I was eight years old, along with a Parker pen and several bottles of different colored inks. I was instantly besotted with the lovely leather book and its pale blue, featherweight paper.

I was one of those children who would rather visit a stationery shop than a toy store. By the time I was twelve, I had a collection of fountain pens, various inks, different kinds of writing paper, several seals, and sticks of sealing wax in numerous colors. I wrote real letters to family and friends, as well as letters to characters I met in novels—long, elaborate missives, telling them how meeting them had influenced me.

My father suggested we should post them to each author's publisher. Which we did. When I was eleven, one of my letters, written to Peter Rabbit, addressed to Beatrix

Potter, was printed in the *Sunday Times* upon the publication of her newest book.

I didn't write letters like that anymore, but I still composed them in my mind whenever I finished a novel I especially loved. And all these years later, I still used a Parker pen—but now a Parker 51 with deep purple ink—in the Smythson notebooks my father continued to give me on every birthday.

As I made notes in the small, cramped room, I found myself adding fanciful comments about how the pieces affected me and thinking of what love story I might connect the eye to.

Several times, upon closer inspection, I realized that a piece appeared to be mourning jewelry and not a love token. Since pearls represented tears, a pearl frame or one escaping the eye meant the piece was a memorial. It might have also had a painted tear. If clouds were painted around the eye, that was symbolic that the sitter had gone to Heaven. An angel holding a palm frond in the background of one brooch signified the same.

I decided against including any of the memento mori pieces and put them in a separate tray. While lost love certainly fit the times we were in, I wanted my show to be an uplifting one. A celebration of love.

After an hour, I'd narrowed my choices to sixteen and was examining the last, my favorite.

As I had with all the others, I placed it on a tray by itself and gave myself up to the twilight blue eye surrounded by opals.

The painter of this piece had been a master of his medium. It truly appeared as though the man in the miniature was looking directly at me.

And that he knew me.

And that his knowing was full of passion, possession, and caring.

I turned away from the brooch, shaken once more by the sensation the gaze had caused when I'd first seen it. I looked back again, feeling as if he was not just looking at me but communicating his desire. Devouring me with his glance.

I'd reviewed and analyzed over forty eyes that afternoon, but the *twilight eye,* as I'd begun to think of it, was the only one that affected me in such a profound way.

Through my loupe, I scrutinized it. There were sixteen well-matched opals, at least a half carat each, arranged to make an oval frame around the small painting. Several of the stones were slightly crazed, which happens with opals because of their high water content. They are a mix of silica and water, created millions of years ago as water flowed through rock. The crazing didn't detract from the piece. Two of the opals were loose, though, and the brooch would need to go to the restoration department.

Next, I scanned the portrait itself. First quickly and then slower. Eyes were typically painted in watercolor or gouache upon ivory, vellum, or card stock and then covered with glass. This one was gouache and one of the most precisely rendered I'd seen. The blue eye with its fringe of dark eyelashes, an eyebrow arched just so, as if to suggest intent, and a few wild wisps of mahogany curls were all that could identify the sitter.

Most of the painters of these intimate portraits remained unknown. While leading miniaturists of each period painted the lovers' eyes, they rarely signed their work. Exceptions were the Georgian artists: Richard Cosway, George Engleheart, and Thomas Richmond the Elder. I was choosing the eyes for the emotions they evoked, not for their attribution, but was, of course, checking all the information I could gather on each.

I turned over the yellowed tag hanging from the twilight eye's pin bar and copied down its six-digit number. A file with the corresponding number in the archives would contain all the information the museum had about the piece: how and when it was obtained, authentication details, any records of if and when it had been repaired or restored, as well as when it had been displayed.

I planned to pull the files of all the pieces I was considering the following morning so I could get started writing the catalog.

I remained sitting, staring, stunned by the painting of the twilight eye. It was so evocative of the lover's feelings. His gaze moved me in a way that continued to surprise me.

I could almost hear him whispering his love to me.

I shivered.

I turned the brooch over and examined the back. I was surprised to see it was partially covered by some kind of paint or enamel in a violet color. It was slightly rubbed off in several places, revealing bright gold beneath it. That was odd. Usually, museum pieces were cleaned before they were put away.

Four hallmarks were visible in the area where the paint was rubbed off. A maker's mark, which I didn't recognize; the fineness symbol identifying the gold as twenty-two carat; the historical image of a leopard's head—the town mark for London; and lastly, the alphabetical letter denoting the date.

Each year was given a font, and the capital A on this piece represented 1868, which fit with the pin's tube-type hinge. Next, I examined the fastening mechanism. As befitting the time period, it was a bit crude, consisting of a simple bar pin that notched under a curved catch. I tried to unlatch it, but it seemed stuck. I tried again, to no avail. I examined it more closely—there was no apparent reason it would not open.

Carefully, I tried a third time, finally accomplishing the release. But I pricked my finger in the process, and a bright red bead of blood bloomed. The drop slid off and soaked into my navy skirt before I could catch it.

Another rose to the surface.

I put my finger into my mouth and sucked. I felt a little faint. Was that from the sight of the blood? I supposed it could have been, but I'd never felt that before. More likely, it was from working in such a confined space for so long.

I returned the tray I'd been working with to the shelf, gathered my notebook, torch, and pen, then left, locking the padlock behind me. Once I pulled the files and made certain which pieces I was including, I'd take preliminary photos so I could write them up and then get them all restored. Most just for cleaning, but two, including the twilight eye, needed slight repairs.

On my way out of the vault, I passed a wall clock and saw it read six fifteen p.m. Surely, I hadn't been down there for two hours. I checked my watch. The same time exactly. I hadn't realized how much time I'd spent studying the pieces. Well, if that was the time, there was no reason to return to my office now. It was chilly in the vaults, and I'd worn my coat to keep warm, so I thought I might as well leave.

But since I wasn't due at Sybil's until seven, I decided to say good night to my painting. I didn't know what drew me to *La Belle Dame sans Merci* that particular evening—not that it took much; I loved it so. Maybe because it was so near to closing time. I thought the museum would be quiet and I'd have the room to myself.

When I arrived, I noticed right away that there had been curatorial changes to the room. It had only been a week or two since I'd last visited, but there were different paintings on the east and north walls. A Victorian-looking bench had been moved in front of *La Belle Dame*. And it was occupied. A solitary man sat on it, staring at the Ashe Lloyd Lewis painting, his back to me.

I'd hoped I wouldn't have to share my painting with anyone else, but now that I was here, I wouldn't let him keep me from it.

I walked toward it, standing on the other side of the bench so I wouldn't be distracted by the museum-goer and focused on the work of art in front of me.

There was a poignancy to it that often overwhelmed me.

A longing in the lover's expression that reached out and spoke to me. As if the artist knew me and had a message for me.

I didn't realize I had started to cry until a low voice asked, "Might I offer you this?" A proffered handkerchief appeared. His voice was low and smooth, like melting chocolate. His hand looked strong, but there was a grace to his long fingers. A light dusting of fine, dark hair disappeared under his starched white shirt cuff.

I was embarrassed that a stranger had noticed my tears.

"No, thank you."

"Please," he insisted.

There was something in his voice, almost as if he was trying to communicate that it was imperative I take the handkerchief. That something monumental was at stake.

I surprised myself by taking the linen and dabbing my eyes with it.

"Thank you."

"Is there anything I can do to help?" he asked.

He was tall, towering more than a foot over me, though I was average height. Shining, dark brown hair fell in waves across his forehead and down his neck where it met his stiff white collar. His eyes were dark blue and oddly familiar. I tried not to stare, but he was looking at me as intently as I regarded him.

"No, no, I'm fine," I said. I wanted to ask him if we'd met before but didn't want to be rude if we had, and I'd forgotten.

I studied his face, trying to remember.

He had a well-groomed beard, a broad forehead, full lips, and expressive eyebrows. He was not classically good-looking, but he had a kind face, and there was a gentleness to his manner that put me at ease.

"I didn't mean to intrude, but when I saw you crying…" He shrugged, and that's when I noted that his clothes were a bit odd. He wore a tan-colored overcoat with a dark facing of silk on the roll that looked quite old-fashioned. As did his hat. I suddenly remembered that it was Halloween. He must be in costume. But why? We weren't having an event at the museum, were we? I hadn't heard about it, but it was certainly possible. We had to be. How else could this man be here after closing hours?

"Yes, well…" I tried to make my voice sound flippant. "It's just this painting. It always affects me that way, and…"

I didn't finish my sentence. Even if we had met in passing, he was still a stranger.

"It affects me, as well." He smiled.

I felt a flutter deep in my stomach at how his eyes smiled along with his mouth.

"But that's to be expected, I suppose," he continued. His voice made me want to keep listening to him. "What isn't expected is how it moves you. I'm flattered."

"Flattered?" I was confused.

He gestured to the painting. "Yes, by how the painting moves you."

"It's moved me since the first time I saw it. It's the passion between the woman and the knight… " I broke off. My comments were too intimate.

"Well, that pleases me."

Why would it please him? Unless…was he a new curator and responsible for the changes in the gallery? The different paintings and the bench?

I asked him if he was.

"No, I don't work here. I'm pleased because I never dreamed I'd see this painting in such an illustrious institution so soon after it was finished and witness someone being so touched by it."

"Soon? This was painted in 1864," I said as I mentally did the math. It had been painted eighty-three years ago.

"It's not long ago at all. When I finished it, I wasn't certain what its fate would be or if it would be received well."

"You didn't know what its fate would be?" I was thoroughly confused now.

The man held out his hand in greeting. "I'm so sorry. Of course, you must think I'm speaking gibberish. I should introduce myself."

As our fingers met, I heard a distant bell chiming. Had someone left a main door open? I'd never heard any of the nearby church bells this deep inside the museum. Was the London Oratory having an early concert?

Had he said his name? Had the bells obliterated it? How to ask him to repeat it without seeming rude? Maybe he hadn't said it yet. He hadn't let go of my hand, and I hadn't pulled away. Our gazes held, as well.

For the first time in a long while—no, for the first time that I could remember—I was trembling from someone's touch. I had never imagined such a feeling could come so easily or in such a public place, and certainly not with someone I didn't know.

How long did we stand there, looking at each other, my hand in his? A few seconds? Minutes? I had no sense of time passing or stopping. Finally, the man spoke again.

"I'm sorry, I was going to introduce myself, wasn't I?" he asked.

I nodded.

"I'm the artist," he said.

"An artist. Oh, of course," I said, thinking I should have known he was an artist from the scent in the air: the faint odors of turpentine and linseed oil along with an inviting, woodsy warmth.

"Yes, an artist," he said, "but specifically of this painting." He tipped his head back toward the wall, and a lock of his hair fell over his forehead.

Of this painting? Ashe Lloyd Lewis had died in 1868. I knew that from art history books. I knew that from our files in the museum. I knew it because I had seen his tombstone.

Clearly, this man was dressed as the artist for Halloween and staying in character.

"I don't blame you for wishing to have that kind of talent."

"I'm flattered yet again, but I am not impersonating him. I am Ashe Lloyd Lewis, and it is a pleasure to meet you," he said, waiting for me to tell him my name.

But for the moment, I couldn't speak.

CHAPTER 9

"And you are?" the man claiming to be Ashe Lloyd Lewis asked me.

"Jeannine Maycroft, Keeper of the Metalworks here at the museum." I spoke automatically while my mind tried to make sense of what this man had said.

Lewis had died at age forty, seventy-nine years ago. Had he not died in the fire, that would make him one hundred and nineteen years old now. No one could reach that age. Even if it was possible, the man standing before me was obviously no more than forty years old. There were some expression lines at the corners of his eyes and mouth, but otherwise, his skin was smooth. And his deep blue eyes, looking back at me so intently, were those of a man still full of vigor.

It must be that he was related to Ashe and named after him. It was not at all unusual for relatives to be named for their forefathers. But for a descendant to pretend to have painted the picture? That was bizarre. And then I remembered yet again that the day was October 31st. This had to be a Halloween prank of some kind. Perhaps one even set up for my benefit by someone who knew my affinity for the painting. But did anyone but Clio know that? And she was long gone.

"I hope more of my paintings wind up in these hallowed halls," the man mused. "I'm working on portraits now to pay the bills, but I hope to get back to larger compositions soon."

"So, you are following in your ancestor's footsteps?"

"I am. My grandfather and his father were all portrait painters. Originally from Sweden. Now, Mrs. Maycroft, please tell me why you were crying. I never intended for this painting to bring anyone to tears."

"Why are you pretending to have painted this work specifically? I'm sure your works are wonderful, as well, but I know everything about the artist and when this was done, and you couldn't be the one who painted it."

He looked offended. "Without meaning to be disrespectful, I don't see how you could know more about it than I do. I spent much time working on it. Even when I had other commissions that dragged me away, I kept coming back to *La Belle Dame*, knowing it wasn't yet perfect. Rossetti kept telling me that it was finished and that I was going to ruin it by overworking it. And then, when I finally decided it was done, he told me he'd been wrong, that I had improved it. He is the one who pushed me to submit it to the Summer Exhibition and who threw me a fete when it was admitted. I just didn't realize that it would be given to the museum so quickly. It's such an honor."

I was angry now. Yes, this man knew a lot about the time period, but that wasn't difficult. Many books had been written about the Pre-Raphaelites that he could have studied. I had read most of them.

"Mr.—"

"Ashe Lloyd Lewis," he repeated as if I had forgotten.

"I don't appreciate you making a fool of me."

"Mrs. Maycroft, please, believe me, the very last thing I am doing is making a fool of you. I'm simply telling you about the painting and about Mr. Rossetti taking such good care to encourage me since becoming his assistant and—"

"Lewis was one of a kind. Someone who accomplished so much in such a short time only before he was so—" I stopped myself. I didn't want to waste any more time with this man. My career was in jeopardy, and I had more than my share of problems to work out.

"It was nice to meet you." I couldn't bring myself to use the name he'd given me. It felt sacrilegious somehow. "The museum is closing now. I'm not sure why the guards didn't warn you to leave, but I'll find one now who will see you out." I didn't want to leave the building with him.

He looked bemused. "That's all right, Mrs. Maycroft. I'll see myself out," he said and then began walking toward the gallery's exit. He stopped at the door, then turned and looked back at me.

"Thank you."

"For?"

"Caring so much about my painting. I hope one day you can see some of the others."

"There are no others," I blurted out.

"Of course, there are," he said. "There are half a dozen paintings, and that many more drawings I'm currently preparing for a show."

"No, none of them survived."

"You must have me confused with some other artist. I'm quite sure of what I've created." He seemed to be the aggrieved one now. He nodded to me formally and then exited without another word, leaving me alone with my confusion and the painting that had given me so many hours of joy. I looked back at it but wasn't seeing the figures and colors or absorbing its atmosphere anymore. I was thinking about the man's deep blue eyes and the certainty that I'd seen them before.

CHAPTER 10

I didn't depart the museum right away. I was too disturbed. Not just because of the man pretending to be Ashe Lloyd Lewis but because I wanted to look at the other paintings that were new to me. It appeared the gallery had been changed more than I realized in the two weeks since I'd last visited. The museum often updated its galleries, but we were usually told about changes in the weekly memo sent to all the department heads.

While the Lewis painting was in the same place, half the other paintings that used to hang here had been replaced with others I knew less well, if at all. I studied each, wondering at the choices the Keeper had made. These weren't the best examples from the mid-1800s. Not in the slightest. I sat on the bench in front of *La Belle Dame sans Merci* and wondered why it wasn't upholstered. It wasn't nearly as comfortable as the old one. As I tried to find a more agreeable position, I felt my foot kick something. Looking down, I saw a leather-bound book on the floor, just underneath the bench.

I picked it up. It smelled of turpentine and—I sniffed— yes…linseed oil. The same scents as the man in the Halloween costume. He must have left it here. It was such a fine journal.

Perhaps he would have his name—his *real* name—and address inside.

Opening it, I read the following on the frontispiece.

A.L.L.
16 Cheyne Walk
London
"Fine art is that in which the hand, the head, and the heart of man go together."
John Ruskin

The initials were those of Ashe Lloyd Lewis. I flipped through and saw the most amazing sketches. Masterful, powerful pencil drawings. Moments quickly capturing the lines of a woman holding a jug, a man lifting a child into the air, a couple dancing. These certainly looked like Ashe Lloyd Lewis drawings. How did the man I'd met have a notebook that surely should be displayed in the museum? If this belonged to Lewis, it was a valuable and important artifact that could shed light on an enigmatic painter. Or was it not the artist's at all and just a clever prop for the man's costume? If so, was the address really his? Or had he researched where Lewis had lived? I knew Rossetti had lived at 16 Cheyne Walk, a blue plaque on the house identified it. And I'd recently met the woman who owned the home now. She'd brought me the Pre-Raphaelite jewelry prop. Was she the wife of the man I'd just met?

If the journal had once belonged to Ashe Lloyd Lewis, then the address made sense. It might be something else Mrs. Whitfield had found in the home. If the man who'd been masquerading as him carried it as a prop, he might not have anything to do with number 16 himself but had just been good at doing his research and thorough in creating the facsimile sketchbook.

Either way, I was due at Sybil's at 51 Cheyne Walk in an hour. I supposed it made sense for me to stop by number 16 and see if this book was their property.

Even if I had not been taught to pay attention to the unexpected, I would have thought this was one too many coincidences. I thought about what Grandmother Imogine had promised me. When I was surprised by what seemed impossible, I would be led where I needed to be if I followed its path. Not where I *wanted* to be, necessarily. But where I needed to be.

It had happened with meeting Clio when I was just a girl and led to me getting my job. Other than that, there hadn't been many other instances of magick in my life.

Yes. I'd drop off the notebook on my way to Sybil's.

I recalled the man's eyes and how he had looked at me. I remembered not the discomfort I'd felt at who he was pretending to be, but how I'd been drawn to him before I knew his name. And it seemed, he to me. It had felt as if time had slowed, and the elements had realigned to allow for the meeting. As if it had been planned somehow, and once we set eyes on each other, a key turned a lock, and its tumblers slipped into place.

If he was Mrs. Whitfield's husband, I had to laugh at my overactive imagination. I had read too many romance novels, watched too many love stories at the cinema, spent too many hours listening to my grandmother, Imogine, talk about the notion of soulmates. She never doubted that I'd meet mine one day. She used to tell me that time was circular and that I kept looking for love as if it were linear.

I never understood what she meant and when I'd ask her to explain, she'd winked at me in that way she did as if she had a secret she wasn't ready to share.

Oh, how I missed her. She'd died four years ago, not war related at all but of old age.

Truth be told, I was tired of missing people. Which was

part of the reason I didn't want to date and eschewed Sybil's pushing. Falling in love would mean risking more loss. And I'd had enough. In fact, I hoped the man in the gallery was Mr. Whitfield. Then there would be no temptation. No fantasy.

I left the gallery and proceeded through the quiet, darkened hallways of the museum toward the exit.

After hours, the museum's atmosphere was always more weighed down with history. As much as I was at home in this building during the day, it was different at night, and I preferred it. Night was not a time to inspect arts and crafts and marvel at the talent it took to create them. It was a time to simply be thankful for the fact of the museum. To take solace in the civility of saving and protecting objects of beauty, importance, and curiosity. To marvel at the history entombed within these walls.

I could have lingered in the great hall for hours but hurried out. There was a sign I needed to follow.

It was pouring outside, but there were always staff umbrellas stashed in a hidden closet by the entrance. A custom that had begun in the 1850s when the director at the time hadn't wanted to walk through the miles of hallways to return to his office to get one.

Outside, the visibility with the fog and the rain made it difficult to see more than a few feet in front of me. From Exhibition Road, it was typically a twenty-minute walk to Sybil's. I'd done it dozens of times, but the rain was unrelenting, and the fog was so heavy I was loath to walk. Except, given the weather, I knew my chances of finding a taxi were slight. Maybe I'd find one along the way. So, I started off on foot. The streets were eerily empty, but given the storm, I wasn't surprised. It was that hour when most people had already gone home from work but were not yet out for the evening. There would normally be more revelers out on Halloween, but given the weather, that activity would be delayed.

As I continued on, hunched under my umbrella, the atmosphere reminded me of nights during the war when we'd been confined to our cellars and basements or the underground and then how, right after the air raid ended, we'd emerge to empty streets to inspect the damage the German's had wrought.

As I turned the next corner onto Thurloe Place, I became aware of a stench. Rotten eggs? Offal? A sewer must have backed up somewhere nearby. I gagged from the odor.

Hurrying on, I passed a couple in costume, also huddled under umbrellas. He was in a top hat and tails, and she wore a Victorian evening dress. I didn't envy them their cumbersome costumes in this weather.

I was turning right on Fulham Road a few minutes later when I suddenly saw the most unusual sight of a horse and carriage coming toward me. Because of the fog, I hadn't seen it at all until it was almost right on top of me. I jumped back to avoid it. As it rumbled by, I watched in astonishment—my heart beating heavily—as I realized how close a call it had been. A *horse and carriage*. Someone had really gone all out for Halloween.

Continuing on, the streets remained relatively empty. On Old Church Street, I saw yet another costumed family as disheveled as I was, fighting the storm without umbrellas.

I finally reached Cheyne Walk and headed to number 16. I was just at the gate when my heel slid on a slippery patch of stone, and I tripped. As I landed, I felt my ankle twist violently.

The impact knocked the breath out of me. As the shock wore off, and I tried to calm my labored breathing, I realized I was soaked through now. Damn. I'd arrive at Sybil's a mess. I looked at my right foot. Already swelling. Of course, it had to be the same ankle I'd broken during the war, which had never fully healed. I still got twinges. And now, I'd fallen on it again.

Pain radiated up my leg. The rain continued to pelt down on me.

I needed to move, but I couldn't figure out how. Going on the last time I'd injured this foot, I didn't think I'd be able to stand.

"Are you all right? Let me help," a woman cried out. She was carrying an umbrella, running down number 16's steps and through the gate. For a moment, I was so confused—she was dressed so oddly. Then I remembered. Halloween.

"I should be fine," I said and tried to rise, but even the smallest pressure on my foot was agony, and I collapsed back down. This was the worst time to have hurt myself. "I just need a second."

"You are sitting in a puddle and drenched. And in the dark, no less. You can't be out alone, not even here. Let me help you up."

"Did something happen here?" It wasn't at all unusual for me to be out alone at dusk or later, and this was one of the better neighborhoods in London, yet this woman seemed so concerned.

"Well, yes. You've fallen. I was closing the drapes when I saw you." She pointed behind her to a building. "Your costume caught my attention. One second you were there, and the next you weren't. We can do all the talking you want inside." The woman grabbed my arm. "Let's get you up."

Tentatively, I put a tiny bit of pressure on my foot, but it immediately buckled beneath me again. "I'll grab you and lift. Put your foot behind you, don't put it down."

The woman's fingers gripped my upper arm tightly and held me upright.

"Lean on me and hop," she said as she led me toward the house.

"I don't want you to go to any trouble. I'm due at a friend's house just down the street. I can hobble."

She looked at me with raised eyebrows. "Hobble? I don't

think so. You couldn't put the tiniest bit of pressure on your foot just now."

"I'll use my umbrella as a cane."

"All right, let's see you do that," she said. "I won't let you go without being certain you are all right. Especially at night, in a storm no less."

I positioned the umbrella and put my foot down. The pain shot up through my leg and I began to tilt, but she'd been ready and grabbed hold of me again.

"I don't think you'll be hobbling anywhere but inside with me so we can tend to your injury." She reached down and picked up my pocketbook, tucking it under her arm. "You won't want to be leaving this on the street. Now, let's get inside so I can fix you up."

"What an imposition. I'm so sorry." I despised needing help. "I hate to bother Mrs. Whitfield."

"You're not making much sense, but no matter," she said as she repositioned herself to be a crutch. "Just keep your foot up behind you and hop on your good one. We'll go as slow as you need."

The woman was shorter and rounder than I was but strong. She had a kind smile and smelled of butter and sugar.

"Ready?" she asked.

"Yes."

We took a first step—or hop, as it were. Then a second. It was arduous, but we were slowly moving forward. To take my mind off the pain, I focused on the details of the house we were headed toward. We passed through a wrought iron gate and ascended eight steps leading to a central bay.

I was out of breath and perspiring by the time we reached the front door. Despite my pain, I noticed the door knocker was a strange medieval dragon that reminded me of carvings at my cousin's home in Paris. My helper navigated me through the doorjamb, and we entered number 16.

From the front hall, we made a left into a sitting room

and toward a couch. I took in what was one of the strangest rooms I'd ever seen. On the walls were mirrors of every size and design; my disheveled form reflected back at me what seemed to be hundreds of times. Where there were no mirrors, there were drawings and paintings.

My savior helped me onto the couch.

I let out a deep sigh.

"Now, let's just elevate your ankle." She placed a cushion at the end of the sofa.

I held my breath, knowing that lifting and lowering my leg would hurt. And it did.

"There now, the hardest part is done. You just rest here, and I'll get you a blanket, compresses, and a tincture for the pain."

I closed my eyes as the throbbing continued. I heard a clock chime somewhere in another room and counted to seven. I needed to call Sybil and tell her I would be late for helping her with the flowers, if I made it at all.

The pain was terrible, and I opened my eyes. If I concentrated on my surroundings, maybe I could forget about it for a bit.

Opposite me was a paneled Chinese black lacquer mantelpiece with birds, animals, flowers, and fruit carved in gold relief. Flanking a finely wrought brass grate and matching irons and a fender were blue Dutch tiles. The colors were repeated in a corner china cupboard, filled with Spodeware.

The woman returned with a tray holding an old-fashioned green bottle, a silver spoon, a china bowl of water, and cloths.

"I'll see to your ankle now."

"Before you do," I asked, "could I use the telephone?"

"The tele-phone?" she pronounced it oddly.

"Yes. I know you're being so kind in helping, but before we get started, I would like to tell my friend that I won't be at her house in time and see if she could perhaps send her driver around."

"You can send a note. I'll ask the boy to take it round."

"But calling would be so much less trouble."

"Calling? You can't call on her no—you can't manage even a few steps."

"I meant telephoning would be so much easier."

"I'm not at all sure what you're talking about, but let's get some of this medicine in you and this cold compress on your foot. Then we can work out the note."

She studied my foot. "Oh, my. It is more swollen than I thought. I think I'm going to need to take off your shoe."

I nodded. I was wearing a stacked heel, lace-up Oxford in black leather. She unlaced it gingerly and then examined it carefully as she pulled it off.

I held my breath against the pain.

"What an usual heel. And so high, too," she said. "No wonder you tripped."

I looked down at her feet but couldn't see her footwear under her long skirts.

She wrapped my ankle in a cool, wet cloth and then lowered it back onto the cushion.

"Now for the tincture." She picked up the bottle. On the label was a drawing of an anchor with a nautical rope and the words: *The Anchor Brand.* Below that: *Laudanum.*

I knew what it was—a form of opium used as a painkiller in Victorian times. I'd read many biographies of artists and writers who had been addicted to it. And I had no intention of taking it, no matter how bad my pain.

"I appreciate that," I said, nodding my head at the bottle, "but I get regular headaches and have some powder in my pocketbook—" I looked around for it.

The woman picked it up and gave it to me. I searched in it and pulled out the packet. "If you could just get me a glass of water?"

She was gone but a minute and returned with another tray, on it a crystal glass, a carafe of water, and a silver spoon.

I mixed the draught and drank it down. I handed the glass back to her and thanked her.

"Are you comfortable?"

"Yes, this is so kind, really. For you to bring a stranger into your home, especially when you have a party tonight."

She frowned. "A party? No. And home? Oh, it's not mine." She laughed.

"Oh, I thought you must be part of Mrs. Whitfield's family."

"Mrs. Whitfield?"

"Yes, I was under the impression she lived here."

"I'm Fanny Cornforth. I do some modeling and help keep house for the owner, Mr. Rossetti."

"Mr. Rossetti?" I asked.

"The artist, yes. Perhaps you've heard of him?"

"Of course, I have. I work at the Victoria and Albert Museum and—"

"You work where?"

"At the museum, I'm the Keeper of the Metalworks."

She was about to ask me something else when I heard a door close. Footsteps sounded, and then a shadow crossed the room.

"Fanny? Is everything all right? The gate and the door were left open," a man's voice called out.

"We had a mishap on the street. This is"—she looked at me and smiled—"I don't believe I asked your name."

By now, the man had walked into the sitting room and was staring at me with surprise.

"It's Mrs. Maycroft, isn't it?" the man who called himself Ashe Lloyd Lewis said as he approached. "We've met." He turned to Miss Cornforth and then back to me. "But how are you here?" he asked, clearly confused.

I reached for my pocketbook again, opened it, and pulled out his notebook. "You left this at the museum. As I was calling on a friend nearby, I thought I'd drop it off. But I seem to have tripped at your front gate. Miss Cornforth was kind enough to bring me inside."

"Let me get you some tea, Mrs. Maycroft," she said.

"Would you like tea?" the man asked. "Or would you prefer brandy or sherry? You must be in some shock."

"Actually, brandy would be lovely," I said.

"I'll get it," he said. "Meanwhile, Fanny, could you see to the fire? It's a bit chilly in here."

He went off to get the drinks while Miss Cornforth fussed at the fireplace, adding a log and poking at the embers.

I watched her work with fascination. I had read about the model named Fanny Cornforth. I knew the names of all the Pre-Raphaelite Brotherhood's favorite models. And she did look similar to the woman in the paintings, but she could have been wearing a wig to replicate the red hair the group so admired. Yes, with a wig styled that way and some artful makeup, she would certainly have looked enough like the woman in the paintings.

What had I stumbled upon? A living tableau of the 1860s set up as some elaborate masquerade for a Halloween party?

I looked around the room. Everything was period perfect, including the furnishings. Surely, they had not been recreated for tonight. But no, the other way around. The people who owned this house had chosen these characters and time period for the party since the house suggested them.

My eyes took in the décor with delight, the Arts and Crafts examples were exemplary. The dark green walls were covered with paintings and drawings from the period and were so well done I would have guessed they were originals if I hadn't seen half of them in museums. All done by master painters of The Brotherhood, I recognized several Gabriel Dante Rossettis, Hunts, and Millias. Four were done in a style that suggested Ashe Lloyd Lewis had painted them, even though I'd never seen any of them before.

I wanted to get up and study them closer, but even if I

could have, the light wasn't bright enough. That's when I noticed that, in addition to all the other perfect touches, there were no electric lights in the room. Instead, there were gas lamps and a profusion of candelabras and candlesticks.

Why, I wondered, would anyone re-create a Victorian tableau to this extent?

"Miss Cornforth?" I asked.

She turned. "Fanny, please. Can I get you something?"

"No, I had a question. Did I hear you correctly before that this is Mr. Rossetti's home?"

"Yes. Mr. Dante Gabriel Rossetti lives here. Along with his assistant, Mr. Lewis. There are some other people who come and go. The poet, Mr. Swinburne, often stays for quite a while."

"You mean Rossetti lived here when he was alive."

"Was alive? He is very much alive, Mrs. Maycroft. He left not a half hour ago for an engagement."

I was looking beyond her to the right of the fireplace, staring at a painting I knew was in the Tate Museum. *The Annunciation.* And to its left another piece I recognized. *The Blue Closet.*

I knew that Henry Tate had been a patron and collector of Pre-Raphaelite artists and donated sixty-five of his paintings to the National Gallery, including the two I was staring at, both of which had been installed in the museum that carried his name in 1897.

They were there. I had visited them often.

"Here you go." Mr. Lewis returned and handed me a cut crystal balloon. He had brought one for himself as well, and sat opposite me in a wingback chair.

"To your recovery," he said and lifted his glass to me. I tipped mine back and took a sip. It burned my throat, but a welcome warmth followed.

"I owe you a debt of gratitude for returning my notebook, Mrs. Maycroft, but I am so sorry your kindness has resulted in your injuring yourself."

"You're welcome. It's all my fault. The rain made the sidewalk slippery, and I wasn't watching. "

"Then it's the rain's fault, not yours." He smiled.

I had the same reaction to him I'd had in the museum. There was little or no subtext to his words, but I felt another conversation going on between us. One made of sensations, that same dramatic pull I'd felt before, and an intensity of glances that spoke volumes. It was an attraction that felt like combustion. I looked away from him to the fireplace. The flames seemed less fiery than what passed between our eyes.

"Is Mr. Maycroft at home waiting for you? We can send a note."

"No, I'm a widow," I said.

"I am so sorry," he replied.

I nodded. "Thank you. As for the note, I asked Miss Cornforth if I might use the telephone to let my friend Sybil know I'm here, so she could have someone come get me. Maybe you could help me do that?"

"The telephone?" Mr. Lewis gave me the same confused expression the housekeeper had. "I'm afraid I don't know what you mean."

"Damn it all." Another man's voice rang out. "There was a fire in the kitchen at my brother's house, and rather than—" He walked into the room and took in the sight.

"Who is this?" he asked. "And how did you get hurt?"

"Gabriel, this is Mrs. Maycroft, she works at the Victoria and Albert," Mr. Lewis said to the newcomer. "She tripped on our sidewalk."

I stared at a man I'd seen before in many photographs. A balding male with dark, brooding eyes and a very high forehead. Despite him being in his sixties, there was a rakish air about him.

The man who called himself Ashe Lloyd Lewis turned to me. "And this, Mrs. Maycroft, is the esteemed artist and poet,

Dante Gabriel Rossetti."

The fire was warm, and the brandy had gone straight to my head. The man whom I recognized from photographs we had at the museum, Mr. Rossetti, reached out his hand to me. And then my world went dark.

CHAPTER 11

When I opened my eyes, I found myself looking up into familiar blue ones.

"I didn't think I'd find you," I said.

I realized I'd just spoken out loud what I'd been dreaming. In my foggy fantasy, I was lost in an overgrown forest not unlike Highgate and trying to find him.

"You'll be feeling all right in a moment or two," the man said, giving me a smile brighter than the candlelight and warmer than the fire. I felt it deep inside. I had a sudden desire to reach out, take his hand, and tell him that, of course, I felt all right now that we had found each other. What was I thinking? I shook my head as if I could make sense of the nonsense in my mind. This was not the someone I had been searching for; this was the annoying man pretending to be Ashe Lloyd Lewis.

"I'm sorry, I have no idea what I'm saying. Did I fall asleep?" I was embarrassed.

"You fainted. I gave you some smelling salts to revive you," he said. "Would you like to sit up? Let me help you."

He took my arm, and I had the same reaction I'd had earlier—it was as if I'd touched a shoddy electrical wire.

I saw from his face that he had felt it, too.

I sat up, reached for the brandy, and took a sip. And then another.

"I have quite a few questions," I said finally.

"And I hope I have satisfactory answers."

"The first is very simple. You believe you really are the painter, Ashe Lloyd Lewis?"

"I don't *believe* I am. I know I am. But you clearly don't believe me. Is there a reason for your doubt?"

"The same man who was born in..." I pictured the tombstone in Highgate. "1828?"

"The same."

"And you live here in this house with Dante Gabriel Rossetti?"

"I do. I am his current assistant, and in exchange, I have a room and a studio in the garden."

"Do you have a copy of today's newspaper?" I asked.

"A newspaper? Right now?" He looked at me strangely.

"Yes, please."

He left the room and returned a few moments later holding *The Times*.

He handed it to me, and I looked at the date on the banner.

Thursday, October 31, 1867.

I read it once and then again.

"So, what is going on here is an elaborate Halloween party pretending it's 1867—from your costumes to the paper."

"Costumes? There's no Halloween party here tonight. I didn't even realize today was Halloween. And there's no pretense. It is 1867. Why would you think it wasn't, Mrs. Maycroft?"

I took another sip of the brandy. I looked back down at the newspaper in my hand and then around the room again. This time, I looked for outlets on the wall down by the baseboards but saw none. First, Fanny, and then Mr. Lewis seemed not to know what a telephone was.

"It really is 1867," he repeated.

"And the man who came in before really was Dante Gabriel Rossetti?"

Mr. Lewis nodded.

In my heart, I had known it was Rossetti. I had studied all of his works. I'd seen photographs and paintings of him. And I knew Fanny Cornforth from Rossetti's paintings. I thought about the walk to number 16. How everyone I'd seen had been dressed in Victorian garb. Halloween was a children's holiday. Certainly, some people dressed up, but they wouldn't have all been dressed in costumes from the same era.

I tried thinking back to when I'd started to notice the oddities. It was in the museum. When I'd come out of the vaults after working with the lovers' eyes and had gone to look at the *La Belle Dame* painting. The gallery had been arranged differently from how I knew it.

I shut my eyes.

This was all impossible.

It could not be 1867.

My father was an avid science fiction reader and had introduced me to the genre. We'd read all the best books together and had long discussions about them. We both especially liked time-travel stories. Among our favorites were *A Christmas Carol* by Dickens, *A Connecticut Yankee in King Arthur's Court* by Mark Twain, *The Time Machine* by H.G. Wells, and E. Nesbit's *The Story of the Amulet*.

He'd even introduced me to ancient texts having to do with the subject. One of the first known examples of time travel in literature appears in the *Mahabharata*, an ancient Sanskrit epic poem compiled around 400 BC. And a story from the first century BCE about a Jewish miracle worker who goes to sleep under a carob sapling only to awaken seventy years later to find the tree fully mature and fruitful.

I'd even read two time-travel tales written by Pre-

Raphaelites: *A Dream of John Ball*, written and illustrated by William Morris, and a disturbing short story by Rossetti himself called *St. Agnes of Intercession*, which he started to write in 1850 but remained unfinished at his death. I'd read it at university and believed it to be more a story of reincarnation—a subject that fascinated Rossetti—than time travel. Still, either was possible since he never completed it. Hugh and I had even discussed it once.

In the tale, an artist falls in love with a woman while painting her portrait and then is told by a friend that the woman in his painting resembles the woman in a fifteenth-century work of art by a painter named Bucciuolo Angiolieri.

The artist travels to Italy, tracks down the older portrait, and sees for himself that the two women are, in fact, identical despite having been painted over four hundred years apart.

Had he known another incarnation of this woman in a previous life and recognized her across the centuries when he met Mary Arden? Or had he traveled back in time, fallen in love with her, and then found someone who looked so like her he'd become enamored again?

Since the story remained incomplete, its meaning remained a mystery. Nevertheless, it had impressed and aroused my curiosity enough at Oxford that I'd never forgotten it.

Now, being in the sitting room of Rossetti's house on Cheyne Walk, having met a man who appeared to be the owner himself, a woman who was well known to be his model, and an up-and-coming artist, there were only two explanations.

One, despite what the man claiming to be Ashe Lloyd Lewis had said, this was a phenomenal theater piece. Or two, these people were indeed living in 1867, and I had somehow traveled back eighty years.

"Mrs. Maycroft, you've lost all your color. Here, please, take another sip of the brandy. Perhaps I should ask Fanny to fetch the doctor and—"

"No, no, that's not necessary. I think I'm just in shock."

"Are you sure you are all right?"

"I'm not really sure of anything except that I don't need a doctor."

"Perhaps you hit your head when you fell?"

"I don't think so. I don't feel any pain."

"Then why have you just turned white as a sheet?"

"Well, you are sure to question my sanity when I tell you this, but before you do, remember that I have been questioning yours since we met. When I walked into the gallery at the V&A earlier to look at—"

"The V&A?" he interrupted

"The museum where we met."

"The South Kensington Museum," he said.

I remembered that the museum had not been named for the queen and her consort until 1899.

"Yes. When I walked into the gallery at the South Kensington Museum to look at…"—I hesitated but then said it—"your painting, it was October 31…"

He nodded.

"In the year 1947. I live in London in the year 1947."

"Even though you don't remember, you *must* have banged your head when you fell."

"I know that's what you think. What you need to think. That I've lost my mind. But I haven't. I live in 1947. That's why I've been acting the way I have. I haven't believed you any more than you believe me now, but it's true. I was born in 1910. I work at the museum, now called the Victoria and Albert Museum, as the Keeper of the Metalworks. I studied history and specialized in the history of art at uni. I've lived through two World Wars you have never even heard of."

He smiled. "And you expect me to believe that you somehow traveled back in time to today?"

"I don't expect you to believe me. I'm not even sure *I*

believe what I am saying. But if you are truly who you say you are, if this house is owned by Mr. Rossetti, and it is indeed 1867, then there is simply no other explanation."

"I'm starting to wonder if you have escaped from a hospital for the disturbed." He smiled. "Except other than this preposterous theory, you seem completely sane."

He appeared utterly serious, and I had a horrible thought that he might take me to one of the infamous Victorian sanatoriums I'd read about and leave me there. I would be forever lost if I had traveled through some warp in time.

I had to leave. Find help. Protect myself. Return to my time.

"I've bothered you enough—" I started to stand, but my ankle buckled under me.

Ashe Lloyd Lewis caught me.

"What are you doing?" he asked.

"I can't let you take me to a hospital for the insane." I struggled to right myself.

"I would never do that to you."

He said it in such a curious way—with a caring voice that made no sense for a man speaking to a stranger.

I'd heard it, and so did he.

"I don't know why you should, but please trust me. I will do everything I can to help you recover from whatever strange waking dream you are having, but you know there's no such thing as time travel."

"If I can prove it, will you believe me?"

"If you can prove it, I'll have to, won't I?"

I reached for my pocketbook and brought it onto my lap. I rifled through it and found what I was looking for—my most recent train ticket receipt. I handed it to him.

"Look at the date, please."

He stared at the piece of paper in his hand.

"And look at this," I said. I had found something else in my voluminous bag, a program from a play I'd seen at the

Palace Theater—one as preposterous as what was happening to me now, *Finian's Rainbow*. It even had my ticket stub inside.

"Well, this does say 1947," he whispered, raising his head to meet my eyes. "Surely, this is some kind of joke prepared for me. Some trick of having the program printed up. Who put you up to this? Rossetti? Between the seances and his beliefs in reincarnation that he's always talking about, this is quite a stunt."

All at once, my bizarre circumstances and the pain in my foot suddenly felt like too much. Tears filled my eyes.

He pulled out a handkerchief and handed it to me. "Keep this up, and I'll run out of handkerchiefs."

I laughed and sobbed at the same time.

"We'll figure this out," he said reassuringly, and even though I had no reason to trust him, I did.

"If this is a trick of Rossetti's, I like the shorter skirts he deemed to be the fashion of the future," he said with a twinkle in his eye. "Do you think…?" He hesitated. "I know this is presumptuous, but I would love to sketch you when you are up to it. Would you allow me?" he asked.

To have Ashe Lloyd Lewis sketch me? What an amazing thought. "Of course. I'd be honored."

"He chose you well if it is a trick. You have the look all of us clamor for, with your full lips, strong jaw, and your hair…the color is the holy grail among our set."

I felt myself blush.

"You're a true Pre-Raf model," he said.

"Yes, you all did prefer redheads, didn't you?"

We were both quiet for a moment, then he added, "It's so strange to hear you talk about Rossetti and our friends in the past tense."

"It is the past. And I promise you, I am no more a joke planned by Mr. Rossetti to trick you than you are one planned for me."

"So, you believe we didn't have a newspaper printed with

a false date on it and set up the house to resemble what it might have looked like in 1867? And you did not have a theater program and train ticket printed with those dates on them for me? That only means one impossible thing."

"I'm not sure I can believe in the impossible."

He nodded. "Nor can I."

"I'd like to go home," I said, suddenly teary again.

"I wish I could make that happen for you," he said.

We sat in silence. As strange as everything was, the unreality of my situation was oddly mitigated by the man beside me. For no rational reason, I sensed that whatever might happen, he would protect me. Feeling safe wasn't something I was used to.

Since I could remember, I'd always felt as if the bottom of my world was about to fall away, and I'd be lost.

Now, the bottom *had* fallen away, but I felt as if I'd been found.

CHAPTER 12

It was time for dinner, and I managed to hobble to the dining room with Ashe's help—he insisted I use his first name. I told him to use mine, as well.

There were five of us around the table. In addition to Rossetti and Fanny, another painter was present: George Frederic Watts. His presence stunned me—if I could be any more stunned. I knew his work well. He had been associated with the Pre-Raphaelites until the 1870s, when he became interested in comparative religion and focused on exploring life's tentative and transitory qualities.

I felt as if I was drunk, even after just those few sips of brandy. How was it possible that I was eating cottage pie with these men and one of their muses? What could Sybil possibly think since I hadn't shown to help her with the flowers and the cuff links? Fanny had agreed to send a note, but when the boy got to number 51, the woman who lived there had said she'd never heard of Sybil.

Of course, she hadn't.

Surprisingly, I was hungry, and the food was good. Creamy potatoes and a savory lamb filling with carrots and peas. The red wine matched perfectly and went down a little too easily. Between my swollen ankle—which, thank goodness, had stopped throbbing—and the bizarre situation, eating and drinking seemed so normal.

The conversation centered around an issue the men had clearly discussed often. Should art focus on the serious problems facing people in their industrial age—poverty, hunger, and disease—or instead offer a respite and give viewers an escape into beauty?

I listened, fascinated, forgetting my problems for a while, caught up in their thoughts and arguments. Being given this insight into a world I'd only read about was better than any lecture I'd attended at university.

"My goal is to sell enough paintings so that I always have enough money to give to those living in poverty," Watts said.

"Charity is admirable, George. I'm not arguing that. It's how you depict the squalor of reality in your paintings that gives me such pause," Rossetti countered.

"How else can we ensure that the terrible conditions so many people are enduring are brought to light *but* by using our paintings to illustrate the issues?"

After dinner, Rossetti and Watts retired to smoke. Ashe said he'd join them once he helped me upstairs.

I was surprised when he lifted and carried me up the center staircase. I'd expected him to suggest I lean on him and hop. While this method of transportation was much easier, it made me uneasy. I was too aware of his arms underneath me, of the heat generated where they met my body and the pressure I felt through my clothes. Granted, a man had not held me since my husband—and Samuel had been at war without leave for almost two years before he was killed. I'd forgotten what contact felt like. How comforting it could be, and at the same time, how exciting to experience the sensuality of touch.

Ashe carried me to a guest bedroom wallpapered with a

William Morris pattern I was familiar with, pimpernel—a study in sage, bay-leaf green, and gold. I admired it, and Ashe was surprised I knew its name and history.

"While this period in art isn't all that popular now, I've always been drawn to and studied it."

"Why aren't we all that popular?"

"Styles come and go, and Victorian and Arts and Crafts design hasn't been rediscovered yet. The war—" I shook my head.

"I don't actually know how wise it is of me to tell you too much about my present." Everything seemed impossible. "This really is 1867, isn't it?" I asked him.

"It is, and I'm sorry about how troubled you are by that. But I'm glad we're the ones who found you. There are a lot of unsavory characters out there that would take advantage." He glanced at my watch and then the pearls around my neck. "Robbing you blind would be the least of it…a woman with your countenance."

I smiled. "Thank you for the compliment, but is it really that dangerous? Fanny said something like that, as well."

"It is. Sadly."

"I read something about the crime during this period, but I didn't think it was so widespread that I wouldn't be safe in Chelsea."

"A woman alone isn't safe anywhere."

"That's so hard to reconcile with the London I know." I looked around. I felt the bed under my fingers. I examined the face of the man sitting in the chair by the desk.

"I wonder if I'm actually awake. Maybe I fell down at work, hurt my head, and am actually hallucinating while lying in a gallery at the V&A. Perhaps I will be discovered hurt or even dead in the morning."

"I can assure you that you are awake, and this is not a hallucination. But if it assuages you at all, I'm equally perplexed. I admit that even with your clothes, the tickets, and the theater bill, I've wondered if you aren't quite mad and making up everything you are telling me."

"What have you decided?"

"Your eyes are not mad, Jeannine. There is nothing in them but curiosity, intelligence, and passion."

"You've made a study of reading eyes?"

"I have, actually. I've been hired by quite a few clients to paint portraits of their loved one's eyes."

I sat forward, excited, the pain in my foot ignored, my strange circumstances forgotten for the moment.

"Lovers' eyes? You have? I'm doing a Valentine's Day exhibit for the museum and came across a vault of jewelry that features eye portraits. Very few people know much about them. The museum hasn't displayed them for years, and I just started researching them."

"I can tell you whatever you need to know. My grandfather painted them, as well. They were popular in his time and have once again become so now. I have at least half a dozen commissions coming up in the next few months."

I sat back against the pillows, amazed by Ashe's revelation.

Fanny came into the room carrying a glass of cloudy liquid on a tray. She had a nightdress draped over her arm.

"You can go now, Ashe. I need to help Mrs. Maycroft undress for bed."

Ashe stood. He seemed hesitant and lingered. "I will bid you good night, Jeannine," he said finally. Then he walked over to me, took my hand, and brought it to his lips. "I hope that despite the strangeness of this evening and the situation you find yourself in, you sleep comfortably. Tomorrow, we will do what we can to straighten this out and make plans to restore you to your time—after I've done those sketches, if that's all right?"

I wanted to protest that nothing mattered as much as me getting back to 1947, yet at the same time, I wanted to know more about where I was. I wanted to talk to Rossetti about his work. I wanted to see his studio. I wanted to speak with other members of the Brotherhood. And I wanted to sit for Ashe and have him look at me again like he had this evening.

Despite my bizarre and inexplicable situation, I managed to fall asleep thanks to what Fanny called a *sleeping draught,* which I discovered later contained laudanum.

I woke to rain pelting the window and, for a few moments, thought of the odd dream I'd had. That I'd somehow wound up in a stranger's house in Cheyne Walk inhabited by artists I had admired and studied for years.

And then I opened my eyes and felt the shock anew. I wasn't home. My ankle throbbed. I had tripped on the street and was brought into this house. I'd met Ashe Lloyd Lewis, Dante Gabriel Rossetti, and one of his muses.

Was I now living one of those fanciful stories my father and I used to argue about? Was time travel possible? Was time circular? He and I had debated the meaning of concepts put forth by great thinkers of the time, but I'd never thought I'd experience them.

"What is eternal is circular, and what is circular is eternal." – *Aristotle*

"There is Eternity, whence flowed Time, as from a river, into the world." –Plutarch

"What then is time? If no one asks me, I know; if I want to explain it to someone, I do not know." –St. Augustine

During the war, when London was being bombed, when I was sitting in shelters with strangers, and we were all wondering what we would find when the air raid was over, there were moments when it seemed that reality was impossible. That we couldn't have gone from the complacent lives we had been living to what was happening. I had known what nervousness was before the war, but not in the way I learned about it during. I had never been a calm child or an easygoing adult, but the fear of not knowing what might happen next made me overly anxious. It was the lack of control. Many of us felt it. Suffered because of it. And justly so. We were living under siege, with no idea when the nightmare might start again. I endured and taught myself to disappear by escaping into reading ancient history. By focusing on a piece of art I had studied. Or a pyramid I'd visited. I used the expanse of history and the survival of objects to refocus my thoughts. To prove to myself that things endured. That they had strength. If only I could find some within myself.

And now, in Cheyne Walk, a mere fifteen minutes and eighty years away from my life, I desperately wanted to talk to my father, tell him what was happening, and get his opinion on what had befallen me. But he was...my father had not even been born yet.

I stared out the bedroom window down into the garden. Rain was still pelting down.

Who could I go to for help? The Daughters of La Lune had access to arcane and alchemical knowledge. Each could delve into the mysteries that would frighten some people and were met with total disbelief in others.

Our story began with the tale of the Witch of Painted Sorrows, a sixteenth-century courtesan, and continued down through the ages via her female descendants. I started doing the math of who could be living in 1867.

My great-grandmother Eva Verlaine would be alive. She was another famous courtesan they called L'Incendie because of her fiery red hair and flashing topaz eyes—traits I'd inherited. But if I remembered correctly, she'd eschewed the La Lune legacy. What about her children?

Eva had two illegitimate children. My aunt Sandrine Duplessi's father, who wouldn't be of any help if he was alive since males could only pass on the gift; they had no magick themselves, and so wouldn't have access to the secret knowledge I needed.

The other child was my grandmother Imogine, born in 1845, when Eva was just seventeen and embarking on what would become an infamous career. She kept the pregnancy a secret until she could hide it no longer and then went to visit her sister, Adeline, who had moved to England and lived in London.

After Eva gave birth, she left my grandmother to be raised by Adeline, a healer and herbalist with a private practice, using the herbs and plants to create potions said to be magickal.

Imogine followed in her aunt's footsteps, which led her to meet and marry Walter North, a botanist at the famed Chelsea Psychic Garden, created in 1673 by the Worshipful Society of Apothecaries.

Imogine worked there alongside her husband, even though women weren't officially employed by the gardens until 1877. My grandparents had one daughter—my mother—and three sons.

I used to spend a lot of time with my grandparents, especially when my father was on site in Egypt. I loved tending their beloved garden with them and receiving lessons on the plants and how to mix remedies and salves to do all kinds of things, from curing headaches to increasing appetites.

Grandmother Imogine tried to teach me some of her magick, but even though I had the same La Lune blood running in my veins, I didn't have her affinity.

Of everyone I could think of, I imagined she'd have an idea of how to send me back to my time. But she had died seven years ago, when she was ninety-five years old, sitting in her garden among plants she'd cared for and nurtured her entire life.

But no, I reminded myself. I was getting confused again. That was the whole point of this exercise. This wasn't 1947. It was 1867, and my grandmother was very much still alive, and only a young woman herself now. She'd be twenty-three and newly married to my grandfather.

I had to find her and ask her for help. As a Daughter of La Lune, her ability had been as a healer. I wasn't ill. I was lost in time. But wasn't that a sickness of a kind? Surely, she would know how to cure it.

CHAPTER 13

The following day, Fanny came to check on me, holding a silver-handled ebony cane. My foot was still swollen and sore, but with the cane, I could put some weight on it. She suggested I stay off it for another day, but I told her I didn't want to stay in bed. I very much wanted to go out and try to find my grandmother.

Fanny offered to help me dress and went to fill the bath. Returning fifteen minutes later, she led me, hobbling, to the bathroom, which was filled with steam that smelled of lavender.

The night before, I had been delighted to learn that the house had an indoor bathroom, complete with a flushing toilet. From my history studies, I knew that while not rare, indoor plumbing was considered a luxury in the 1860s. There was no roll of toilet paper, but paper squares were available. While they were much rougher than I was used to, I was grateful the Rossetti household had evolved—most still relied on newspaper.

I was a bit embarrassed to undress in front of Fanny, but I had no choice since I couldn't manage getting in and out of the tub on my own. I settled into the hot water, which felt better than any bath I could remember. Sliding down, I let it wash over me and soak my hair.

When I surfaced, I asked Fanny for some shampoo, and she seemed confused.

"You have the soap." She nodded to the bar.

"Yes, but liquid shampoo is so much more efficient. You don't have any?" I asked.

She looked at me with an expression I'd come to know well in the last twenty-four hours. Half confused, half amused. There were so many things I was used to or took for granted that were unknown to her. It was almost like we were speaking a different language.

Once I was out of the tub and dry, Fanny helped me dress. She said my clothes were still damp, not to mention not in keeping with the style, so she gave me some of hers. She'd laid out a frock that looked familiar, which struck me as odd, but before I could ask her about it, she held out a pair of clean, white cotton drawers and a chemise.

Working at the V&A and reading history, I was familiar with the complicated dressing of the era, so when Fanny set to putting a corset on me, I refused. I knew how difficult they made breathing and movement—especially to someone as unused to them as I would be. So, we skipped the corset, and I held up my arms for her to pull a shirtwaist over me. It had a pale yellow top with a rich amber skirt. It was only a bit too large—at least I looked presentable. I still didn't completely believe I would really find everyone else dressed like this when I went outside. Part of me still wondered if this was an elaborate game.

"The colors are flattering," she said as she put up my hair. "But without the corset, you don't look quite right."

"It will do," I said, smiling at her consternation. "I won't be attending any important functions."

At last, after all the absolutions, which took longer than they did at home, Fanny helped me downstairs to the dining room for breakfast.

Ashe was already there, sitting alone, reading the newspaper.

Seeing us, he smiled as he stood and pulled out a chair for me.

"Would you like tea?" Fanny asked.

"Yes, please," I told her, and she went to fetch it.

"I wondered if you were a dream," Ashe said once she was gone.

The words resonated with me. For a moment, I was silent and not sure how to answer. Before I could, he broke the spell by asking how my foot was.

"It's better, thank you. My shoe even fits today." I pointed my toes but winced. That hurt. "I know I look odd— these shoes with this dress, which doesn't really fit that well, and my hair is a mess without my curling iron."

"Your what?"

"What I use at home to curl my hair." I touched my unruly waves that had escaped Fanny's efforts to tame them.

"I think your hair is quite glorious," he said. "So does Rossetti."

And that's when I realized what it was about Fanny's clothes. "I think I've seen this dress in one of his paintings," I said.

"The coloring suits you. I'll ask Fanny to have the seamstress come over today."

I remembered what I'd read. "Aren't there some ready-made clothes shops here in town?"

"Yes, but they're mostly for men's and children's clothing. I would think you'd want something more to your tastes. Besides, you should stay off your foot today and give it a chance to heal." He gestured to the sideboard. "Are you hungry?"

"I am, yes." In fact, I was surprised by how hungry I was.

"Let me get it for you so you can sit."

Ashe filled a plate with broiled tomatoes, mushrooms, eggs, and sausage, then placed it in front of me before filling one for himself.

"I was waiting for you," he said as he sat and picked up his fork.

"Were you?" I asked.

He looked at me for a moment. The air in the room suddenly seemed electrified.

"As a matter of fact, yes," Ashe said. "Like Rossetti, I draw from life with models. But no matter how many I see, as lovely and interesting as they are, I have always felt as if I've been waiting for one face. Rossetti has had so many muses—Lizzie Siddel, Jane, Fanny. But I've never found mine. Quite a few times, I thought I saw her in my sleep. Occasionally, I've caught glimpses of her on the street—the color of her hair or the set of her jaw or the sway of her neck—but she never turned out to be the woman in my imagination. She always remained elusive."

He paused.

I realized I was holding my breath.

"Until yesterday. When I saw you in the museum."

Our eyes held. The enormity of what he said silenced me. I had thought him familiar when I saw him, as well.

How could this be?

"Jeannine, you might be an actress hired by Rossetti to inspire me. Or you might be mad. Or you might really be from a time in the future. But none of that matters. Yours is the face I have been waiting to paint. Would you be willing to sit for me? Not just for a drawing but for a painting?"

I hadn't taken a bite of food yet. How to tell him that his voice echoed inside me in a way that defied logic? When you listened to a marching band, there was a certain way the drum sounded inside you—as if beating from within you and not coming from without. The reverberation caused an almost sexual response. Ashe's voice was like that for me. I knew I was hearing it through my ears, but at the same time, I felt it was an instrument arousing me. His eyes moved me, as well. I'd fallen asleep thinking not about my predicament but about sapphire-blue eyes that seemed to see more of me than others. I'd thought it was just because he had the eyes of an artist. He didn't just look. He took me in. As if his eyes were a camera lens capturing me. Memorizing me.

"And I'm afraid that now that I have found you, you are going to disappear," he whispered.

Unexpectedly, I realized I was afraid of the same thing.

I was a grown woman who suddenly felt like a teenager, aware of my body and desires for the very first time. Nothing about my reaction made sense. I'd loved Samuel. I'd even been a bit in love with Hugh. I'd believed I'd known pleasure. But gazing at Ashe Lloyd Lewis across the breakfast table in a house on Cheyne Walk in a time that, unless I *had* gone mad, was decades before I was born, I felt as if I were truly connecting to someone for the first time, and that no one who had come before had truly touched me. I was feeling a kind of passion I'd never felt before. The man speaking to me had been dead for almost eighty years in my time, yet he was sitting here with flesh that I wanted to touch, blood I wanted to feel heating against me, and lips that I wanted pressed against mine.

"I might disappear, and it scares me, too," I whispered back.

He smiled sadly. I so wanted to know what was behind it.

"Ashe." It was Fanny at the door.

The charge in the air evaporated. Ashe turned from me to her.

"Yes?"

"Mrs. Talbot-Crane is here."

"Oh, goodness. Is it time already?" He turned back to me. "I'm sorry, but I have a sitting this morning. I'm doing a study for one of those damnable eye portraits."

"That's all right. I want to take a walk. I need to get my bearings."

"You mean to go out alone?" he asked.

"Yes, why?"

"It's not done."

"Not done?"

"No. There are too many areas where it is unsafe for a woman to be alone, and given you've never been to *this* London before, you won't know where any of them are. Not to mention your injury. Fanny, will you accompany Mrs. Maycroft?"

"Yes," Fanny said to him, then turned to me. "I'll show you where you can go and where you can't."

"And later this afternoon," Ashe said as he rose, "if you aren't too tired, maybe you'd let me start sketching you?"

If I'm still here, I thought as I agreed.

I had been determined to figure out how to get home as quickly as possible, but how could I turn down the chance to have the man who'd painted *La Belle Dame* paint me? I thought about home. My empty flat. My complicated situation at work. Who would worry about my disappearance? My father was in Egypt and wouldn't even know I was gone. Sybil would worry. And Alice, Andrew, and Jacob at the museum would be concerned. But one more day wouldn't cause that much of a crisis.

After breakfast, I told Fanny I'd like to visit the Psychic Garden. Since it dated back to the mid-seventeenth century, I knew it would still be where I expected it to be—less than a five-minute walk away and certainly a safe enough area during the day. I told her I really could handle the short excursion on my own. I didn't want her with me when I met my grandmother—if indeed she was there. It would be complicated enough trying to explain who I was to Grandmother Imogine.

"I can't let you go alone," she said. "I promised Ashe.

Not to mention, your ankle is still bruised, and our cobblestone streets aren't easy to navigate. All you would need is to trip and hurt yourself even worse."

"Well, the truth is, there's someone there I need to talk to, and I think it might be better if I saw her by myself."

"I simply can't let you wander the streets alone. You heard Ashe; it's not safe. There are many things to see at the gardens. I can keep myself occupied while you attend to your meeting, all right?"

I acquiesced.

Fanny fetched her wrap, handed me one and the cane, and we ventured out. It wasn't raining, but a heavy fog blanketed the city. I had been afraid of the fog since I was a child.

To assuage my fears when I was small, my father would tell me stories about Tefnut, an Ancient Egyptian leonine goddess who was the deity of moisture, moist air, dew, and rain. The stories explained that Tefnut needed the fog as a cloak of invisibility to visit the man she loved, whom the king—her son—forbade her to marry.

It wasn't a happy fairy tale to tell a child, but my father didn't believe in giving every story a happy ending. He alleged children needed to know that there were problems to be solved and issues to be dealt with in life.

Fanny and I headed out from Cheyne Walk east to Cheyne Gardens. So much looked the same that I realized how little had changed in eighty years, yet this London was so very different from the one I knew.

"Can I speak freely?" Fanny asked as we turned onto Royal Hospital Road.

"Of course."

"For years, Mr. Rossetti has held seances at the house. He claims we've often been visited by spirits and received messages. I've seen many more strange things than I've understood. Your visit is one of the strangest if what you say is true. Ghosts, I can understand. But time travelers? Your story is none of my business, but Ashe is. He's a very special man who has suffered greatly in his life. So, please, whatever your reasons for coming to Cheyne Walk, tread softly with him, Mrs. Maycroft. Because you will be treading on his soul."

"What has he endured?"

She hesitated as if the story wasn't hers to tell.

"I can be discreet," I offered.

She nodded and began. "He was married and had two dear children: a six-year-old son, and a five-year-old daughter. Two years ago, the family had a trip planned—they were going to Plymouth, where his wife's parents and her sister live. Ashe had a commission to finish, so he sent his wife and children on a few days ahead. Their train met with a terrible accident, and all of them were killed. Ashe's heart died in that crash. He's never really recovered. He works all hours. And like so many others in the Brotherhood, he indulges wildly in drink and women. But while the rest of them are soothed and inspired by their excesses, nothing eases Ashe. He is in turmoil all the time. Or at least he was until last night. And this morning again. Something in him has shifted. He seems alive in a new way. It's not as simple as a spark in his eye, but it is. The way he looks at you and holds you in his gaze is different. The tone he uses to speak to you is different. Please, be careful. I don't know why or how you've managed to give him this relief, but I do know he's not strong enough yet to endure being hurt again so soon."

As she spoke, the fog seemed to grow thicker. I wanted to reach out and push it away from me, but it persisted and weighed on me, as did her story.

"Fanny, I don't know what to tell you. I don't belong here. I'm an anomaly. A trick of light or shadow. I don't know how I got here, but you don't need to worry. I am sure I won't be staying long enough to hurt anyone."

I meant it, but I felt conflicted even as I spoke the words.

How could I leave so soon and not explore where I'd landed and how I'd gotten here?

If I had come back to this time, did that mean there was a way I could go back to other times? To ancient Egypt? I imagined for a moment taking my father with me. Giving him the gift of a lifetime to see his precious Alexandria the way it must have once been.

"Well, if that's the case, then good," Fanny said, but there was suspicion in her tone.

"You think I'm mad, don't you? You don't believe a word of what I am saying."

"Gabriel talks of such impossible things and believes them, but I think it's the draughts he takes. He even wrote a story about a man who was reincarnated and fell in love with the same woman he had loved in another era. He is convinced that man is him, and it is his story. Are you saying what has happened to you is reincarnation?"

"No, it's not that. I'm still myself. But it seems I've somehow jumped back from my time period to yours."

She was shaking her head. "A story just as impossible as Gabriel's."

I knew about that story, of course. *St. Agnes of Intercession.* I had it on my shelf at the office. *My office,* I thought with a pang, because I realized that in 1867, it would belong to someone else. I tried to remember the names of the Keepers who had been there in the Victorian era; I'd read the museum's history. Before I could recall, Fanny interrupted my thoughts.

"Rossetti has been working on the story for years—he's having trouble with the end—and it still isn't finished. But I can show it to you if you want when we get back. He's let all of us read it. And maybe you can ask him to do a séance for you. Perhaps by talking to the spirits, you can figure out how to go back to where you came from."

"Fanny, you don't *really* believe anything I've told you, do you?"

"I might believe it if you did, but you aren't even sure of what you've told me, are you?" she asked.

We'd reached the garden gates. In the distance, I saw a young woman with hair so red it looked as if it was on fire. The same color as mine. I knew before she turned around that her name was Imogine.

I looked at Fanny. "I didn't a few seconds ago, but I do now."

CHAPTER 14

True to her word, Fanny went off to walk the garden pathways and gave me some privacy. Using my cane and being careful of the stones, I made my way to my grandmother. I stopped a few yards away, in the shadow of a tree, stunned, simply watching the redheaded young woman tending to an herb bed. I remembered dates well and knew that she would have been a newlywed and either not yet pregnant or just pregnant with my mother in the fall of 1867. That made this excursion very critical. I had to be extremely careful not to interfere in any way that could affect my grandmother's life, which could in turn affect the future. Mine, as well as hers.

I stepped out of the shadows.

"Excuse me," I said, surprised at how badly my voice shook.

She turned and took me in, not registering anything but mild interest in a stranger coming up to her. "Hello," she said with a smile.

I recognized her voice right away. It had a particular timbre—a little rough, as if sandpaper had rubbed it.

"Hello," I said, not at all sure how to begin.

Seeing the cane, she took the lead.

"Are you here for your injury?" she said with the genuine concern and kindness I knew so well.

She was younger than I was now by a full decade, and she looked at me with the respect that one offers someone older, which was so odd.

I responded to her warmth and felt the same emotion toward her I always had. I wanted to reach out to her. I wanted her to take me into her arms, hug me, give me a peppermint, and tell me everything would be all right. Grandma Imogine had played the part of my mother from the time I was three years old. With my father away so much on digs, she'd been central to my life.

"Can I help?" the young Imogine asked again. She had a perplexed expression on her face as she took in my countenance. I could tell she recognized the resemblance.

"Yes. Yes, I think you can."

She nodded to my cane. "It can't be comfortable for you to walk. Let's sit over there, and you can tell me what I can do."

"How did you know this was an injury?" I asked as we sat beneath a willow tree.

"The cane is too tall for you. If you had a permanent condition, you would have had it shaved down. Its height suggests that it belongs to someone else, and you are borrowing it."

I smiled. Just like my grandmother to take in all the details. She was the most observant person I knew, and the only one who could read Sherlock Holmes stories and guess the endings.

Looking at my face intently, she frowned a bit, then shook her head and smiled.

"You are here for a remedy, yes?" she asked.

I nodded.

"But not for your foot."

"Well, I hadn't thought about you helping with my foot

when I planned to come and see you, but now that you mention it, if there is something that can help it heal faster, I'd be happy to try it."

"Of course, there is. Tell me what you did to it."

I described my fall, and she explained what she would prescribe.

I nodded, remembering the same formula from when I was a little girl and had suffered a similar injury.

"Now, tell me the other reason you came to see me."

How to start?

I looked down at her hands. So young, so strong. I thought back to the last time I'd seen them. Knitting a sweater, fingers thick with arthritis, the skin wrinkled and dotted with age spots.

I reached out and turned over her right hand so her crescent moon-shaped birthmark was visible. And then I turned my hand over, revealing an almost identical mark in the same place.

Every Daughter of La Lune was born with a crescent moon-shaped mark somewhere on her body. They identified us to each other—a secret society of women tied through the centuries, all sharing the ability to make some kind of magick.

All except for me.

Imogine nodded in understanding. "So, you are a La Lune? What is your name? Where are you from? This is so exciting. Most of us are in France. A few cousins in Italy, and one in Spain. Why haven't I met you yet if you are in London?"

She was visibly excited, and it was contagious. My grandmother had always been so enthusiastic about everything life had to offer. She had taught me to be, as well. Even losing her daughter—the tragedy of her life, she called it—hadn't stopped her from finding joy in the world. *I lost that ability*, I thought. The war had robbed me of it. Now, sitting here, I felt a bit of it return. I wanted to share so much with her. There were so many things I wanted to tell her that I knew she would love to hear. But if I told her too much, it could upset the trajectory of her life. And thereby mine, as well. I couldn't be selfish. I had to give her only the most innocuous information.

"My name," I said, "is Jeannine. And I am from London…" I hesitated. Oh, how I wanted to tell her, not just so she could help but also because I wanted her to comfort me, the way only she could. She was the one person in my life who always made me feel that everything would work out.

She searched my face for a moment as if looking for the answer there.

"You can trust me."

"What I have to tell you will seem farfetched."

"Coming from a Daughter of La Lune, that's quite a statement."

I laughed.

"Tell me," she said and took my hand. "It's all right, you can tell me."

I almost wept at the feel of my hand in hers. I'd missed her so much since her death at the start of the war. I closed my eyes for a moment, steeled myself, and then began.

"I seem to be caught in a time warp," I said. Now, I was the one watching *her* face. There wasn't shock, but there was confusion.

"I need you to explain that a bit more."

"I am not from this time, not from your time. I am ahead of you." It sounded less frightening to me to just say *ahead of you*.

She nodded, taking it in, accepting what I said.

"I've heard of such a thing." She leaned forward. "How far ahead?"

"Because I need to be careful not to alter anything while I am here, I don't think I should tell you any more than you absolutely need to help me go back."

"You're right." She nodded again. "How about you tell me what you were doing before you jumped time?"

I hadn't tried to retrace my steps, but I did so then. I explained about being in the gallery at a museum—not mentioning which one—and recounted seeing the man in dress from this period.

"What were you doing right before you entered the gallery?"

I tried to remember. "I was in one of the vaults downstairs, gathering items for a show I am curating."

"What items?"

Could it hurt to tell her? I didn't see how.

"Eye portraits. Do you know what they are?"

"No."

I described the miniatures.

"Oh, yes, I've seen them in the South Kensington Museum."

"It hasn't been called—" I started to correct her but stopped myself. "Sorry, that's something you don't need to know."

"Let's go back to the miniatures. Did any of them date to this time? Now? Here?"

"Yes, several. Why?"

"Usually, there is an item from the time you shift to that allows the jump. Can you remember?"

"They aren't all dated precisely so I don't know exactly, but they are popular enough here in your time."

"Were you touching them? Moving them?"

"Yes."

"Can you describe what you did, in as much detail as possible?"

"I had chosen over a dozen of them and had just examined each to see what kind of repairs, if any, they needed. That was it."

"Are you sure? Think back. Did anything else happen?"

I closed my eyes and thought back again.

"There was one thing. When I picked up one particular brooch, I pricked myself."

She nodded slowly. "Did you draw blood?"

"Yes."

"You are a daughter of La Lune. What is your ability?"

"I'm an anomaly. I don't have one."

"We all have one."

I shook my head. "I don't, and you said—" I stopped myself. I was about to tell her what she had told me when I was fourteen years old.

"I said what?"

I quickly covered my mistake. "You just now said we all have one. But, really, I don't."

"But you were given a spell when you started your menses?"

"Yes."

"Who gave it to you?"

I almost blurted out, "*You did,*" but caught myself again. "My grandmother," I whispered, afraid to even bring the idea of my grandmother into the awkward and astonishing conversation.

"Tell me the spell, lamb."

For a moment, I couldn't speak. Grandmother Imogine always called me *lamb*. It was her pet name for me. Did her using it now mean she had knowledge of the future? Or did Imogine call everyone that? My head was spinning.

"The spell?" she prompted.

"Yes, the spell." I shut my eyes and recited it. "Make of the blood, a journey. Make of the journey, a passion. Make of the passion, life everlasting."

She let out a deep sigh. "Ah. Well, there you have it."

"What?"

"Your ability is spelled out right there. They aren't always so clear. *Make of the blood, a stone. Make of a stone, a powder. Make of a powder, life everlasting*—what ability does that suggest? We have no clear idea from the words. But yours…well it's not that much of a mystery. *Make of the blood, a journey. Make of the journey, a passion. Make of the passion, life everlasting.* Our abilities are set when we start menstruating since they run in our blood, and blood is always central to our abilities. In your case, I think it's even more connected than most. When you pricked your finger on the brooch, I believe your blood and the metal reacted to each other to send you back to the time the brooch was made."

She turned my hand over and inspected my fingers.

"Is that it?" She pointed to a red cut on my left index finger, raw to the touch and fresh after less than twenty-four hours.

I nodded.

"That's the culprit. It's festering a bit, as well. I can give you a salve for that in addition to your ankle. You do need to make sure your finger doesn't become infected."

"Thank you. "

"You always were getting into scrapes when you were little. Cuts and bruises, more than other children."

I was startled. "What? Are you asking? Or telling me? And if you are telling me, how can you be in the present but know about the future?"

"Lamb, you need to trust time. There's a reason for everything. We can't understand it all right away, but you will live your way into all the answers."

And then she put her forefinger to her lips in a gesture I knew so well. It was always her response when my incessant questions and requests for more information exhausted her.

Tears sprang to my eyes. I had my grandmother back again. Suddenly, I wasn't ready to go back to my time.

Somewhere, a bell chimed out eleven peals.

"We need to get you the ointments and potions now. I have deliveries to make and appointments to keep."

"But what do I do about going back?"

"I need some time for that. I have books at home I want to study. Tell me where you are staying. When I find a solution, I'll send word for you."

"And in the meantime?"

"Enjoy your journey." And then she gave me the grin I knew so well that made my heart heavy and delighted me at the same time.

CHAPTER 15

Back at 16 Cheyne Walk, Ashe greeted me and then, noticing my package, said, "That doesn't look like it holds many clothes."

"We never got to the shops. We might do that this afternoon."

"Where were you, then?"

"The Chelsea Psychic Garden."

"A curious choice. Why there?"

"Because I was—"

He interrupted. "Would you like some tea? Come to the kitchen and tell me there. I just finished my session and need one badly. There's nothing tea doesn't make easier to bear."

I agreed. I needed a cup. Some normalcy to ground me after my extraordinary morning. I followed Ashe into the kitchen, where he lit the stove, boiled water, and spooned tea into a pot. He took cups and saucers out, put several biscuits onto a plate, and added a silver creamer vessel and sugar.

After boiling the water, Ashe poured it into the teapot and picked up the tray. I followed him back out to the drawing room.

"So, tell me why you chose the garden to visit."

As he poured, I explained, first about the Daughters of La Lune and then about my mission.

He asked quite a few questions, which I answered as best I could.

"I expected more skepticism," I said when he appeared to accept my story.

"Your background is no more difficult to accept than the idea you have traveled here from the future."

I laughed. "I suppose you're right."

"So, tell me, were you able to find your grandmother? Your own grandmother?"

I nodded.

"And did you tell her who you are?"

"Not exactly. I didn't know if that would be wise. I told her that we were related and what had happened to me."

"Did she believe you?"

"Actually, she did. But remember, she's a Daughter of La Lune, as well. She knows our family history."

I spooned some sugar into the delicate porcelain cup decorated with violets and stirred. I noted that Ashe didn't take any sugar.

"Does she have any idea of how to get you back to your time?"

"No, not yet. But she's going to look into it."

"Well, that gives us a couple of days, at least. I hope." He smiled from under his long, dark lashes. I felt my skin flush. "I don't want to lose you yet, Jeannine."

There was a starkness to the way he looked at me and the tone of his words. I didn't understand the urgency of our connection. As much as it thrilled me, it frightened me a bit, as well. I needed to center myself and took a sip of the strong, black tea, reveling in the familiarity of it. The last twenty-four hours had been fraught with emotions. Landing here. Meeting Ashe and Rossetti. Going to the garden. Joy at seeing Grandma Imogine. Remembering that I could only see her in this past, that in my present, she was buried in her grave. Suddenly, that made me think about another grave. One in Highgate. That of the man sitting opposite me.

I knew when Ashe would die. And how. It was written in the history of the Pre-Raphaelites. Clio had told me everything she knew about it. What was I supposed to do with that information? Could I...*dare* I warn him about the fire that would take his life and cut short his career? What right did I have to interfere in the past? And yet, how could I *not* tell him?

There was no guidebook for this. I only had the imagination of writers like Jules Verne and Charles Dickens to go on. And was their fiction right? Conceptually, it made sense that even the slightest change might affect a greater one later on, but was that true? I was actually here in the past. Perhaps that was how it was supposed to be.

"What are you thinking about? You look so troubled."

I looked at him, and our eyes held. They say you shouldn't meet your heroes because their humanity will disappoint you. Perhaps his would. But so far, he'd proven to be as sensitive and charismatic as I'd imagined he was.

"Would you postpone your shopping trip and sit for me this afternoon?" he asked. "I don't want to give up a moment of the time we have together."

"Of course."

Ashe had a studio in the garden, a small one-room structure filled with sketches and canvases. As I stood inside for the first time, the evidence of his talent overwhelmed me. I hadn't seen much of his work in the house, but there was so much here. I was speechless, humbled, and in awe of the jewel-toned paintings of mythological scenes, the strong and capable men, and the beautiful, seductive, and intelligent women.

Finally, I found my voice. "Your work is extraordinary. The one painting in the museum is just a taste." I stood silent for another moment, looking from one canvas to the next.

"I always thought what differentiates many Pre-Raphaelites from other painters is that the women are never thoughtless bonbons only important for their beauty. They're thinking equals, if not superiors. Your women seem especially strong and powerful. And every bit as capable as the men."

Ashe came over to where I was and stood beside me. He was so close I could feel the heat of his body. He looked at what I was looking at—an unfinished portrait of a woman sitting by a window, a book in her hand, a simple crown on her head. She was studying the landscape where a knight in armor had just dismounted and stood by his steed. The sky was lit up with a sunset that flashed off the metal of the man's suit and her crown.

"I never realized that before, but I suppose you are right. I'm attracted to the stories where the women have power, be it mystical, physical, or intellectual."

Ashe turned back to me. For a moment, he didn't speak, just studied my face. I knew he was learning the curves and angles of my features as a painter. And then I saw the expression in his eyes change as he did the same thing—learned my face—but now as a man.

Reaching out, he traced my cheekbone with the lightest touch of his forefinger. And then the slope of my nose. Then, my lips. He left a trail of fire when he moved on. Sparks shot through my body, setting me alight. The sensations were so intense I shut my eyes as his finger moved to my jaw, down the side of my neck, and across my collarbone.

"I would know you anywhere, our souls—yours and mine— are made of the same stuff," Ashe quoted a line I remembered from *Wuthering Heights*.

It was just one of the books I'd read where the heroine felt faint at the touch of her lover. I'd always shrugged at what I felt was exaggerated prose. But I was discovering, here in this little studio rife with the scents of oil paints and turpentine, that you *could* feel faint from such a touch. Swooning wasn't purple prose but a very real reaction to arousal.

I still had my eyes closed, and so I sensed—not saw—when Ashe moved closer. Then his arm went round my shoulders, and he pulled me to him. He pressed his lips to mine without hesitation, and I kissed Ashe Lloyd Lewis back with a new kind of desire I'd never known.

I was lost in the kiss. I had no thoughts anymore. I was pure sensation. Pressure and heat built inside me. My entire being was concentrated on the few inches where our lips met. I could tell he was giving me his all with this one embrace. He was totally open to me and what might happen between us, to who I was, and without any judgment or demands.

How long did we stand there kissing? It might have been a minute, two, perhaps ten…I had no idea. But the person I had been before Ashe touched me was different from the one he let go of.

The knowledge of what was possible had altered me. I knew I could not stay here with this man, yet I felt he was my destiny—a contradiction that made no sense.

"I'm tempted to take you over to the couch now and make love to you if you'd have me, but God help me, I'm torn. I'm just as anxious to pick up a brush and capture the look in your eyes. I don't know if I've ever seen someone who, so willingly, showed their passion in their gaze as you are doing, Jeannine. Your eyes were the color of honey. Now, they are like blazing topaz. Electric. As if our kiss has turned them on like the new lights on the Strand."

I wanted to go to the couch and explore him, too, but Ashe had decided for us. He wanted to paint me, and I had to admit the enticement of that excited me, too. To sit for the painter I had admired since I was a little girl was almost too hard to believe.

He sat me in a chair and pulled a second one up so he could sit closer to me.

"This isn't going to be a formal portrait," he said. "I'm not even going to paint your whole face today."

Then, he arranged a tray of gouache paints, a fresh jar of water, and several very thin paintbrushes. With pins, he affixed a thick sheet of velum, no larger than a page in a book, to a board and then sat beside me.

"Wait, I've never had my portrait painted. I've never posed for anyone. What should I do?"

"Just relax and think about our kiss."

"It's all I can think about," I said softly.

"Me, too," he answered.

Then there were no more words as his eyes went from me to the vellum and back again.

After about thirty minutes, he put down his brushes and said he was done for the day. Indeed, he looked exhausted but satisfied—how I imagined he would after making love.

"Can I see?"

He turned the vellum. He had painted only my eye and two errant curls that had escaped my updo.

"Once you are done with this, I want to kiss you and then have you paint a portrait of your eye for me," I said. "It's only fair I have one of you if you have one of me."

"Absolutely. And there's nothing I'd like more than to have you kissing me again. But do we have to wait until tomorrow for that? I have another appointment now that I can't do anything about. But there is tonight."

"Yes, tonight," I said.

"What is wrong?" he asked.

"How do you know there's something wrong?"

"I told you. Your whole soul shows in your eyes.

Depending on what you are thinking, the color even changes. It's subtle. Not something I'd imagine many people would notice, but I'm trained. I saw the shift. What were you thinking just now?"

"I felt sad for a minute. It's as you said. You and I have been looking for each other for a long time. I've even dreamt about you. When I was little, I created an imaginary friend I now realize was a forethought of who you are. And now that we've found each other... I won't be able to stay here, Ashe. Not for long. Once my grandmother helps me figure out how to get back, I have to go."

"Once she finds the solution, the timing of when you use it will be up to you, won't it?"

"Yes, of course," I said with certainty, but little did I realize it wouldn't be up to me, Ashe, or Grandmother Imogine when I left.

CHAPTER 16

The next morning, both my ankle and the pinprick on my finger were greatly improved, thanks to Imogine's salves. Once we breakfasted, Ashe went back to the studio to prepare for a sitting, and I returned to the Psychic Garden to see if my grandmother had figured out what I needed to do to return home.

I knocked on the cottage door, and a man answered. I had a hard time holding back my tears when I saw him. He was a young version of my beloved grandfather, who had died when I was just twenty.

"Can I help you?" he asked in a familiar voice.

"Yes, I'm here to see my…to see Imogine."

"Are you Jeannine?"

I nodded.

"She's out but should be back soon. Would you like to sit and have a cup of tea?" he said.

"Yes, please."

I watched him make the brew, basking in the familiarity of his actions.

"She said you are related. A cousin, perhaps? She wasn't quite clear on the family connection."

My grandfather, the man I knew, was cognizant of the Daughters of La Lune legend and quite accepting of my grandmother's abilities, but I had no idea how much he knew when they were so young and newly married.

"Yes, we're related," I said, somewhat obliquely. If he noticed that, he didn't react.

"I'm not sure I understand it at all, but if Imogine believes you are here from another time, who am I to question it? I've seen her do things that defy all logic. But working with plants and flowers, I've seen *many* things that defy logic. Did you ever study a single rose? The way the petals unfold, their scent, the way they blossom? We take so much for granted that is absolute magick. Just how the seasons change. How the world goes from day to night. How water flows. If you just sit back and pay attention, magick of all kinds is all around us."

I smiled and hoped he couldn't see the tears in my eyes. I had heard him talk like this so many times in my life. Oh, how much I'd loved my grandfather. I had missed him so for the last eighteen years. And here he was, talking to me about his favorite subject. A conversation so familiar, I could fill in his next sentence without having to guess. This man had helped form how I viewed the world, and listening to him now, I realized that lately, at least for the last few years, since the war had taken its toll, I had become remiss in looking around me, dwelling in the simple things, and glorying in the mystery and magick the Earth had to offer.

"To dwell in the simple things," he said, "is how one stays at peace."

"I love how you look at the world," I said to him, not thinking that it might sound strange. For a moment, he did look confused, but then he seemed to accept what I'd said.

"Since you are family, don't forget, if you need anything while you are in London, come here, all right? We don't have all that much"—he gestured around the simple cottage—"but we can make sure you stay safe and are well fed. London can be a cruel place for a woman, especially an unmarried one."

"I'm actually widowed," I said.

His eyes showed concern.

"I'm so sorry. Imogine didn't mention that. Only that you were alone."

"Well, yes. I am very much alone."

"How long ago did you lose your husband?"

"Five years ago in the—" I was going to say *war* but stopped myself. I had no idea what the last war was to someone living in 1867. "In the countryside...in an accident."

"Death is cruel, but you must remember that life is for the living," he said. Another of his favorite sayings.

I took a sip of my now-tepid tea. It was sweet, just the way my grandfather had always made it. I floated between times, remembering the person this man had been. Which here and now was the man he was yet to be. The way authors had written about time travel did it short shrift. Clearly, none of them had ever experienced it themselves.

I heard footsteps outside on the gravel path, and then the door creaked open. Imogine came in carrying a basket of herbs on her arm. I recognized the basket. It was the same one—albeit newer—she'd always used in my timeline. I felt a catch in my throat. The memories were like pellets of hail—hitting, hurting, haunting.

My grandfather jumped up and took it from her, gentlemanly and concerned.

"You shouldn't be working so hard. You should be careful."

Was she sick? *She looks more than healthy*, I thought. She actually glowed. I was about to ask when she tutted at him and said, "Get on with you. Women have been having babies since time immemorial. The midwife told me that if I feel well, I can keep doing everything the same. And I don't just feel well, I feel wonderful."

I stared at them. I'd known it was possible that she might

be pregnant with my mother at this time, but I hadn't prepared for the dizzying effect the reality would have on me.

My grandmother noticed.

"Are you all right?"

"Yes, fine."

"Hmm. You look a little peaked. All this traveling." She reached for my teacup and felt its temperature. "Let me make something better for you than lukewarm tea." She looked at my grandfather. "Didn't you notice her tea had gone cold?"

She put the kettle back on and, while she waited for it to boil, took three bottles off a shelf. Once the water boiled, she filled a cup and then added three parts violet leaf tincture, one part skullcap leaf and flower tincture, half a part Oriental poppy, and a teaspoon of honey.

"Drink this up now," she said, handing me the cup. I took a sip gratefully, recognizing the smells embracing me. This was her restorative brew whenever anyone was wan. Since she'd died, I often made it myself using her recipe, but it never tasted quite the same as I remembered. This time, it did.

The familiar drink went to work right away, soothing me. It was so familiar that it made me smile but also ache a little at the same time. I wanted this time with my grandparents to go slowly.

I watched as Grandmother Imogine returned the tinctures to the shelf. There were at least two dozen dark brown bottles, all identical except for labels written out carefully in her distinctive hand.

I knew each one, what it was used for, and how to mix it. She'd started teaching me when I was old enough to reach the stove. I'd loved cooking up the potions in her kitchen—much bigger than this one—because by then, my grandfather was a well-known botanist who had written a dozen important books on the subject and was quite successful.

I finished the drink.

"There, you already look much better," my grandmother

said. "The color's returned to your cheeks. Are you feeling well enough to discuss your predicament? I've been doing some research."

"Yes," I said, feeling a surge of anxiety.

My grandfather stood. "I'm going to take my leave now. There's work to be done in the gardens. It was a pleasure meeting you, Jeannine. I hope to see you again while you are in London."

I so wanted to get up and hug him. To have him hold me and forget for a few more moments that he would be gone again once I returned to my time.

A lump formed in my throat, but I forced it down.

"Thank you so much. It really was my pleasure."

Despite my efforts, my voice cracked a little on the last word, and he smiled at me as if sensing something. He came over and knelt in front of me. "You take care of yourself, all right? And pay attention to the little things, yes? The magick of the flowers and the sea and how the hummingbirds hover in the air."

I nodded, now unable to speak. He seemed to understand and took my hand in his, squeezing it. Even though he'd just met me. Even though it was overly familiar for a man in his time to do such a thing, some instinct had guided him, and I was so glad. I squeezed his hand back twice, in the secret way he'd devised for me when I was little and scared. If I squeezed twice, he knew that something was bothering me and would take me aside, no matter where we were, and find out what was wrong.

Something flashed in his eyes for a moment, but then it disappeared. He seemed surprised to find himself on the floor and holding my hand and rose brusquely, kissed my grandmother on the cheek, and made his way outside.

"Drink some more of that. This is all quite difficult, I know," she said kindly.

I wanted to ask her what she knew but didn't. I wanted to

believe that she knew the truth—who I was to her and where I came from. If I didn't ask, I could go on believing that instead of finding out I was wrong.

Grandmother Imogine pulled out a thick leather-bound book and began leafing through the pages. "This is one of our family grimoires—the one most associated with my abilities."

I had grown up seeing the book on her desk. Our family had dozens of volumes full of magickal spells and invocations, one dating back to the original sixteenth-century courtesan and self-proclaimed witch, La Lune.

"I've been reading about your predicament, and there seems to be a potion that can help. Unfortunately, I'm afraid I don't have all the ingredients here. Some are very obscure, and finding them will take me a few days."

I had the odd sensation of being thrilled and disappointed at the same time. A few days would give me more time with Ashe and my grandparents. A few days would also impede my work on the Valentine's Day show.

"That's all right. I would be happy to stay. Is there a pub nearby where I can take you both to lunch? To thank you for the work you are doing for me?" I asked, not wanting to leave yet.

"Why bother with mediocre fare? I have a soup on the stove, and pudding ready. Why don't you stay here and eat with us?"

My grandmother had been a wonderful cook, and our meal was delicious. The soup was another familiar memory. It was her hearty beef soup laden with carrots, parsnips, and peas. The bread she served was a freshly made cottage loaf with butter from a local dairy. It was as delicious as my grandmother used to tell me it was when I was little and she'd complain about never finding a dairy as good as Nigel Green's after he passed away, and it shut down.

Eating with my grandparents was bittersweet. I tried to savor every bite and bit of conversation, knowing it was a gift.

Once we were done with the bread and soup, Grandmother Imogine served a syrupy sponge pudding. It was a typical and simple dessert, but instead of using store-bought golden syrup as most did, she made her own syrup flavored with the essences of raspberries and roses, which she grew in the garden during the summer and then used all year long.

I took my final bite, savoring the taste, knowing I'd never taste this ambrosia again once I was back in 1947. Even when I tried to make it, it never came out the same. I could buy the roses and raspberries and cook them down the way she'd shown me, but it never tasted as good. I knew that was part of her magick. The things she could do with what she grew in the garden—from food to medicines—couldn't be reproduced with a recipe. There was some otherworldly essence, the La Lune part of her, that made everything more special. More delicious if it was food. More healing if it was a tincture, salve, or powder.

When lunch was done, Grandfather went out to the gardens to work again, and I helped Grandmother Imogine clean up. While we put away the dishes and silverware, she asked about my life.

"What year exactly did you travel here from?"

I hesitated. Was there any reason not to tell her? I couldn't think of one.

"1947."

She did the math. "Eighty years from now." She thought for a few more seconds. "Even if I live to a very old age, I doubt I will make it to one hundred and two. So, I won't be able to see the world you see every day."

"Maybe you will live to one hundred and two. You're a very good herbalist. You can keep yourself healthier than most, whip up a potion or two."

She laughed. "Then I'll be a very old crone, and people can travel from far away to buy my *eternal youth* elixirs."

I couldn't tell her how close she was to describing the

very way she would live. She watched my face.

"You look so sad suddenly, lamb. What's wrong?"

How could I tell her that I was thinking of her and my grandfather and how much I missed them. About their beautiful graves and how often I visited and the flowers I'd planted.

Well, I could tell her part of that truth.

"I was thinking about my family and how much I miss them all," I said, hoping it was an innocuous enough answer.

"While you are here?"

"No. I miss them because they've passed away."

"Who is gone, lamb?"

"My mother, my brother, and more. Also, my mentor, and my husband."

"Oh, I'm sorry. How long have you been a widow?"

I told her.

"And you had no children?"

"No. We were only married for three years, and my husband was in the service almost the whole time and not home very often. During those years, we probably spent less than thirty days together."

"And you have no aunts or uncles?"

"I do have some, and cousins, but none of them live in England." *And not all of them made it through the war*, I thought but did not say. "I'm sorry if I'm holding back. I don't know if it's wise to talk too much about the future. I'm afraid if I do, I might change something." I didn't say the rest of what I was thinking. I didn't know if I should talk about the daughter not yet born to this woman.

"Yes, yes. That's wise. I'm so curious, though, about the world you are living in. Is it very different than this one?"

"In some ways, yes, but in others, not as much. For instance, this garden is exactly the same."

She smiled. "That's good to know. Are things easier?"

"Again, in some ways, yes. Medicine is much more

advanced. So is plumbing and transportation. London smells so much better, and it's much safer for women. I don't think anything of taking a walk by myself, even at night."

"Well, that's something to look forward to."

There was a knock at the door, and Grandmother Imogine went to see to it.

"Hello." I heard a man's familiar voice.

"Hello, can I help?" my grandmother asked.

"I'm Ashe Lloyd Lewis. I was told Jeannine is here."

"She is indeed. Come in."

I turned around in my chair to see Ashe enter.

"How did you know I'd be here?" I was surprised.

"Fanny told me, and as my session ended and I had some errands, I thought I'd stop and see if you fancied taking a walk with me. The gentleman outside told me you were here."

"What a lovely invitation," my grandmother said and then winked at me. "You go on now. Have a good time. I'll send word as soon as I have what you need."

"Thank you for lunch," I said.

"Oh, that was nothing." She leaned forward, hugged me, and whispered in my ear. "I get feelings about people, Jeannine. This Ashe is a good man. He sees you exactly the way you need to be seen. Don't be afraid of him."

I couldn't believe what I was hearing. They were the exact words my grandmother had said to me so many times when I was growing up. Whenever I'd wonder what the future held, she'd always tell me that, one day, I'd meet a good man who would see me exactly the way I needed to be seen. I'd question her, and she'd give me a cryptic smile and say, "There are great adventures in store for you, lamb. Just remember not to be frightened of them."

And here we were, in 1867, a time before even my mother was born, and Grandmother Imogine was watching the moment she would predict years in the future.

"What did she whisper to you?" Ashe asked once we'd

left the cottage and were walking through the garden toward the exit. "You had such an expression of disbelief."

Without telling him the exact words so as not to be embarrassed, I explained the gist of what my grandmother had told me and how it was exactly what she used to tell me all the time.

"Does that mean she remembered meeting you now when she was just a young bride?"

"It suggests so, but that's so confusing—" I stopped suddenly.

"What is it?"

We were walking by the water. To the left was the Thames. I walked over to the wooden railing and gripped it tightly. I watched the water flowing and thought about time flowing and how complicated it was.

"What is it, Jeannine?"

"I told her my name. When I first met her, I told her my name. Jeannine Maycroft. Will she remember that? Will she tell her daughter about meeting me? Is that why I'm called Jeannine? Grandmother Imogine met my husband. She knew his name, of course. Did she know I would marry him? And that he would leave me widowed?"

"Did she ever say anything to you to suggest she knew the future?"

"Of course, that was one of her abilities. She could read the future from scrying—staring into a bowl of water that she infused with certain herbs. I just don't remember if anything she told me or pushed me to do was part of this."

We continued walking, turning left onto Lupus Street where Ashe found a carriage that took us on to Buckingham Palace road, then into Mayfair and onto Regent Street. I was fascinated by how many landmarks were exactly the same, yet how different London felt.

It was difficult to navigate the streets with all the horse droppings and garbage. There were no signs of the war, of course, and that was refreshing. Not for the first time, I had the experience of dual emotions battling in me. I was both fascinated and frightened.

Ashe, sensing my emotional overload, distracted me by telling me about our destination. We were going to Ackerman and Co., the shop where he bought art supplies. He told me that it dated back to the early 1800s.

We were there to purchase paints and paper he'd run out of. His portrait business of eye miniatures was doing so well, he was low on supplies.

We entered the shop, and a salesman who knew Ashe by name greeted us, asking how he could help. While they went over Ashe's list, I looked around and found a display of various watercolor sets. My mother had been a watercolorist, and while I hadn't inherited her talent, I had inherited her love of painting. Except for me, it was a hobby. I examined the mahogany and brass box. It had three lift-out sections and multiple compartments filled with pastels, watercolors, brushes, colored pencils, and various china pots for holding water.

I heard the salesman tell Ashe the price of his long list of supplies and was surprised at how little it came to.

Ashe found me still examining the box, wishing I could purchase it, wondering if I could take it back with me when I returned to the present.

"Can you ask how much this is?" I asked him.

Ashe asked, and the salesman quoted a number. It was very expensive compared to the amount of Ashe's supplies, but so little in 1947 pounds that I thought it was worth it to try and see if I could take it back.

"I'd like to purchase this," I told Ashe. "I have pound notes." I pulled out my change purse, which I'd put in the pocket of the coat Fanny had lent me that morning.

"They won't do you any good," he whispered, pushing my hand back. "And please, be careful not to let anyone see them, Jeannine. They're dated in the future. They'll think you're trying to use counterfeit money."

Quickly, I returned the notes to the change purse.

"But I'll buy it for you if you've your heart set on it."

I shook my head. "No, I don't know if it will travel well, and it's too dear for you in today's prices."

Outside the shop, Ashe asked if there was anything I'd like to see before we got a carriage back home.

"Everything. Is it all right if we walk?"

"What about your ankle?"

"It's so much better. Grandmother Imogine's salve is a miracle remedy." I smiled, thinking how true that was. "We could walk and see how far I can get, can't we? Then take the carriage."

"Of course, my lady. Your wish is my command." He looked around, thinking. "I have a better idea, though. I know the perfect place to walk, but it's a bit far, so let's get that carriage. We can stroll once we get there."

Only a minute later, we were on our way to an address on Bayswater Road that I didn't recognize until we arrived. We were on the edge of Kensington Gardens.

We disembarked and headed toward the entrance.

"To take pressure off your ankle, take my arm," he offered. "I don't want to tire you out before we even get there."

Little did he know that I would have been happy to take his arm without the excuse of needing support. As soon as our limbs touched, even through our coats, I felt a tingle go down my back at being this close to him.

We entered the gardens by Buckhill Lodge, a stand-alone Victorian cottage that I was familiar with. It was one of the many lodgings originally built for the groundskeepers and was still standing in my time. I'd used this entrance myself on my long, solitary walks.

"Are we going to the Italian Gardens?" I asked.

"We are. Since they opened, I love to come here and sketch."

We had reached the elaborately laid-out trees, raised terraces, fountains, urns, and geometric flower beds.

"Prince Albert is said to have had them designed to be similar to Osborne House on The Isle of Wight, where the royal family spent holidays."

At the same time, we both said, "The queen's and prince's initials—"

I let him finish.

"Are on the walls of the pump house."

And then I laughed.

"I'm so glad you brought me here," I said.

"Then so am I. You don't have that faraway look in your eye that I've seen so often. I want to see you happy, even if that means losing you, but I'm hoping that won't happen too soon. Might I dare a little part of you feels the same way?"

"Yes, Ashe, yes. It's so complicated, but I'm not ready to leave you yet, either."

He lifted my head with a finger under my chin and looked into my eyes, then leaned in and pressed his lips to mine. This time, my arms went around him before his went around me.

CHAPTER 17

"When did you first know you wanted to be a painter?" I asked.

We were back at 16 Cheyne Walk, and Ashe was working on my eye portrait again now that he'd replenished his paint supply. I sat in a place I had never even been able to imagine: Ashe Lloyd Lewis's studio. I had so many questions about his technique and the subjects he chose. It was heady to sit with him and ask anything I wanted. I thought about how Clio would have loved hearing about this.

"My father is a thatcher. When I was a little boy and school was out, he would bring me to help him on jobs. I was in training to follow in his footsteps. It's a good business. Hard but steady work. Necessary. He never had to worry about putting food on the table for my sisters and me.

"I was about nine years old when we went to re-thatch a house and a smaller building for a man named Cuthbert Bell."

"The illustrator?" I asked. "I know his work. We have some of his paintings in the museum."

"Yes, one and the same. It was an accident that I even met him. I was climbing a ladder to hand something to my pa, who was on the roof. As I climbed up, I passed a window. I couldn't help seeing inside. The walls were covered with paintings of his fantastic, magical fairy and fantasy worlds. I didn't know it then, but I was seeing illustrations for a new edition of stories by The Brothers Grimm.

"I was so entranced that I failed to notice a pile of old thatch sliding off the roof. It hit me and knocked me off the ladder. I fell to the ground, and the ladder toppled down on top of me.

"The noise brought Mr. Bell outside. Once he saw what had happened, he insisted that my father bring me into the house where he could attend to me.

"I'd been knocked out. When I came to, I thought I'd died and gone to a magical kingdom. I was inside Mr. Bell's studio. I couldn't stop staring at the paintings.

"Once my father ascertained that I was all right, he prepared to take me back outside, but Mr. Bell insisted that I spend the rest of the day inside with him. He told my father he was working on a series of illustrations and could use me as a model instead of drawing from memory. He even offered to pay my father for my time. He refused any payment but agreed to let me remain in the studio.

"As Mr. Bell drew me, I asked him all sorts of questions about how he worked. I had always loved to draw, but my father treated it as a childhood game. I knew my mother's father and grandfather were painters in Sweden, but of stuffy portraits—or so I thought at the time—that hung in our house. Given her family, my mother often indulged me in the idea that I had real talent and treated me to art supplies for Christmas and my birthday.

"Once Mr. Bell realized how interested I was, he gave me some pastels and paper and let me draw while he sketched me. Occasionally, he gave me pointers. He could tell from my enthusiasm how much I loved what I was doing.

"When it was time to leave for the day, Mr. Bell offered my father a proposition. He could use a model. In exchange, he'd give me art lessons. Mr. Bell's son had two daughters around my age, and he said they were there often, so I'd have playmates.

"My father was uncertain. He told Mr. Bell he was training me to be a thatcher. '*But he has real talent. If you allow it, I can train him to be an illustrator,*' the artist told my father. It was the first time I'd thought maybe I could create art for a living instead of doing the kind of hard work my father did. It took my mother cajoling and me begging, but my father and I eventually reached a compromise. I could work with Mr. Bell for the rest of the school year. If Mr. Bell couldn't sell one of my drawings, I'd return to my apprenticeship. No matter that I was still a child. My father wanted proof of my talent.

"For the rest of that year, I went directly to Mr. Bell's studio after school instead of my father's toolshed. It was Mr. Bell who bought one of my drawings that June. He hung it in his studio. I continued studying with him long after I grew too big to be his model, and once I was finished with school, I became his assistant. His son had not followed in his footsteps, and Mr. Bell took me under his wing as if I were his own flesh and blood."

Ashe grew quiet. He was no longer painting my eye but had a faraway look in his.

"When did he pass?" I asked, recognizing the expression of grief.

"Ten years ago. I had already gone out on my own, but I still worked in his studio alongside him. He told me he liked the company. That man changed my life. He was as important to me as my parents. I never stopped learning from him." He was quiet again. "I'm sorry," he said, coughing away what I guessed was a lump in his throat.

"Don't apologize. Missing is what happens when we don't have anywhere else to put our love."

Ashe nodded. "Well said. And you're exactly right. I know too much about grief," he said. "Far too much."

I remembered what Fanny had told me about Ashe losing his wife and children. I endeavored to change the subject.

"Do you have any of Mr. Bell's work with you as the model? I'd love to see you as a little boy."

"I do, actually. When we're done here, I'll show you."

Ashe continued to paint my eye for the next thirty minutes and then said he was finished for the day. He hadn't forgotten my request, and once we were back in the house, he suggested I come with him and he'd show me the Cuthbert Bell illustrations he had.

I followed him upstairs to his room. It was in some disarray. As someone here to help Mr. Rossetti in exchange for lodging and food, Ashe was probably responsible for taking care of his own quarters. While Mr. Rossetti was well known and successful, I'd read enough to know that his finances fluctuated from year to year and had noticed he didn't employ much help. The only regulars were a cook, Fanny, and a young maid who always seemed harried and overwrought.

Ashe turned his back to me and opened a drawer in the armoire. While he rummaged through his things, I looked around, my gaze eventually landing on the bed. It had been hastily made. I couldn't help but see how the quilt had been pulled up only so far, and the sheet below was still visible. And there was an impression of Ashe's head, still on the pillow. I wanted so badly to lean down and lay my cheek against it. An intimate desire that, like so much else now, bewildered and confused me.

Ashe turned back around, holding a leather portfolio tied with a string. As he took in my expression, he looked from me to the bed to the portfolio, which he then put down on his writing desk. He took the five steps over to me.

I held my breath. I wanted him to kiss me again despite how dangerous it might be for both of us. I heard Fanny's warning in my mind: Ashe had been hurt. He had lost his wife and two children.

Yet I felt drawn to this man in a way I hadn't felt before, with a heady, almost giddy joy. I felt untethered to reality, and it felt damn good. For so long, at least since the war, there had been no real pleasure that wasn't tinged with grief or pain.

Ashe stood only inches from me—as close as possible without us actually touching. I felt the heat coming off his body and wondered if he could feel it from mine. He reached out and drew a line across my cheek down the slope of my nose and then outlined my lips with his finger. It seemed he left sparks wherever he touched. There was more—deep, deep inside me were little explosions. I took the last step to close the distance between us, and his arms went around me fiercely. We were pressed against each other so tightly there was no space left.

Feeling his lips on mine, tasting him, I inhaled his scent of turpentine, peppermint, and verbena and tried to memorize it. *One day*, I thought, *I will be back in my own time and will crave this scent. I will want it desperately and won't be able to find it.*

I was all too familiar with loss and how it ached. How it robbed you of every other feeling and surrounded you like fog. Even as I knew I was setting myself up for a yearning I would not be able to squelch, it didn't matter.

I wanted Ashe, now, for as long as we could have each other.

I began to unbutton his shirt, pushing it off his shoulders and revealing his warm chest. His scent grew in intensity, rising around me, now mixed with the musky smell of his body.

I buried my head in his neck and ran my hands down his bare back. I luxuriated in the feel of his muscles. It wasn't enough to touch him with only my hands. I needed to feel his flesh against mine, and I started to pull at the shirtwaist I wore. Unfamiliar with Fanny's clothes, getting out of the layers she'd dressed me in was a struggle.

Ashe started to laugh. "Let me help you," he said, his

voice in a deeper register than I was used to. It was the sound of desire, and it stirred up even more in me.

Finally, I was out of the ridiculous underclothes and pressed my breasts to Ashe's chest, luxuriating in the deliciousness of our first coming together.

As if I were a featherweight, he picked me up, carried me to his bed, and gently laid me down. I sank into the down comforter and pillow and watched as he moved beside me and took off his pants and underclothes until he stood naked before me.

"I want to draw you like that," he whispered as he remained standing, his state of undress tantalizing me. "The expression on your face. If I could capture it on paper, every man who saw it would be desperate to own it. If only to imagine that one day, if he was very, very lucky, a woman would look at him with that much desire."

"Later," I said in a husky voice I barely recognized as mine.

"Yes, later. The truth is, nothing could make me stop and pick up a pencil now, Jeannine. Not with you lying there like that."

"I'm glad," I said and opened my arms.

He came to me.

Having been married, I thought I knew what to expect. I had been titillated by Hugh's kisses. I'd enjoyed sex with my husband. Looked forward to it, even. But this was nothing I had known. Being with Ashe was an explosion. A volcano. A storm. This was a meeting of two souls on another plane. Ashe was the same kind of artist in bed that he was in the studio. His attention to detail. His bold colors. His ability to create. He did all that to me as if I were the canvas, and he was painting a whole world that had never existed before on my skin. I had an energy I never knew, a hunger I'd never felt, and when he finally and at last entered me, I lost my ability to think, which had never, ever happened to me. With Ashe moving inside me, his fingers wrapped in my hair, his lips pressed to mine, I felt only the sensation of swirls of want, need, and the scarlet waves circling and drawing me into its vortex. I was drowning in passion. Craving more before I had even been satiated. And once I was, overwhelmed by what the two of us had done with each other's bodies. How had we climbed to such an exhausted place in such a short time? How did he know my body better than my husband had? How could Ashe see inside me and touch me exactly how I needed to be touched? How did he know my body's reactions when I did not even know them?

We lay there, exhausted, slick with sweat, and breathing hard. I didn't know that I was crying until Ashe reached out and wiped away my tears.

"What is it?" he asked.

I didn't know the words to describe how I was feeling. How could I have found this man only to have to let him go?

"Jeannine, I've been with other women since the accident, but I haven't made love to anyone since my wife was killed. Until now. Thank you."

I felt a drop of wetness on my chest and realized that I wasn't the only one in tears.

CHAPTER 18

The following day, Ashe was in his studio working on his commission, and I was in the drawing room rereading Rossetti's reincarnation story, but this time from the original manuscript. At ten thirty, Fanny interrupted to tell me I had a visitor and escorted my grandmother in.

Once she was settled with the tea Fanny had delivered, my grandmother told me she thought she'd figured out how to help me get back home. I smiled and thanked her, while inside I felt my heart ache. If she noticed anything strange about my reaction, she didn't question me, she was too excited about her discovery.

"What I read is very esoteric and complicated—writings that go back to the sixteenth century and John Dee. Do you know about him?" she asked.

"He was a famous alchemist and philosopher, wasn't he?"

"Yes, yes. An astrologer and mathematician. He was said to be able to speak to the angels and was the owner of England's largest library at the time, which supposedly held over four thousand books and seven hundred manuscripts. That library disappeared during his lifetime, but some collectors believe they have found some of the books. A very learned man I've studied with has several of them, and I went to speak with him. Do you have the clothes you were wearing from your time?"

"Yes, upstairs."

"Can you show me?"

I took Imogine up to my room and laid my clothes and pocketbook on the bed, the shoes on the floor.

"Do they look any different to you?" she asked.

"Different how?"

"This sounds unbelievable, but from what I read, they could be disassembling. You can take things from now back to your time, and they will remain intact because they already exist, but anything you bring here from your present won't remain intact indefinitely because it does not exist here yet. So, look at your clothes closely. See if they seem the same to you."

I did what she asked.

"How do they look?" she asked.

"The same."

"Hmm. That's curious. Maybe try them on. Perhaps you'll be able to tell better if you are wearing them."

I was confused but did as she asked, removing Fanny's cumbersome outfit to return to mine.

"Do they feel the same?"

Now, I wasn't sure. Looking down at my skirt, it did seem like the color might have faded a little. I rubbed my hands on the wool. Perhaps it felt thinner.

I told Imogine.

"Can you check that everything you brought with you in your reticule is still inside?"

I smiled at her old-fashioned word for pocketbook as I picked it up, opened it, and looked in.

"I can't be sure, but I think so."

"Now, one last thing. Show me the cut on your hand."

I held it out for her to see.

Imogine nodded. "I think you're ready, then."

"For what?"

"To return."

"But I—I'm not ready. I haven't told Ashe about the fire or—"

"Jeannine, if you wait, you might not be able to get back at all. You could be stuck here."

"I just need a little more time."

She shook her head. "I don't advise it. It's very risky for you to be here at all."

"I need to talk to Ashe, warn him." I felt tears spring to my eyes at the idea of leaving. She wiped one away. It made my heart hurt. I wouldn't just be leaving Ashe; I would be leaving my grandmother, as well.

Imogine smiled at me. "All right, but after you've talked to him, you have to leave. The time is right, but it might not be for much longer. Your cut has healed. From what I read, that's key. "

"All right, once I tell him, I will leave, but how do I do that?" I wiped away another tear.

"Do you remember your spell? Tell me, and I'll explain."

"Of course."

I thought of the spell. *Make of the blood, a journey. Make of the journey, a passion. Make of the passion, life everlasting."*

Then, a wave of dizziness hit me. I'd felt that before, hadn't I? I tried to think. Yes, in the vault when I'd pricked my finger. A feeling I'd attributed to my aversion to seeing the blood.

I realized what was happening.

"You tricked me," I told my grandmother, hearing my voice echo as if I were in a tunnel.

"I'm sorry, Jeannine, but you don't belong here. And if…" Her voice was becoming faint, as was her visage. Darkness crept in as if twilight was turning to night.

"But I didn't even…" I wanted to tell her that I hadn't said goodbye to her yet either…or my grandfather…but my words stopped coming as if trapped inside me, and I was stuck inside a narrow tube of black. And then, I was spinning.

Suddenly, all movement stopped. For a moment, I just stood where I was. Eyes closed. Afraid to open them. Minutes passed. My breathing was ragged. I tried to pinpoint the scent I smelled. Dusty. Stale.

And then I knew. With a sob, I opened my eyes. I was in the locked room in the basement of the Victoria and Albert Museum. A tray of lovers' eye jewelry in front of me.

As if no time at all had passed.

I looked at my finger. There was only the faintest mark where the pin had broken the skin—the kind that takes days to form, not a fresh wound. I had been gone for three days. I knew it. And yet, from where I stood, I had not been gone at all.

I closed my eyes again. I pictured Ashe. His eyes. I tried to conjure his scent. I had not warned him about the fire. And then I wondered if all I'd imagined had truly happened. Maybe I'd just scratched my finger a little, not really cut it as I thought I remembered. Perhaps it was all a dream. I took a step, and my ankle twinged just enough to prove that I'd twisted it—there was no question.

I felt sick to my stomach. I reached into my purse and found the ginger candies I always kept handy since my stomach took it hardest whenever I got nervous. I put one in my mouth and then slid down the wall to sit on the floor, crying so many more tears.

CHAPTER 19

Somehow, it was still Friday night, October 31, 1947. Halloween. Sybil had been expecting me to bring the cuff links and help her arrange flowers. Even if it wasn't so late, I couldn't go. I couldn't see her now. I was too confused, too distraught. I was feverish, and the dizziness returned every time I turned my head.

Once back in my flat, I called her and told her I'd come down with something and was so sorry but couldn't make it. I told her I would have a messenger deliver the cuff links in the morning.

"I was worried about you when you didn't come or call."

"I'm sorry, I…" I wasn't a good liar. I didn't know what to say.

"I was getting ready to call hospitals around the city. It just wasn't like you not to show up or call."

"I know."

"Jeannine, what's wrong? You don't sound like yourself at all."

"I got caught in the rain and twisted my ankle. It took me so long to hobble home…" I stopped making excuses.

"Well, I am coming over there tomorrow. I want to see

for myself that you are all right. I'll pick up the cuff links then."

"No, really. You have too much to do. I'm all right. Just sorry I'm missing your party tomorrow."

"You have to promise me that if you aren't better by Sunday, you'll call a doctor."

I promised, even though I knew no doctor could help what ailed me.

Once we wrapped up what was a far more difficult conversation than I'd imagined, I poured myself a few fingers of scotch and sat on my living room couch, trying to make sense of what defied all logic. What was I going to tell Sybil when I finally did see her?

For hours that night, I lay restless in bed, reliving the last three days over and over until, finally exhausted, I drifted off around three in the morning.

I woke up on Saturday, no longer dizzy but with a terrible headache.

It was raining hard, giving me the excuse I needed to stay inside. Instead of continuing to obsess about what I believed had happened, I decided to write down everything I could remember about the last three days in hopes of answering three questions.

What exactly had occurred? How? And why? No matter how much I wrote, I only came up with more and more questions. And I missed Ashe. I yearned for the smell of him, for his touch. For his quiet ways and comforting manner. And for the fiery passion just beneath the surface, so quickly aroused that so quickly aroused *me*.

Despite the clouds threatening yet more rain on Sunday, I walked to the Chelsea Psychic Garden. I needed to somehow connect my present to the past I'd just experienced.

Although I knew the route very well, I felt lost. The

familiar was no longer familiar. The expected was unexpected. I traversed the streets, wondering who was walking these same streets in the parallel universe I'd lived in for three days. What was Ashe doing right now, eighty years in the past? What had he thought when he came to look for me and discovered I was gone? Had he wondered if I was real? Had he looked at the only proof there was of my having been there at all—the portrait he'd done of my eye? Had it given him solace, or did it cause the same pain in him that I felt? I was homesick for a man, a time, and a place I never should have known.

Reaching the garden, I meandered its paths, trying to merge the reality of this day with what now seemed like the fantasy of my last visit here when I'd had lunch with my grandparents.

Or had I really been there? Was there any chance that what I believed had occurred had not? Could I have fallen in the small, poorly ventilated underground room while examining the eye miniatures? What if I'd twisted my ankle there, hit my head, and suffered hallucinations? Then I'd come to, believing it had all happened, when in reality just an hour had passed.

I reached the home where the head botanist lived. I stood outside and stared at it. When I was a child, and my grandmother had brought me here, she'd told me stories about what it had been like living in the cottage and bringing up my mother in the gardens. I had those stories embedded in my memory. *It wouldn't be unusual*, I thought, *for my hallucination to include a visit here to meet my grandparents when they'd lived on the grounds.*

I wanted to peek inside a window and see if it looked the same as it had a few days ago. But did I dare? What would the current botanist say if he saw me? I took a few steps closer and tried to peer in, but there were curtains on the windows, and I couldn't see a thing.

It was only noon. I'd resolved nothing and was just as

uneasy as I'd been since Friday night. Instead of going home, I took the underground to Highgate Cemetery. As I always did, I bought a posy of violets from the young woman selling them at the lych-gate and then returned to buy two more.

My first stop was our family plot, where my grandparents and my mother were buried. My brother's body had not been recovered, but he had a cenotaph here. I placed the posy at the foot of the family marker and sat on the stone bench that faced the monolith. As befitting the burial place of a botanist and an herbalist, the gravesite was carefully landscaped, and my father paid for perpetual care to keep it pristine. Whatever the season, there were dozens of flowers and bushes in bloom. Even now, in early November, there were violet lily turf spikes, pink Peruvian lilies, and fuchsia and light pink chrysanthemums, along with holly bushes with their bright red berries, and English ivy curled over the iron grave fence. And, as a nod to my grandmother, there were herbs planted here, as well. This time of year, the rosemary, with its lavender flowers and miniature bay trees, scented the air.

I closed my eyes, inhaled, and thought about the young couple I'd met days ago and how, now, just days later, I was sitting at the foot of their graves.

Overwhelmed with exhaustion, confusion, and longing to see the people I'd loved so much and lost, I felt myself close to tears. I'd always hated crying. Tears were useless. They had never helped me understand anything, and that was what I needed. To understand. Resolving not to fall prey to my emotions—it seemed I'd never cried as much as I had this weekend—I stood. I had one more stop, and then I'd go home and call my cousin Opaline in France. She was the family's matriarch now, and I needed her guidance.

The walk from my family's plot to Clio's was twenty minutes, and I spent the time preparing myself for what I knew I would find there.

Due to the storm, Ashe's stone was covered with so

many orange, red, and yellow leaves it looked as if a fire was burning. I bent and brushed the debris off, my fingers finding and then lingering, tracing the outline of his name carved into the granite.

I laid the posy down.

"It was real, Ashe. I know it was," I whispered to him, across the minutes, days, weeks, months, and years. "I miss you," I whispered across time, willing him to hear me.

My determination not to cry abandoned me. This man was still so very much alive to me, even though I was standing in a cemetery on this dreary November afternoon staring down at his grave.

On Monday morning, I arrived at my office on time and greeted my staff, who responded without surprise. From the calendar on the wall, it was Monday, November 3, 1947. They'd last seen me on Friday after Mr. Gibbons' four p.m. meeting about Michelle Auriol's visit and had been busy preparing for that.

I settled at my desk and was about to begin work when Alice walked in with a telegram. It was from my father, who was working on his beloved excavation in Egypt.

Have been contacted by the Midas Society regarding items we stored during war years. Very concerned. Am detained here. Can you contact them and find out what this is about?

My father and I were members of the somewhat secret Midas Society of jewelers, curators, collectors, antique dealers, auction house owners, and the like. Dating back to the Renaissance, it had been founded by an Italian prince horrified by his father's looting practices.

The prince named the group after King Midas, a greedy man who destroyed everything he cared about by turning it into gold. First, his precious roses, and then his even more precious daughter. Only when confronted with the dangerous and addictive power of avarice, did he learn from his mistakes and beg the gods to reverse the power.

Midas Society members took an oath that if an object came across their desks they believed to be stolen, be it coins, paintings, sculptures, jewels, or other objets d'art, they would not sell it but rather do everything in their power to restore it to its rightful owners. If they couldn't be found, members agreed to put the item into safekeeping until the time came when they *could* return it.

The Society also employed private detectives, often called in by individuals to investigate lost, missing, or stolen works.

I reread the telegram and then looked at my watch, calculating the time difference between London and New York where Jules Reed, a jeweler and the vice president of the Society, worked. We were contemporaries, had met several times, and I trusted him to help.

Being five hours earlier in the States, I'd have to wait until the afternoon to place the call.

The rest of the morning passed without incident, but I remained unnerved by my father's telegram. His reputation was beyond reproach. What kind of investigation could the Society be opening? It worried me. I well knew they didn't get involved in frivolous cases.

Besides, we were members ourselves.

How could storing art at Woodfern during the war be part of any investigation?

Just as Operation Pied Piper had moved more than one and a half million people out of London to keep them safe, national treasures were taken out, as well. Our national museums, archives, and libraries used quarries, tunnels, prisons, and caves. In addition, many families who owned estates at least two miles away from major cities, factories, towns, and points of danger, volunteered to help store treasures in their homes—including my father, who offered Woodfern as a storage facility to the Ministry of Works. Because of my association with the V&A, it was decided that Woodfern would take our museum treasures not being kept in the quarries or the steel-reinforced vaults under the museum's architectural courts.

During those years, I spent every other month at Woodfern, watching over the holdings. On alternate months, my father stayed. Occasionally, we were both there at the same time. Once, during our dual residence, there was an incident involving intruders that put both of us in mortal danger.

Two thieves, knowing some of England's greatest pieces of art were being stored in houses throughout the Royal Forest of Dean, were making the rounds, burglarizing random properties. Ours was the last of a dozen houses attacked, including our dear friend Barbara's. Caught unawares, my father was captured, bound, and held at knifepoint, ordered to take them to the treasures. I had been outside cutting roses of all things, but thankfully saw the encounter through the window. I ran around to the kitchen, pulled out our housekeeper, Mrs. Cendriff, and told her to bicycle to get the police.

Then I went back around to the front of the house and walked in through the front door as if I were just coming in with no idea what was occurring. My father already had a cut on his cheek where the thief had hit him when he refused to share where the collection was hidden.

Now, the thieves threatened to hurt my father worse if I didn't tell them.

When we first took in the cache, my father and I had planned for what we would do if this ever happened. I wasn't sure why he hadn't implemented it. It was up to me.

I tried to keep calm as I agreed to do what they asked and

led them out of the room.

There were two basements in the house—one under the east wing and one under the west. The treasures were under the east wing basement in a wine cellar. I led the thieves to the west wing basement, which we had set up for exactly this scenario, taking advantage of a secret door built into the wall during the seventeenth century as an escape route. It could be locked from the inside or the outside.

I knew they would make me go in first, which I did. There were no electric lights in the basement, but there was a torch at the top of the steps. I grabbed it and climbed down.

"All the artwork is in the area to the left," I said.

Both men hurried down. I waited until both had reached the last step and were peering into the darkness, anxious to start their search.

"You go first," one of the men ordered.

"I'm coming," I said.

My father and I had rigged a rope from the door at the bottom of the stairs so I could pull the door shut from below. As I tugged the rope, I dropped the torch, hoping the sound would distract them from the door shutting.

The crooks didn't seem to have realized anything except that the torch had fallen.

"Pick that up and show us where these things are," the man barked.

"It's all in here," I said as I led them into the second part of the basement, which was filled with crates of old furniture and paintings—nothing of value, just the debris of centuries of our family home being refurbished and refurnished over the years.

While they attacked the piles, I leaned against the wall, quietly watching and waiting until I was sure they were fully engrossed in their activity. Once I felt they were, I pressed on the stone that opened the hidden door, slipped through, closed it, and then bolted it behind me.

I climbed up to ground level, let myself out, ran back around to the front of the house, double-bolted the door to the basement, and then went to see to my father.

He hadn't been hurt badly, but I cleaned the cut, applied some salve, and then we both waited outside for the local police to arrive.

Helping protect the nation's treasures during wartime and hatching such a clever plan against the men who tried to take it were among the many reasons my father was honored by the king and knighted.

So, what kind of investigation could there be? My father was a hero, as was I, something he always reminded me of. I had a medal from the king to prove it.

I spent the morning writing copy for the Valentine's Day catalog, a harder task than anticipated as I was preoccupied, alternately with my excursion into the past and my father's telegram. And then yet another distraction occurred when I saw Hugh escorting Madame Auriol through the hallway. From my desk, I overheard him gallantly—in French— offering her information about the purpose of the department I was impressed that he'd done such a thorough job since his return of learning about the most important new acquisitions we'd made.

"We have one of the most comprehensive collections of metalworks of any museum in England. Among the objects I will be showing you are a reliquary of St. Januarius that supposedly held his head. It won't be too gruesome, I promise, it's empty now."

I heard the president's wife laugh and wasn't surprised, Hugh was such a natural flirt. I put down my pen. I was still miffed that he was conducting the tour. I was the Keeper, after all. At least, for the time being. *Plus, he's not the only one who can speak fluent French*, I thought as I walked out of my office.

"Madame Auriol," I said as I approached and introduced myself. "While you have the most gracious host, I know that jewelry is one of your passions. We have recently obtained some medieval jewelry that I think you'd find fascinating."

"We've already been. And you're right, I did find them fascinating," Mrs. Auriol said.

I glanced at Hugh, who gave me a little shrug. *He's trying to show me up*, I thought. And then she added, "Monsieur Kenward told me how you were personally responsible for putting the collection together. Quite impressive. And that you are the only female Keeper at the museum. That is impressive, as well."

I didn't look back at him but kept my gaze fixed on the president's wife. "Thank you," I said, a bit embarrassed that I'd assumed the worst of Hugh. Again. "I'm glad you were able to see the jewelry before the exhibit is dismantled," I said to her.

And there I was, confused yet again about Hugh's methods and motives. I wished I could talk to Clio, but I'd call Sybil later. I needed her objective opinion and advice on how to deal with this man who was either a charming rake or a calculating usurper.

Finally, at two that afternoon, I was able to call Jules Reed and ask him what the telegram had been about.

"Apparently, at least one item stored at your country house during the war is missing from the museum. The Society has been asked to look into it," he said.

"Oh, Jules, you have to tell me more than that."

"It's premature for me to share anything else. While I personally find it very hard to believe that one of our own members could be guilty of any infraction, it is in the Society's charter to fully investigate any accusations."

"Seriously? My father is under suspicion? He opened his home to the government to help during a terrible time in our country's history. And while doing so, he lost his only son to the war. My father is still grieving. Percy followed in his footsteps, was everything my father could have wished for.

His death was a blow he hasn't yet recovered from. He can't possibly be at fault for anything but risking his life to protect the treasures under his care."

"I wish I could tell you more, Jeannine, but I simply can't. Do understand we are going to be completely thorough and careful here. I personally believe it has to be a mistake. I know that this won't help much in the moment, but please know we are doing everything in our power to not only expedite the inquiry but put our very best investigator on it. And please pass my concern on to your father."

I didn't bother asking him to explain further. I knew the way the Society worked, and confidentiality was the hallmark of their investigations. I would just have to reassure my father the best I could. I hoped he wouldn't have to come home. Egypt was where he was happiest, even as he struggled with grief. He had his crew and his friends there. Here in England, without being on a dig, his memories would haunt him even more mercilessly.

CHAPTER 20

I didn't have to wait as long as I'd thought I would to learn more about the investigation. The whole senior staff was called to Mr. Gibbons' office at four o'clock—his favorite time for having meetings, as Hugh had sarcastically pointed out on Friday.

That afternoon, Gibbons stood behind his desk, hands by his sides. One might have thought he would have been in a better mood given how well the private tour for Mrs. Auriol had gone. There were rumors that the president's wife was planning a dinner with all the major museum directors throughout Europe to be held at her home in Paris, and Hugh had already been invited. Was it true? If so, that would be a major coup for him and work against me in our competition.

I looked out through the window into the gray drizzle. Mr. Gibbons' expression was just as dour. There were over a dozen Keepers and assistants in the room, plus Hugh, who was still unassigned as yet, though he did have both an office and an assistant.

"It's come to our attention that an important item is missing from our inventory. It was moved out of the museum during the war. As you all know, Clio Oxley was in charge of all transfers, and her detailed paperwork shows that the item in question was taken to Woodfern Manor." The director looked directly at me, and everyone in the room followed his gaze. Under scrutiny, I crossed my arms in front of me and lifted my chin higher. Grandmother Imogine used to tell me it was a bad habit:

"Sometimes, you have to listen, even when you don't want to hear what someone is saying, and not act as if you are automatically right and they are wrong."

Grandmother Ruth also considered it a bad habit but for an altogether different reason. She said it made me look angry, and, as she said, angry people are not attractive.

"The item in question is a painting, which does not seem to have been returned," the director continued. "We are hopeful it was not stolen during its storage or in the transportation process but rather returned and somehow mismarked, getting lost in our vast holdings."

So, it was a painting the Society was investigating. Except nothing was missing, I was sure of it.

Clio had been in charge of the team that removed the objects from Woodfern and oversaw their safekeeping. As her assistant, I was involved in every step. Once the items were secure at our house, whether or not my father was in residence, Clio and I had taken turns staying at Woodfern. One of us was always on watch. After Clio died and I inherited her job before the war ended, I was responsible for the collection's return to the V&A.

I knew for a fact that not one box, crate, or parcel had ever been opened during its stay at Woodfern. I had logged everything as it was taken from the museum with Clio. Alice, Andrew, Jacob, and I logged everything back in after the war—sadly, without my mentor.

I was certain nothing had been lost or misplaced at the estate, in transit, or when it was returned to storage.

"According to the paperwork, it appears the crate with

the *Smeralda Bandinelli* by Sandro Botticelli was checked back in. Two weeks ago, we decided to put it back on display but have not been able to locate it."

I was stunned. It was a very important painting that I knew quite a bit about since it had been purchased by one of my beloved Pre-Raphaelites, Dante Gabriel Rossetti. My mind was racing. What were the chances there would be a connection to him so soon after my—what to call it—*voyage* to the past? Had the painting been in 16 Cheyne Walk while I'd been there? I didn't remember seeing it. I knew Rossetti had purchased it from Christie's for only twenty pounds in 1867. I'd been there at the end of October and the beginning of November. When had the 1867 auction taken place?

The Botticelli was a prized possession of the V&A, but the painter had not been popular in 1867, which allowed Rossetti to buy it at such a minuscule price. Very shortly afterward, in 1870, the painter became fashionable again after the art critic, Walter Pater, published a full-length article about him. Ten years later, in 1880, Rossetti, in need of funds, sold the Botticelli to one of his patrons, the Anglo-Greek stockbroker Constantine Ionides, for a very large profit.

Ionides, who had commissioned Rossetti's *The Day Dream*, collected many Pre-Raphaelites, as well as Renaissance and Dutch masterpieces and left more than a thousand one hundred and thirty-eight pieces, including the *Smeralda*, to the V&A when he died in 1900. This bequest made up a very important part of our paintings and drawings collection.

"We are assuming," the director continued, "and hoping the crate was stored in the wrong department. Or even put inside another somehow. We've begun a thorough search. Considering how much was moved out and back and is still not unpacked, it means the search will take time. But we also need to allow for the possibility that there has been a theft. The problem there is we have no idea when it might have occurred. There is a period of seven years from when the painting was first moved to Woodfern to when we realized it was missing.

"I am asking all department heads to institute a search of your storage for the missing crate. No crisis of this magnitude has occurred before at the V&A. This won't be an isolated activity. Our board of directors has decided it is wise to institute an investigation of all our holdings that were moved out and supposedly checked back in to make sure nothing else is missing. This will go on for months and be quite disruptive to our operations, but there's nothing we can do about it."

Mr. Gibbons rubbed the back of his neck and shook his head.

"Given our security, if the painting isn't in the wrong crate somewhere in the museum, don't you think it's most likely the painting was taken while at Woodfern Manor?" someone asked.

I turned in the direction of the voice. I wasn't sure, but I thought it sounded like Hugh.

"I've been in touch with the authorities. They will be talking to Sir Balfort," Mr. Gibbons said.

Hearing my father's name mentioned angered me. There was no doubt in my mind that the painting, as well as all the other treasures stored at our home, had been carefully protected. My father was, after all, a scholar, an archaeologist, an art lover, and a collector in his own right. He had been knighted by the king for the part he played during the war, safeguarding treasures that belonged to both the V&A and the Imperial War Museum. He was one of the least likely people in all of England to be cavalier about his responsibility. Only our most trusted staff had been allowed at Woodfern Manor during the period we kept the pieces there. Surely, Mr. Gibbons could not imagine my father had been lax in his duties. But from the director's tone of voice and the fact that he'd contacted the Midas Society, he was suggesting exactly that. Or worse.

I wanted to shout and defend my father, but I knew better. If the painting was missing, there was another explanation, and I'd get to the bottom of it.

We were dismissed.

I walked back to my office with Byron Larson, the Keeper of the Furniture. He was in his seventies and had been one of Clio's dearest friends. They'd been lovers, too, though she'd never told me outright. I'd gotten to know him through her, and we'd become close through our shared grief since her death.

"That all sounds very suspicious," he said. "I don't for a moment think the painting was misplaced. Or that anything else was. We don't misplace things here. I suspect there is a thief who pilfered it either on its way to or from Woodfern. Or, I suppose, while it was there. "

I bristled. "No. Between my father, Clio, and me"—all of whom are or were members of The Midas Society, I wanted to say but didn't—"the cache at our house was never left unguarded and was extremely well hidden. And no one but Clio and I knew what was actually there. Everything was coded. This could only have happened once it was brought back here. I hope it is just misplaced and you're wrong, because it's chilling to think that someone here, someone we work with, might be a criminal."

"Oh, I've always assumed people who work here are criminals or could turn to crime if pushed," he countered. "Most people are capable of dastardly deeds. A thin line separates right from wrong, and myriad circumstances might push a person from morality to immorality. We saw the very worst of what people are capable of during the war. Fathers, husbands, school teachers, lawyers, doctors, educators, previously upstanding citizens from all walks of life, all committing unspeakable acts of horror. Compared to those infractions, the theft of a painting sounds quite innocent."

"I do know what you mean," I said. "But at the same

time, a painting like this is a precious masterpiece created by an artist who is no longer alive to create another. A moment in time that was preserved and placed in these hallowed halls to show the greatness men are capable of. And isn't that why the museum and its contents matter so much, now more than ever? As a lasting repudiation of the ugly, unholy acts that others have perpetrated? Every drawing, painting, piece of jewelry, book, fabric swatch—everything someone creates that is beautiful—proves that some of us are capable of greatness. That there is something to aspire to. That not all God's creatures are evil."

We'd stopped at the elevator. Before the doors opened, Hugh joined us. "Bad stuff, eh?" he said.

"Yes, terrible," Byron agreed.

"Well, hopefully one of us will turn it up and be a hero," he offered.

"Sounds like you have your job cut out for you," I said. While I'd managed not to lace the sentence with vitriol, it was in my heart. I knew that he would turn over Heaven and Hell to be the one to solve this puzzle. Anything he could do to make points, he would.

But so would I.

So, what did that make him? Or me?

I went back to my office in a foul mood. I was on edge. We all were. The news about the missing Botticelli disturbed everyone. While the staff hoped it would turn up as being mismarked, we were all too aware of the possibility of theft and wondered if it was a coworker. That caused a kind of unusual anxiety throughout every department.

For me, it was more serious than just anxiety. Woodfern was my father's home. If the painting didn't show up at the museum, and the investigation moved on to Woodfern, that could go public. Even if he ultimately wasn't found culpable, my father's reputation would be sullied. He still hadn't recovered from losing my brother, and I feared a blow like that could do him irreparable harm.

As well as me—whether it was found at Woodfern or elsewhere. Clio was gone and couldn't be held responsible. Any blame would fall on me. If the painting had been stolen at Woodfern or in transit, or was in fact lost, my job would certainly be in jeopardy.

That would please Hugh, I couldn't help thinking. As I walked home, my mind ricocheted between the problem with the painting and my personal crisis of still not understanding what had happened to me.

I saw a taxi and hailed it. I wasn't going home. I had another idea.

CHAPTER 21

I had to see Ashe. Or at least I had to try to see him. Part of me knew this was a hopeless mission, but I couldn't just go on as if nothing had happened.

"16 Cheyne Walk," I said to the taxi driver.

It was still drizzling, there was quite a bit of traffic, and it was taking so long to get there, but I had no choice but to sit and be patient.

I started to think about my grandmother and how she had tricked me into saying my spell and how I should have been on the lookout because that was so like her. To think she knew what was best for me and do whatever she had to do to make it happen. I had always loved her for it, but it had also been our bone of contention. We'd fought over her interference more than once. And despite myself, I'd inherited a bit too much of her belief that she always knew what was best.

The cab pulled up in front of the now-familiar house. I felt a surge of relief. It looked exactly as I remembered. Maybe once I stepped over the threshold, Ashe would be inside. Perhaps he'd always been there and would be still. Was it possible that time moved differently inside the house?

I carefully walked up the walkway since the stones were once again slick from the rain, then climbed the steps, reached the front door, and rang the bell.

I waited.

A moment passed. And then another.

Finally, I heard footsteps. The door opened, and I found myself looking at a familiar face, but not the one I had expected. It wasn't Fanny. This woman wasn't dressed in Victorian garb but in modern-day clothes.

"Hello, Mrs. Maycroft," Mrs. Whitfield said.

I was looking at the woman who'd brought the Pre-Raphaelite accessory she'd found cleaning up her garden to the museum. Was that only a week ago?

"Can I help you?" she asked, sounding confused.

I felt a lump in my throat. Of course, Ashe wasn't here. I'd indulged in wishful thinking. It was 1947 on the street *and* inside the house. I'd been foolish to come. I knew full well who lived here. What was wrong with me?

"No," I said. "I'm sorry. I—" I broke off. I couldn't possibly explain my mission to her. She'd think me mad.

"Are you all right?" she asked.

I couldn't even imagine what I looked like at the moment. "Yes, I'm fine. I'm sorry…"

"I think you should come in. Let me make you a cup of tea. You look positively shocked."

I should leave, I thought, but at the same time, I desperately wanted to go inside. Even if only to prove to myself once and for all that it wasn't Rossetti's house anymore. To convince myself that what I had experienced was…what? Did I want it to have been a dream? Did I want to find Ashe or discover that I was suffering from some delusion? Maybe I'd had a fever, and the whole experience had been a hallucination. We'd all heard of fever dreams.

"Do come in," she repeated, and I followed her inside.

The front hall was different. So was the drawing room

she led me to. The space was laid out in a similar manner, and even the molding remained. The windows looked out on views I remembered. But nothing else bore any resemblance to the house Rossetti lived in. That Ashe lived in. I desperately wanted to go upstairs to his bedroom and see if any of his scent was trapped in the walls, but I could no sooner ask her that than I could ask if he lived here.

Ashe Lloyd Lewis had been dead for eighty years.

I was so lost in thought, I hadn't noticed that Mrs. Whitfield had left the room until she returned carrying a tray of tea things.

Not the service Fanny had served us with.

"Milk? Sugar? Lemon?"

"Lemon, please."

"And I think a little sugar, yes? You seem to have had a shock."

I didn't respond. I still didn't know what to say. What to tell her. I only knew I couldn't tell her the truth.

I took the proffered cup. "Thank you."

She poured one for herself.

I took a sip. The hot liquid was comforting. Something real. Something I understood—a cup of tea.

"I am so sorry to have shown up on your doorstep," I started. "I was given this address and didn't put it all together. I forgot you lived here. Clearly, there's been a mistake. I was told a portrait painter lived here."

"A painter? Not now, no. As far as I know, not since Dante Gabriel Rossetti. But who is the artist? I don't know all our neighbors, but perhaps I've heard the name and can help you find the right house?"

I blurted out the first name I could think of. Harris Balfour—my paternal grandfather's name.

She thought, then shook her head. "No, I haven't heard his name before. Perhaps you'll have to start your search back at the beginning. It is quite a coincidence, though, that your efforts brought you to my doorstep."

"Indeed." I was thinking of what I had been taught, of the expression every Daughter of La Lune uttered—*there are no such things as coincidences*. I'd learned that when something seemed to be one, it held a deeper meaning that merited attention.

"It must be amazing living in a house with such rich history," I said. "Finding things in the garden the way you did. Have you found other things in other places besides what you brought me?"

"Yes. During a renovation we did before the war, we found a cabinet that had been walled up. Inside were a lot of drawings. Not all of them by Rossetti, though. It seems he was a voracious collector."

"Yes, he was. Famous, especially for his support of other painters. He had a serious porcelain collection, as well."

"Blue and white porcelain, right? I've found shards of it in the garden, and a small cup in the back of a shelf when we repainted the kitchen."

I pictured the cabinets full of Rossetti's treasures prominently displayed and began to feel dizzy.

I took another sip of the tea, unaware I'd drunk almost all of it until Mrs. Whitfield asked, "Can I freshen that?"

I nodded. "Thank you."

While she poured, I gazed out the window. There was something reassuring about seeing the familiar maple tree, its leaves turning that same bright yellow Ashe had called *fire yellow* instead of its real name, cadmium yellow.

I felt a lump forming in my throat. I was altogether too prone to tears lately. I hadn't cried for years. Even since Clio died. But now, I seemed always on the verge. I took another sip of the tea as Mrs. Whitfield talked on about the renovation of the house and other objects she'd found from after Rossetti's time.

After ten more minutes of chitchat, I put the cup down.

"I've taken up too much of your time. I'm so sorry for disturbing you, but thank you for the tea."

"Of course, you haven't disturbed me. I'm just sorry I couldn't be of more help."

I rose, and she followed, leading me toward the door.

"I do have one last question about the history of this house, though," I began.

"Yes?"

"You said you did a lot of gardening."

"Yes, it's one of my greatest pleasures."

"Do you know if there was ever a studio in the garden? Have you found any remnants of it?"

"Yes, I do know that, as a matter of fact. There was a small studio there that burned down in 1868. I still come across bits of charred wood occasionally and glass in the garden. A paintbrush once."

I felt sure I would start to cry and turned away so Mrs. Whitfield couldn't see my face.

She sensed my discomfort and put her hand on my arm. "There's something else, isn't there?" she asked. "Something sad. Do you want to see the garden? I can show you where the studio was."

"No, no. Thank you. I really am so sorry to have interrupted your evening. I'm fine, really. Just a story I once heard about that studio and the artist who used it. An associate of Rossetti's. One of my favorite painters."

"You know of Ashe Lloyd Lewis?" Mrs. Whitfield asked.

I felt chills on my arms hearing his name spoken aloud.

"Yes. I'm surprised you do. He's not that well known."

"No, he's not, but he's part of the history of this house. In fact, I have some of his work. When I mentioned that cache of drawings we found, his were among them."

His drawings? Could I take up any more of this woman's time and ask to see them?

"It's so curious that you are looking for a painter here on

Cheyne Walk and were given this address where several painters once lived."

"Yes, very curious."

"Two coincidences," she continued. "First, that you and I had already met, and that your favorite painter was in residence. Do let me show you the garden." She took my arm.

I followed Mrs. Whitfield out of the foyer and down a hallway that had been wallpapered in a chrysanthemum pattern in various shades of green when I'd been here last. Now, it was painted cream. The floor had been hardwood, where now it was carpeted. I reached out and let my fingers trail along the wainscot railing, something to anchor me to the moment.

When I had last been here, it had looked so different. Smelled different. Felt different. I had been someone other than who I was now, and this woman had not even been born yet.

We reached the end of the hallway and a mudroom, surprisingly unchanged, with several Macintoshes, various hats hanging on hooks, and wellingtons in different sizes lined up under a bench.

And then we were outside. My eye immediately traveled to the right, to where the studio had been. That was where I'd sat for Ashe. Where he'd drawn and then painted my eye for the lovely miniature. Where was that painting now? Destroyed in the fire, along with so many other of his fine works?

I started toward the spot where the structure had been, which was now just another area of a well-established and carefully laid-out garden. There was a pergola where the studio had stood, with thick ropes of wisteria climbing through it, now nothing but twisting bare bark. I stood under it and put my hand on the trunk of the vine. There had been wisteria growing on the outside of the studio, trained up a wall of trellis. Was this the same vine? Had it survived the fire that Ashe and his work had not? I wanted to ask Mrs. Whitfield, but she couldn't know.

"It's lovely, isn't it?" she asked.

"Yes. It must be so beautiful when it blooms. I've always loved the scent." My grandmother had called it a magickal scent and showed me how best to cut it and try to keep it alive once put in a vase—a hard task.

"So very beautiful, yes, and its perfume is divine. We found some old photos of the garden dating back to the mid-1860s, and this vine was here then. Many of the trees were, as well."

"And that bench," I said, pointing. And then I realized my error. I shouldn't have known that. Had Mrs. Whitfield recognized I'd said it so definitively, as if I knew, when I should have asked it as a question?

"Yes, the bench, as well. Would you like to see the photos?"

I told her I would. She turned to go inside, but I remained under the pergola for another moment. I had been in this very spot with Ashe not four days ago. He'd looked into my eyes and opened my heart. Time was playing with me. My grandmother was playing with me. I had been yanked out of what had been and thrown back into what was, and I missed what I'd found. I wanted to talk to Ashe again. I wanted to touch him and breathe him in. I wanted him to kiss me and stroke me, and I wanted to feel that exquisite pain of opening up to him and surrendering completely.

"Mrs. Maycroft? Are you all right?"

With a horrible start, I realized that a tear had made its way out of my eye and was tracking down my cheek. This woman must think me mad, invading her home and crying in her garden.

"My grandparents were gardeners and botanists. They had a pergola just like this one," I lied. "I was just thrown back to their garden and realized how much I miss them," I said as I wiped away the traitorous tear.

She nodded. "Oh, I understand. I lost my husband in the war. Just when I think I've dealt with it and am fine, the sadness overwhelms me sometimes and catches me by surprise."

I told her how sorry I was and shared that I'd suffered that same loss. I asked her how and where her husband died. Though it was a sad topic, at least we had moved on from my odd reaction in her garden.

Back inside, she pulled out a cordovan photo album that she placed on the couch beside me.

"This is a history of the house. My father-in-law put it together. His family has owned this house since Rossetti died. My father-in-law was a publisher and had great respect for history. He found some of these photographs in the house, in a box in the attic. Others, he was able to track down in printshops and the like. Besides the pictures of the garden, for my renovation efforts, I haven't really examined it, but feel free to peruse. I just need to talk to Cook for a minute. I will be back. Are you all set? Do you want more tea?"

"No, I'm fine. Please, don't let me interrupt your evening any more than I already have. I'll be out of your hair in a minute."

"Take your time. I'm not in any rush. In fact, I appreciate the company. My brother lives here, as well, but he's abroad, and I have felt quite alone."

I opened the book to some very old photographs of 16 Cheyne Walk that had yellowed with age. I was looking at the old, car-less street view I'd seen just days ago. And then photographs of the sitting room and dining room of the house the way I remembered them. The familiar wallpapers. The furniture. The paintings hanging on the walls. I turned the pages, lost in the images of an interior that no longer existed anywhere but in my mind.

Then I turned a page, and a small "*Oh*" escaped from my lips. It was a photograph of a group of people sitting at the dining room table. I recognized Ashe right away. A small, grainy image of him, to be sure, but it was him. To his right was Rossetti. Then a man I didn't recognize. Then Fanny. There were also three other men and one woman I didn't know.

My eyes went back to Ashe.

I reached out, and even though I knew better, being an art historian, being a Keeper at the V&A, knowing it was the very last thing I should do, I touched Ashe's face with my forefinger and felt a stab of longing so strong it was an actual pain deep inside my chest.

Would Mrs. Whitfield mind very much if I took this one photograph? There were at least fifty others in the book. She said she had really only spent time examining photos of the garden. She didn't know these people. I did. I had nothing from those days with Ashe. It would mean so much to me if I could just have this one photo.

Carefully, I removed it from the black corners holding it in place. Would Mrs. Whitfield ever notice? When was the last time she'd inspected the book? And it wouldn't be the only empty space. I'd seen other blanks on previous pages. But to steal something?

I could hear murmurs in a faraway room. How could I do this? On the very day when the Midas Society had opened an investigation into a possible theft from Woodfern Manor in which my father might be implicated.

But this was one of fifty old, yellowed photos that no one cared about. What harm would I do if I took it?

And then I had an idea. I'd borrow it. Have it photographed so I had a copy, and then return it somehow. I'd come back here under some pretense and slip it under the couch for her or her maid to find.

Resolved that I was only borrowing it, I slipped the photo into my pocketbook and quickly moved ahead several pages in the photo album so I was almost at the end when she returned.

"Was it interesting?"

"Very much, thank you."

"I'm glad. I'm keeping it for my son. I'm not one for rooting around in dusty histories, but he takes after his grandfather, and I think he'll appreciate it."

I handed it to her, and she replaced it on the high shelf in the bookcase. I was almost breathing normally. From where she'd put it, I guessed she wouldn't be looking at it anytime soon.

"How old is your son?"

"Fourteen. His sister is twelve. They should be home from school shortly."

"And I should go. I've stolen so much of your time. I can't tell you how much I appreciate you opening your door and home to me."

CHAPTER 22

The location of the Midas Society offices are kept secret. There is one in New York City, one in London, one in Rome, one in Greece, one in Paris, and one in Buenos Aries. The headquarters are in Cannes. When you become a member, you are given only the city and country name of the office closest to where you live, but no address until you need it. And even then, it is not written down. You are always escorted to a Midas Society office by a senior member.

I had been to the London office twice, under much more pleasant circumstances than that Tuesday in early November when one of the Society's members, Eloise Harvey, drove me to the meeting I'd been asked to attend.

On a non-descript street in a fancy part of London, there was a row of standard red brick houses with white trim—the kind of innocuous homes you'd find all over town. Using a key, Eloise let me inside one of them. The foyer was as ordinary as the house: white walls, worn Oriental carpet, yellowed and aged family portraits, and dark brown furniture. We took a flight of stairs down to a wine cellar, where Eloise used her keys again to open a small oak door behind a wall of shelving. This led to a cold, damp tunnel. We walked for about five minutes through the narrow passageway until we came to another door, where she used a third key.

We were in a crypt. The ancient burial place was abandoned, once part of a church that no longer existed except for the underground stone reminder. A spiral stone staircase stood in the corner. As we ascended, the cold seeped into my bones.

I was nervous. It felt like I was on my way to an inquisition. And in a way, I was.

We climbed. One flight. Two. Three. And then we were in a turret-like room with arched, stained-glass windows. I saw an old rectory table with four chairs around it. Other chairs lined the wall to accommodate more people. Shelving on two of the walls overflowed with books. A small desk abutted one wall. Nothing was on it but a black telephone. Another door in addition to the one we'd come through led to the residence of the head of the London branch of the Society, Mr. Althorp.

No one ever used the door but him. And no one who worked in their residence knew that he could make his way here from a secret entrance in that house—nobody but his wife was privy to that information.

Mr. Althorp was a distinguished man in his sixties. He had a full head of silver hair threaded with black, and a beard of the same combination. From his brogue to his well-worn corduroy jacket and flannel pants, he looked every inch the history professor he was. Although his name at the college where he was on the faculty was not Mr. Althorp but yet another pseudonym. No one but the head of the Society and his closest friends knew his real name.

I was not one of those friends. But my father was. One of his very closest. Which was another reason this meeting was so fraught with anxiety for me.

"I wish we were meeting under kinder circumstances,

Jeannine," he said.

"So do I."

"Thank you for agreeing to come in."

"Of course." My heart was beating too fast. I reminded myself that I had no reason to be nervous. I knew neither I nor my father had done anything wrong. We had not stolen or misplaced the Botticelli.

"I have quite a few questions, so should we just get to it? This is as unpleasant for me as it is for you. I told Mr. Gibbons that I doubted there was any chance of impropriety on your or your father's part, but he seems stuck on the idea that the painting must have disappeared while under your care."

"So I've heard."

"Can you take me through the procedures surrounding the painting? When it left the museum, how it was moved, who was involved in its transport? And then while it was at Woodfern, who knew it was there? And then tell me about its return."

His voice was calm, his countenance non-threatening. I knew Mr. Althorp did not believe we were responsible for the missing painting, but I was still highly agitated. The fact was, the painting was missing. It was invaluable. And it had been under our care.

It took me the better part of thirty minutes to explain all the particulars. Once I was done, Mr. Althorp had numerous additional questions, all of which I answered without hesitation. The more I explained, the more I was sure the painting had been returned to the Victoria and Albert and its disappearance had occurred afterward.

"What is your relationship with Mr. Gibbons like?" Mr. Althorp asked.

That was the first question which surprised me. "He's not easy to work for, but he's always been fair."

"Are you sure?"

"Yes, why?"

"When you told me he has always been fair, you hesitated."

I smiled. Althorp's reputation as an investigator rested on his acute ability to notice the most minute clues.

"Well, he's putting me through a rigorous test right now that doesn't feel fair at all." I told him about the contest between Hugh and me.

"When is the show opening?"

"February 14th."

He wrote the date down.

"Has Mr. Gibbons talked to you much about your father over the years?"

"My father?" I didn't understand the question.

"Yes, they were both at Oxford and joined the Society of Antiquaries of London at the same time. "

"Oh, yes, right. I did know that. My father once mentioned they'd been contemporaries but not friends." I had a vague memory of something else about that conversation but couldn't recall what it was.

"Was that all?"

Was it? I didn't know. I shook my head. "I think so. What else could there be?"

"On your father's part, I doubt anything else. We've been in touch, and his letters about this situation are quite clear. But when I met with Mr. Gibbons, I got a feeling—mind you, it's just a feeling—that there is something else. And I am concerned. If the painting isn't discovered in the extensive search he is doing at the museum, and word of it being missing gets out, this loss will put Mr. Gibbons in the spotlight. It will be seen as his responsibility, and I get the very clear impression that he's not the type to accept any blame. He'll need a scapegoat, and you and your father are the natural choices. Once he goes public with his accusations, it will be very damaging for both of you."

"It will destroy Father."

"And seriously hurt your career."

I nodded.

"So, you see, if there's something else, anything else that you know about Mr. Gibbons—or can find out—you need to tell me. And I would make finding the painting your priority now."

CHAPTER 23

For the rest of the week, I immersed myself in two tasks: searching for clues about Mr. Gibbons and the missing Botticelli and doing research for my show in the museum's library.

For the first, I enlisted Sybil's help. Though she wasn't in the art or museum worlds, she was amongst the circle of high society people Mr. Gibbons aspired to be a part of. Did she know about any social clubs he was in or tried to get into? Business deals he'd attempted with men of the higher ranks? Was he having money problems?

"There has to be a reason Mr. Althorp suspects Gibbons," I said. "What motive would Gibbons have to steal a painting from his own museum and send his entire staff off looking for it?"

My friend promised to go to work immediately. This kind of snooping around was right up her alley, and I knew she'd be better at ferreting out information than I could possibly be.

With her on the hunt, I could devote my time to my quest for the most beautiful words ever written about love. While it was for the exhibit, it turned out to be a salve for my soul. Ashe Lloyd Lewis was lost to me, but the feelings he had ignited in me still simmered. I dreamt about him every night. Not reenactments of our time together, but scenes of a life we'd never lived. I'd awaken with them so fresh and real that I wondered more than once if I was seeing a world that might have been had I stayed in that long-ago place.

On Thursday, I set up a meeting with the museum's photographer. He would shoot each lover's eye separately for me so I could write up the catalog descriptions, plus work on an idea I had for the catalog's cover. It would be expensive, but I still had some money in my budget that I could appropriate. Once we had that all worked out, I would get the jewels to restoration so they could be cleaned and repaired before the final shoot.

I met Wilson Lennox in his studio, a large room on the museum's top floor. The space was crammed with shelves of equipment—lights, props, and rolls of backgrounds and fabrics. He placed the case of jewels I'd brought up on a worktable and began the process of unrolling a deep red velvet bolt of fabric and setting it beside one of black. We had discussed trying both.

We arranged the fourteen chosen brooches in a large heart shape. It was a difficult still life to light because of the crystal and glass covering so many of the miniatures, but he managed to both avoid glare and still get the gemstones in the frames to shine.

My idea was to die-cut a smaller heart shape in the middle of the main heart, revealing a drawing of the heart-shaped lover's-eye brooch I was making the ghostly hero of the exhibit—the Marie Antoinette eye that hadn't been seen in almost two hundred years.

When you opened the catalog, that brooch and a poem written by Dante Gabriel Rossetti that Ashe had shared with me would appear.

It was an unusual choice. A drawing of a missing lover's token and a painter's poem. But this was a time for romance.

My goal was to enforce the idea of true love not only lasting but being *ever*lasting. Defying time.

I wanted museum visitors to see the jewels I'd chosen and the one that was missing, read the accompanying text, and be moved and transfixed.

I'd found a literary passage, love letter, or poem to assign to each of the lovers' eyes in our library, using the most enduring, hopeful, and moving words I could find.

To go with a pearl brooch with a pale blue woman's eye, I chose John Keats' poem to Fanny Brawne, an original draft of which we had a the museum.

Closer of lovely eyes to lovely dreams,
Lover of loneliness, and wandering,
Of upcast eye, and tender pondering!
Thee must I praise above all other glories
That smile us on to tell delightful stories.

Lord Byron was the owner of a lover's eye, which he kept secret. For a very old lover's eye ring set with rose-cut diamonds, I used one of his most famous verses.

She walks in beauty, like the night
Of cloudless climes and starry skies;
And all that's best of dark and bright
Meet in her aspect and her eyes:
Thus mellowed to that tender light
Which heaven to gaudy day denies.

This poem was not in his hand but from a 1842 edition of his poetry given from Prince Albert to Queen Victoria, and I knew it would be a highlight of the exhibit. Their love story was always a favorite, especially in the museum named for them.

We spent two hours working on the photographs and were finishing up when Alice came rushing into the room.

"Mr. Gibbons needs to see you as soon as possible."

"I need to finish up here and—"

"He said now."

I couldn't leave the jewelry here. It was my responsibility. Mr. Gibbons would have to wait long enough for me to replace each piece in the case and bring it with me.

When I arrived at Mr. Gibbons' office holding the case, his secretary waved me in.

The director was sitting behind his desk in his usual imperious manner, Hugh in one of the two chairs opposite. Both of them looked grim. Usually, Hugh looked relaxed and confident, but not today. He looked different to me. His posture was slumped. His hair ruffled as if he'd been running his hand through it over and over. Even his suit seemed wrinkled.

"There seems to be a problem," Mr. Gibbons said.

"Yes?"

"Someone stole Mr. Kenward's notes for the show."

"That's terrible," I said.

"Yes, isn't it?" Hugh said sarcastically.

"Excuse me?"

"Well, it's very convenient that my notes have been taken and we are in competition with each other. It's very possible, isn't it, that someone might want to know what I am doing so they can copy me and win."

"Are you suggesting I went into your office and looked at your notes?" I was outraged. I found this especially odd since I had been sure that someone had been in *my* office looking at my notes, but I had never thought of going to Mr. Gibbons with my hunch. I wondered if this was Hugh's way of deflecting suspicion.

"I am going to have to ask you to tell me your plans for the exhibit, Mrs. Maycroft, so that I can ascertain that nothing going on here is untoward."

I was so glad I'd protected myself. Once I had suspected Hugh had been in my office, I had been leaving notes out detailing plans that were nothing like what I was actually doing. While I had no proof to show that Hugh was spying on me, at least I was protecting my concept.

"I don't feel comfortable doing this here and now," I said.

I was not going to make this easy for the director. I was being tested when Hugh should have been.

"How will you know that Mr. Kenward hasn't stolen my idea?" I asked.

"Given the circumstances, that is highly unusual—" Hugh started.

I turned on him and interrupted. "Hardly. The circumstances are that last week I found my desk rifled through. I wrote down what happened and had it notarized with the date of discovery. I can get that dated letter if you'd like." I looked at Mr. Gibbons. I was challenging him, but so be it.

My father and I were already under suspicion for the missing painting. I would not endure more about my integrity over the Valentine's Day show, as well.

"This is turning out to be very unpleasant," Mr. Gibbons said with his typical understated tone. "I expect to see both of you back here in the morning. And please, bring the letter, Mrs. Maycroft."

"Absolutely. With pleasure."

I picked up my case and started out of the office. I was halfway down the hall when Hugh caught up with me.

"You are playing a dangerous game here, Jeannine. One I don't intend to let you win. I never had anything but respect and admiration for you, but you never believed that, did you? Well, now we're here. This will all go down easier if you just admit defeat now. I'll be a very good boss to you." He reached a hand toward my face. I wasn't sure what he was about to do, how he planned to touch me, or why, but I wasn't about to let him and backed up.

"We had good fun all those years ago when I first came to the museum," he said. "We could go back to being friends. Become *office lovers*, as Mrs. Auriol suggested to me after meeting you." He grinned, and his eyes twinkled.

Unbelievable.

"There's no fraternization allowed here now, just as there wasn't then. You put me in danger. Clio even thought you were doing it to try and get me fired. I defended you to her. But now, I think I was wrong not to pay more attention to what she said. You were trying to get rid of me then, weren't you? And you are trying now, which I am sure isn't behavior consistent with museum management. And lastly, you have no idea who you are dealing with. I'm no longer a young research assistant but a woman hardened by war, a seasoned curator with a letter describing my notes and the date they were tampered with. I doubt you'll be able to counter my proof."

Hugh's grin had faded. He looked down and quietly said, "I, too, am seasoned and hardened by war, Jeannine."

And with that, he walked past me.

I stared after him. When I no longer heard his footsteps echoing on the floor, I returned to my office with the case of eye jewelry.

I locked my door and opened the lid. The jewels gleamed up at me. I sat for a few minutes, disappearing into their glow and enjoying the sight.

Beauty is cleansing. It takes over for a moment and gives you room to breathe, to escape, to float on its wings of delight. There were so many pieces in the museum that I found transportive, but these had proven to be special in their own way.

Art is created for so many reasons. Religious, educational, functional, commemorative…but these eyes were all pained to freeze a feeling. To take love, passion, devotion, and forever keep a memento of it. Looking into each of these painted eyes, I felt that love bubbling up and surrounding me, soothing me, reminding me and promising me what could be.

And of all of these, one spoke that message to me the deepest. I lifted the eye that I now believed was Ashe's, somehow here in the museum all these years later, and held it. At the time of our sitting, he hadn't painted his eye, so I couldn't be certain, but having spent those heady days looking into his soul through his eyes, I had little doubt. It was that twilight blue with flecks of gold that intensified when he was kissing me. I didn't understand how it was here in the museum. I had asked him to do a self-portrait for me—had he done it after I left? I hadn't wanted to tell him about it or ask about something that hadn't yet happened in his time. I had wanted to discuss my quandary with Imogine first, but then I'd been transported back.

I thought about the ancient mysteries my grandmother had told me about when I was growing up and how she'd educated me in the magickal world that was our heritage. I recalled the people in history who had known things unknowable about the past and the future. The artists, writers, and scientists who had created objects that must have come from knowledge beyond their time. Were they all time travelers? She'd intimated as much when she talked about them when I was a child. And now that I thought about it, she'd foreshadowed this experience. I realized she'd known exactly who I was in 1867. And she'd kept the secret from me in my present life, only obliquely suggesting it and hoping I'd be at least a bit prepared when it happened. But I'd forgotten until now. I missed her anew. My eyes filled with tears, thinking about the young herbalist in the Chelsea Garden who had helped me. And I missed my grandfather with his knowing smile and hugs. But mostly, I missed Ashe.

I lifted the brooch. Would it be a terrible mistake to put it on? Just to feel Ashe close to my breast for a little while? To remember and revel in what I'd had for those few days. I might never know that passion again, but at least I had known it once.

I worked the archaic clasp on the back of the brooch. I felt a prick of pain. The catch had sprung open again, just as it had before. I put the pin down and inspected the pad of my index finger. There was a bright red spot of blood. I put my finger into my mouth and felt faint. I shut my eyes for a minute to stop the room from spinning.

CHAPTER 24

I'd fallen asleep in my chair, except this wasn't my chair. Mine was upholstered and comfortable; this was hardbacked, and I felt stiff. And this wasn't my streamlined desk but a bulky, scarred one. And none of my things were in front of me. The case of lovers' eyes wasn't there. Panic built deep in my stomach. What had happened to me? Had I fallen asleep in my office and sleepwalked into someone else's? But no one had an office that looked like this.

I turned and looked out the window. Yes, it was the same view I normally looked at.

I put my hands on the edge of the desk and felt a shot of pain. Looking down, I saw a cut on my index finger with crusted blood on its edge. I remembered then: trying to put the brooch on and pricking myself.

It was the *blood* that had transported me. *Make of my blood, a journey.*

I stood and walked out into the hallway, which also appeared different from how it was in my time, but I didn't stop to inspect it. I had someplace more important to be.

Out on the street, I was both surprised and excited to see what I'd seen just over a week ago. Men and women in period dress from the mid-1800s. I was running now, toward Chelsea. It was normally a twenty-minute walk, but I made it in half that time and bounded up the steps at number 16, out of breath and perspiring.

I lifted and let the dragon knocker on the door drop and then held my breath as the door opened.

I so hoped it was not Mrs. Whitfield in 1947.

It wasn't. It was Fanny. I had returned to 1867.

"Hello, Jeannine!" she said as she reached out, took my hand, and pulled me over the threshold. "Come in, come in." Excitedly, she ushered me the rest of the way inside. The hallway wasn't cream; the beautiful green-flowered wallpaper was back.

"You are breathing so hard. Are you all right?" she asked.

I nodded. "I am. I ran all the way here once I realized where I was."

"Well, sit down and catch your breath. Let me get tea. Ashe is out, but he should be back shortly."

I sat on the couch and looked around the room, filled with all the Victorian furniture upholstered in its heavy green velvet. My eyes roamed the walls, taking in the drawings and paintings dispersed in museums in my time. Seeing everything as it had been, with no sign of Mrs. Whitfield's alterations, was a great relief.

Fanny returned with a tray. Cups and saucers, a pot of tea, a plate of scones with clotted cream and jam. She'd added a slim silver vase with a long trail of ivy in it to make it festive.

"You scared us," she said as she poured the libations. You just disappeared. We were all so worried."

"I didn't mean to leave so suddenly, without word."

"Ashe will be happy, so happy you are back. That lovely young girl from the Chelsea Garden came and talked to him, but she didn't make him any less sad." She took a sip of her tea. "You really are all right, aren't you?"

"Yes, quite. And excited to be back."

She was looking at me with her head cocked to the side. "You're wearing your modern clothes. I'll put what I lent you back in your room."

"I want to pay you for wearing them, though. I know how dear they are."

"Don't you mind that for now. Your breathing is still a bit labored. Was getting here difficult? Are you tired?"

"I'm fine. I'll be fine."

And I was sure I would be. I didn't know how long I could stay this time, but at least now I had a second chance to warn Ashe about the fire.

He came home about thirty minutes later. Fanny heard his key in the lock and went to greet him and alert him. He rushed into the room, knelt at my knees, and took my hands in his.

"I was bereft, Jeannine. Please, please don't ever do that to me again."

His grip was too strong and he was hurting my fingers, but I didn't tell him that. Such was my relief at feeling his flesh, smelling his scent, looking into his eyes—his real, blinking eyes filled with tears, not the miniature painting.

"I'll try. But I didn't plan it. I was in the bedroom one minute and back in 1947 the next."

"Do you know what happened? How it happened?"

"I think so, but I need to talk to Imogine. I think it has to do with a miniature I believe you painted of your eye."

"But you couldn't know about that…" he mused. "After you disappeared, I finished your eye and then did something I've never done before; I painted a self-portrait. Not my whole face, but my eye. I did it for you. For us. I kept thinking that if I had both of them, yours and mine, paired up, I'd somehow find you again. It seemed so important, though I wasn't sure why. Imogine encouraged me to do it after you left. She said the strangest thing…"

"What?"

"That it was your seeing me that had brought you to me. That lovers see each other in ways others can't. That our souls had connected through our gazes, and a connection like that was stronger than time. Cryptic, that one." He smiled. "I can barely make sense of what she means half the time, but then nothing about you, about us, makes sense. Except when I'm holding you. Then it makes all the sense in the world."

He wrapped his arms around me and kissed me, and I forgot that I'd been about to ask him what else he and Imogine had talked about.

"Can you stay for at least a while, Jeannine? Will you?"

I shook my head. " I don't know if I can. I'm not sure, but I think this all has a purpose. There's a reason for me being here. A job I have to do."

Then, to myself, I thought, *it may be to save your life from being extinguished too soon.* Perhaps the fire was not supposed to have happened, and fate had sent me back in time to rectify the mistake.

"I'll take whatever time I can get, but I'm not letting you out of my sight."

I laughed. "That sounds a little bossy."

"Yes, I'm going to be a little bossy. Is that all right with you?"

"It never has been before. I've known bossy men and always stayed far away from them. They are always too sure of themselves for my taste."

"How about if I promise only to be bossy about this one small thing?"

"That I can't leave your sight? I don't think that's a small thing. Please don't worry, Ashe. I'll do everything I can to not just up and disappear again."

Fanny had let us greet each other alone, but she returned now carrying another cup for Ashe and a refreshed pot of tea.

Rossetti came home shortly thereafter and was equally welcoming. He had what seemed a million questions about what had happened to me.

"I believe that we're experiencing something in the realm of reincarnation. Not the same thing, of course, but part of the same mystical universe," he offered. "Along with Ashe, I spoke to Imogine when she was here. This is my house, after all, and I want to know if it's hallowed ground."

"What did she say?" I asked.

"That you are the one who has the magick. Not the house, sadly. But she did offer me some herbal remedies for my headaches, and they are truly working. She also read my poetry and told me she is a great believer in reincarnation. I am going to do a portrait of her, with that wild, red hair..." He stopped speaking and looked at me. "The same as yours. I noticed that when she was here and meant to ask her but forgot for all our talk of mystical things. Are you related?"

"Yes, we are."

I left it at that. I didn't mind Rossetti knowing, but I didn't want him telling my grandmother if she wasn't yet aware of it. I had no idea when she would figure it out since I now realized that by the time I turned fourteen, she knew she'd met an older me in this time and place.

The thought made my head ache, and I put my hand to my forehead, willing it away.

"You must be exhausted," Ashe said. "Why don't you go upstairs and have a rest before dinner?"

"I freshened up your room while you were talking to Ashe," Fanny said. "Let me take you."

"Thank you, but don't bother, please. I know the way, and I've put you out enough."

As if this were my home, I climbed the stairs, turned right, and went to the same bedroom I'd occupied before. I took off my shoes and lay on the covers, promptly falling asleep.

Fanny woke me two hours later, bringing the clothes I'd worn the last time I was here. We chatted while she laid them out, and then she left me to dress, urging me to come downstairs when I was ready. She said Rossetti's guests had arrived.

We were eight, with four members of Rossetti's circle joining us, including Edward Burne-Jones and William Morris. I had trouble relaxing at first as we sat around the table. These men were heroes of mine. Their art, along with Rossetti's, meant so much to me. I wanted to tell Mr. Morris how his Green Room at the V&A was still the most beautiful room in all of London. And explain to Mr. Burne-Jones how important his paintings were to those who appreciated the late Victorian period. Instead, I sat and drank in their conversation with more of a thirst than I had for the wine. The talk turned to the new paintings they'd seen at a gallery, including one that depicted the regatta of Le Havre with figures on the beach and the outer harbor covered with small sails. I listened, fascinated as they dissected the work by the young French painter, Claude Monet. I had read that Rossetti and his friends didn't approve of the Impressionist movement, but that was in the future still. In 1867, Monet was still painting realistic landscapes. Even so, the Pre-Raphaelites at the table complained about the *messiness* of Monet's loosening brush strokes and his experiments with his plein-air style. With great vehemence, they discussed what they disliked about it.

I was fascinated by this very inside art world conversation, marveling at the insights.

"Have you seen his work?" Rossetti asked me.

"I have," I said.

"And?" he prompted.

"I like it."

"Because?"

"I think his exploration of light and color is important."

"And if he pushes ahead with that and becomes even less formal, you are saying people will respond to it?"

I had to be careful here. Imogine had warned me about

telling too much about the future. I could make these men's children and grandchildren wealthy if I told them to buy as many Monets as they could in their lifetimes and put them away for the next eighty years.

But I didn't.

"There's no telling how tastes will evolve," was all I offered.

The conversation shifted. Rossetti asked Mr. Morris something about a recent wallpaper design he was working on while Mr. Burne-Jones, who sat on my left, leaned toward Ashe on my right.

"I have a commission for you," Burne-Jones said.

"Too difficult for you to take yourself?" Ashe joked.

"I wish I could take it. There's good money in it. But not my style. Mable Carruthers would like to have one of those eye miniatures done. It's all quite hush-hush, she said, and asked me if anyone could execute such a piece and keep quiet about it. I have a feeling it's not for her husband."

"That doesn't surprise me. Her husband is well known to be a brute," Fanny said.

I'd heard the expression, *having your blood run cold*, but I'd never experienced it before that moment. Carruthers was the name of the man who'd set fire to the studio in Rossetti's garden in 1868. The fire in which Ashe Lloyd Lewis died trying to save his paintings.

"You—" I was about to blurt out *you can't take it* but stopped myself.

Mr. Burne-Jones, Fanny, and Ashe all looked at me.

"What is it?" Ashe asked.

"What name did you say?" I asked Mr. Burne-Jones. I had to be certain.

He repeated it.

"I don't know them. I must have misheard the name. But Ashe, should you take the job if the husband is a brute?"

"Well, he's not a brute to artists," Mr. Burne-Jones said.

"Both he and Lady Carruthers are great art patrons and have kept many of us from going hungry at one time or another."

"That's the truth," Ashe said. "Besides, I won't be dealing with him at all if this is hush-hush, now, will I?"

As good as dinner was, I'd lost my appetite and couldn't finish the curried cod, carrots, and turnips on my plate. I had no trouble finishing my glass of white wine, though. I had to figure out how to stop Ashe from taking the commission that would bring about his demise.

CHAPTER 25

After dinner, Rossetti invited us all to see his latest purchase. I followed with the others, and he led us across a hallway I had not traversed on my last visit and into his studio.

On the easel was a rectangle covered with a white sheet.

"This is it," he said, pulling off the fabric.

I gasped. In front of me was the painting that was missing from the Victoria and Albert, *Portrait of a Lady known as Smeralda Bandinelli*. It was the piece Clio had overseen moving out of the V&A in 1939. The painting that Mr. Gibbons claimed had been lost or possibly stolen by my father. The prize the Midas Society was investigating, putting my father's reputation—and possibly mine—in jeopardy.

I couldn't stop staring at the lady, trying to understand how I could be looking at it here, and how it could be lost in 1947. I simply couldn't make sense of what was happening.

Was this really the exact same painting? It had to be, but still, I examined it. The pale, strawberry-blond-haired woman from the fifteenth century looked out at me boldly, holding my gaze. I had read that, at the time of the painting, women were supposed to keep their eyes lowered, signifying modesty and obedience and were thus shown that way in portraits. But

Botticelli had refused and painted Smeralda Bandinelli looking out. His challenge must have made this a most controversial work.

The painting had to be the same one. Smeralda wore a white cap, a pale pink-lavender flowing—but not overly sumptuous for the era—gown with maroon and gold embroidered edging. The detailed lacework on her sleeves, modest for the Renaissance, looked identical to what I remembered from the last time I'd seen this work. Her simple gold necklace of three rows of open-work links gleamed. The lace handkerchief in her graceful, elongated fingers could only have been painted that way by Botticelli.

Without any heraldic devices in the painting, with lovely but not overly elaborate clothing or jewelry, there was very little to tell the viewer about Smeralda Bandinelli's stature. Because she was painted at all, she must have enjoyed an elevated status, but what exactly it was, remained unknown.

"She's extraordinary, isn't she?" Rossetti asked.

I didn't trust my words, so I just nodded. I was mesmerized by the very fact of this painting of a pale beauty looking at me from her upper-story window.

I had studied this portrait often at the museum, in awe of Botticelli's power to engage the viewer. He'd employed several devices to force your eye where he wanted it to go. The diagonal lines of the architectures—the window ledge, shutter, and shadows—all converged on the lady's face with her right pupil almost exactly in the composition's center. Having been drawn in, you are met with her shocking, forthright gaze.

There was speculation among art historians that the perceived boldness of the lady's glance may have led to the vandalism of her right eye, which, together with her mouth had, at one time, been scored through by an unknown hand but since repaired.

"It's criminal that Botticelli has been forgotten, swept into the past in lieu of Michelangelo and da Vinci," Rossetti told us. "I was able to pick this up at Christie's for twenty pounds, can you imagine?"

There were murmurs of surprise from Ashe, Mr. Burne-Jones, and Mr. Morris.

"I've been cleaning her headdress," Rossetti continued. "Which revealed her fabulous red hair. I'm going to do a series of portraits inspired by her."

"Did you not change her hair color at all?" I asked Rossetti the question so many at the V&A had wondered. A scholar had found a letter from Rossetti to his secretary, Charles Augustus Howell, and one line suggested an alteration.

I have been restoring the headdress, but don't mean to tell.

"Change it? Not at all. I cleaned it. And I whitened the cap a bit, but don't tell anyone. It still looked dirty and I couldn't bear it."

This little piece of information was just thrown in, and yet I couldn't help but think how scholars would relish it. I should be keeping a journal. When Clio and I had packed the painting, the Keeper had told us it was believed that Rossetti had repainted the woman's hair and made it redder to conform with his obsession for redheaded beauties. He'd said Rossetti and the other Pre-Raphaelites reveled in painting redheads because women with red hair were considered evil in medieval times.

I knew that only too well from my family's history. My ancestor, the courtesan La Lune, had been said to beguile so many men because she was a witch, and her red hair proved it.

After all the guests had left, I asked Ashe if I could talk to him privately, and we went up to his room. He sat me on the bed and immediately took me in his arms.

"I'm so very glad you have returned. But what's wrong, darling girl? At first, you seemed so happy to be back, but since dinner, you've appeared worried."

I pulled back and looked at his face. Into his trusting twilight-colored eyes. What to tell him? *How* to tell him?

"Yes, it was something Mr. Burne-Jones said. You need to promise me you'll listen to what I have to say and not interrupt until I get to the end, but then not ask me any questions."

"That's a fairly large ask."

I took his hand and held it in mine, tracing the outline of his long fingers that held me so tenderly and a paintbrush with such force. I thought about the painting in the Victoria and Albert and all the others in the studio that I had never seen in my time because they would be destroyed in six weeks. I thought of the kisses and caresses that I might enjoy if I found a way to stay here in this time and place and save him. I thought about all of it disappearing forever because of Mable Carruthers' need to titillate her lover and make her husband jealous.

"You can't take that commission from Mable Carruthers."

"Why ever not?"

"I told you, no interruptions, and no questions. You simply have to promise me that, no matter what happens to me, no matter how long I stay here or can't, you will never paint a lover's eye for her."

"Are you jealous of her?"

I laughed at that one. "Oh, goodness, no. Nothing so silly as that. It's so important, Ashe. You have to promise me. It's for your own good. Truly."

I didn't realize how tightly I'd been gripping his hand until he extricated it.

"You're crying," he said as he wiped away my tears. "Why?"

I hadn't realized I'd started crying.

"I can't tell you."

"You have to give me some reason for turning down such a lucrative job. Don't you see? If she likes it, she might add me to the list of artists she collects. That could be the break I need. She's very influential in the Salon, and she alone could be how I finally get accepted."

"I can't give you a reason or explain it. Just please promise me."

He looked away from me and out the darkened window. He was silent for a few moments, then seemed to make a decision. "All right. I promise. I'll send a note to Burne-Jones tomorrow."

"Thank you," I said and then leaned forward to kiss him.

It was a bittersweet embrace. I couldn't stop thinking about the commission I knew he wanted.

"You're still preoccupied," Ashe said as he pulled away. "What else is disturbing you?"

"My job is in even more jeopardy now than it was before," I said. I hadn't planned on discussing this with him, but now, I wanted to. Maybe he could give me some advice. So, I told him about the Botticelli, my father, and the whole mess.

"If you could take the painting back with you to your time, it would solve everything, wouldn't it? You'd be a hero. Your job would be saved."

"I suppose so, but…"

"Rossetti only paid twenty pounds for it. I'm sure he'd be willing to let you take it with you when you return, especially if you agree to sit for him. He's quite enamored with your hair."

"Could I take it back? I mean, is it possible for me to travel with it?"

"Did you take anything back last time?"

I thought about it. I'd changed out of Fanny's dress to put on my skirt, blouse, and jacket. So no—and then I remembered. "Yes, I had on Fanny's slip and stockings. I never changed out of them."

"And?"

"They are at home in a drawer."

"Intact?"

I nodded.

"Then we'll arrange it."

"I'll need to plan to have it with me when I go back. Last time, I didn't even know I was going to return. But now I know that my blood being drawn by your eye painting took me back, and my La Lune spell returned me. So, I can choose when I go."

"But a painting seems more complicated than the clothes you were wearing."

"You're right. I can't have the painting on my person," I agreed.

"Imogine might know more. Maybe you can talk to her tomorrow."

I nodded. "Perhaps."

"There's only one problem, Jeannine."

"What is it?"

"I don't want to let you go."

He leaned in, took hold of me, and kissed me. I returned his kiss and felt as if I was floating on the sensation.

"I don't want to leave you either," I whispered. I felt the heat emanating from his body as he pulled me closer—as close as we could get.

But could I stay? Was it even possible? Even if it was, I had to go back and save my father's reputation. Then I could consider which life I wanted to continue with.

"Stop thinking, darling girl. I can hear your mind whirling. Leave it for tomorrow when you go see Imogine. For now, just let us be here and now in this glorious bliss."

I did as he suggested.

CHAPTER 26

"Yes, I believe what brought you here was the blood you shed when you cut your finger on the clasp of the miniature portrait Ashe Lloyd Lewis painted of his eye. The connection between you just needed that small push, and there you were."

I listened with wonder as my grandmother explained what else she had been able to figure out about my visit to 1867.

"And when the cut healed, you were ready to be transported back to 1947," she said.

"So, as soon as this new cut heals, you think I'll return again?"

"I do."

"Just in the middle of a sentence when the wound has closed."

"No, I don't think it's that arbitrary. I asked you to put on your clothes, and then I asked if you remembered your spell. You said you did. You didn't say it out loud, but were you thinking it? Do you remember?"

"Yes..." I thought for a moment. "I was thinking it. Every word of it. So, that's what you think I have to do to travel? Use the spell?"

"Once the wound is healed, yes. Let me see your hand."

I showed her.

"Do you have any of the salve I gave you last time? I'm afraid this one has become infected, as well."

"Yes, upstairs. But what if I don't want to go back? What if I want to stay here? Do you think I can?"

"Before we even get to if you can or can't, it's a question of if you should or not. It's not the natural order of things for you to go missing from your present that way."

"Other than my father, though, I wouldn't be affecting anyone. Except for Sybil, of course. But here, there's Ashe, you, and my—" I was about to say *my grandfather* but instead said, "Family."

"Except there are things waiting for you back home you don't know about yet. A future you can't even imagine. One that has its consequences. As would you being here have its own consequences. Maybe Ashe is meant to do certain things and meet particular people that your being here would prevent. And one of those small acts might have grave repercussions we can't even guess at."

She was right, of course, but to leave Ashe?

"You need to believe me," she said.

"I know." I shook my head as if dislodging the thought. "It's too soon to think about that anyway. I have to go back home at least once to save my father's reputation, and I think Ashe has helped me figure out how."

"What will you do?"

"Mr. Rossetti has agreed to give me the painting in exchange for my sitting with him upon my next return. I'm going to take the Botticelli home and put it in the museum. It's where it winds up anyway."

"Except it's already there."

"Well, yes, but it's missing. So, I'll have it."

"That's so complicated it's making my head spin." My grandmother laughed.

"As it is mine," I said.

"I don't know if that will work," she said, all seriousness returning.

"Nor do I, but I have to try."

"From the look of it, you only have a day or two at the most until your cut heals. This one isn't nearly as deep as the last."

"It's like finding out the day of your death," I murmured, thinking I knew the date of hers, my grandfather's, and Ashe's.

She patted my hand. "There's a future waiting for you. You need to believe that."

"Do you?"

She nodded, "I do, lamb. I know it for a fact."

After Imogine left, I remained in the parlor, in front of the fire, thinking about my plan. I decided that after I took the painting back to the museum and installed it in its proper place, vindicating my father and me, I would return here. For good. No matter my grandmother's warnings. I wanted to be with Ashe.

He returned home while I was still lost in thought. Sitting beside me, he took my hand.

"Did she explain anything further?"

I recounted the conversation, leaving out the part about her insisting I not come back and change the trajectory of my future.

"I have something for you," Ashe said, taking a package from his waistcoat pocket.

He handed me something small, wrapped in white linen. Opening it, I saw a lover's eye. The very miniature I had become besotted with weeks ago at the museum. The portrait of Ashe Lloyd Lewis's eye that had begun this marvelous and strange adventure.

But how could it be here when it was back in the museum? I'd left it there.

"I plan to take it to Bond Street and have it set for you in a circlet of opals, the symbol of hope."

"I thought they signified criminal activity and bad luck?" I remembered Clio telling me as much.

"An old wives' tale, I'm sure. How can a world of color inside a stone be anything but hopeful? But I wanted you to see it first. To know it will be waiting for you when you come back."

"And I will come back. I promise you. As soon as I return the painting. Imogine explained exactly what happened to bring me here, and I feel certain I can repeat the process. I know what to do now."

CHAPTER 27

We decided not to say goodbye. Neither of us could imagine how to do that. I had promised Ashe I wouldn't be more than a few days. A week or two at the most. And he had said he'd hold me to my promise, joking that if I didn't come back, he'd come and get me.

"We belong together, darling girl. I know it in my bones."

We sat on the bed in the room I used when I was there, and we held each other for a long time.

"You'll return, and we'll be together forever," he said.

"Like the lovers in Rossetti's poem," I said.

"Yes."

I had the Botticelli painting rolled up, carefully wrapped and waiting. It wasn't as large as I feared without its frame, only two and a half feet long and half as wide—not even as large as an umbrella. My main concern was for the painting itself. While I had been able to travel back and forth intact—I hadn't tried to take anything from 1867 back with me except for Fanny's undergarments. And while I knew they had remained unchanged for the days I was back in 1947, Imogine had reminded me that we didn't know if the journey had affected them permanently. My theory was that since the painting existed in 1947, I was simply removing it from its hiding place by already having it with me.

Also beside me on the bed was my 1947 outfit, ready to put on. But I didn't want Ashe to see me in it. I didn't want him to watch my disappearing act.

Ashe stared at the clothes.

"Now, go," I said. "Let me do this. I'll be back in just a few days."

He leaned over and took me in his arms. He didn't kiss me. There was no heat emanating from his body as there usually was when we embraced. This was not a touch of passion. There was desire, but it was the desire to stop time. To keep me there. To prevent this trip.

Finally, I pulled away. "I must go."

"I don't know how to let you go," he said, his beautiful, blue eyes turning stormy and glistening with tears. He pulled out his handkerchief and wiped them away. Then laughed sardonically. "After the train accident, I vowed to never allow myself to feel so deeply about anyone again. And here I am. I didn't plan for you to creep into my heart, but it seems you have. And settled in. Ah, Jeannine, what am I going to do?"

We clung to each other.

"You're not leaving me. I'm not leaving you. I just need to save my father's reputation. I'd never forgive myself if I didn't. And then I'll return to you."

He nodded but held my gaze for what seemed like a long time. We both knew there was no guarantee that I could keep coming back. My cousin Opaline had said that in the grimoires she'd consulted—repeated trips to the same time and place were highly unusual. Three seemed to be a limit, and I'd already returned twice.

"There's no changing your mind, is there?" Ashe said.

"No. Just like there will be no changing my mind once I do what I have to do and am ready to return."

He reached out and tucked one of my errant curls behind my ear.

"I'm going to let you change and go. You're right. I can't

watch that. I'd try to stop you. Or come with you."

I'd told him that Opaline had warned me he should never, under any circumstances, try to come to my time. He did not exist in the future and would perish if he tried.

"Safe travels, my love."

I closed my eyes so I wouldn't see him leave the room and shut the door behind him.

I would forever regret that decision.

Once I heard the door click, I changed my clothes. Wearing the suit I'd arrived in while standing in Dante Gabriel Rossetti's house in 1867 felt strange. I was suffused with a kaleidoscope of emotions. I knew myself well enough to know I had to act. If I gave myself any more time to ruminate on the situation, I might change my mind, which wouldn't be fair to me, my career, or my father. He'd lost so much. I couldn't stay here and let my selfishness destroy all he had left.

Dressed, I folded Fanny's clothes on the bed. That's when I noticed Ashe had dropped his handkerchief on the floor. I pocketed it, picked up the case with the Botticelli inside, and recited the words my grandmother had given me when I was fourteen.

Make of the blood, a journey. Make of the journey, a passion. Make of the passion, life everlasting."

Nothing happened.

I sat on the bed, staring at the walls, wondering what I had done wrong and what to do now. The anticlimax of having prepared myself for this and not being able to accomplish it was the final blow. I felt tears spring to my eyes. Crying. Again. The decision to help my father and protect his reputation and mine over staying here with Ashe had been brutal enough. I couldn't bear having yet another chance to change my mind.

I closed my eyes. If only there was a telephone and I could call Opaline and ask for her help. I had no choice. I would have to go see Imogine again. Say goodbye to her and my grandfather again. Then, say goodbye to Ashe all over again.

Reaching up, I wiped away the tears coursing down my cheeks. And that was when I remembered the order of things the last time I'd returned to 1947, and the one thing needed that neither Imogine nor I nor my mantra had included.

My tears.

CHAPTER 28

I opened my eyes in my office at the V&A. I was dizzy, and my head hurt. I ached for Ashe. I had indeed left him again. I reached into my pocket and found his handkerchief, then buried my face in it, inhaling his scent. I felt the stirrings of passion deep inside me that I always felt in his presence. The combination of his cologne and the scents of his paints and skin. But he wasn't down the hall. He wasn't in the garden in the studio where I could go to him. He wouldn't come to my bedroom tonight to kiss me and hold me, and we wouldn't join together to feel all those marvelous swirling sensations.

I had left him to come back here and do what I must—the right thing, the honorable thing—save my father's and my reputations from slander or worse, and foil whoever was actively trying to hurt us.

The tears came yet again. I was tired of crying.

Before the war, I had cried when so moved. But the war and all the death and destruction we'd all suffered had dried my tears. I had been deeply distraught when we learned my brother had been killed in battle, when I found out my husband had died, when Clio had been killed. Each death had sent me into a state of grief in its own way. But no matter how saddened I was, how much I missed each of them, how brutal the loss, there had been no tears left in me.

Why, since meeting Ashe, had I regained the ability to cry so easily? Why were my emotions so close to the surface now?

Was it the passion? The wonder? The laughing and loving? Was it because with the highs came the lows? Had I stopped crying because I'd stopped really living? And now I was very much living again?

I knew then that tears were not just part of *my* journey—what the spell required—but they were also part of everyone's journey, even if that wasn't to travel through time. From each day to the next, in order to feel the joy, you had to feel the sadness.

The dizziness had dissipated. I opened my eyes and looked out the window at the expanse of 1947 London. Then, I looked at the calendar on my desk. Yes, I was back on the same day I'd left. Alice always ripped off the previous day's page when she brought in the mail. I glanced at the clock on the wall. It was ten minutes past midnight. So, I'd only been gone seven hours in the present, but had lived four days in the past.

With a jolt, I remembered the painting. Had it survived the trip? Holding my breath, I looked down at the floor. Yes, it was there.

Now, what about the painting under the wrapping?

Gingerly, I put the package on my desk and then untied the string that Ashe has so painstakingly secured. I unrolled it. There she was. The redhaired lady, resplendent in her pale pink gown, looking back at me and keeping a secret that only she and I knew.

But just bringing her back wasn't the end. I now had to use her to clear my father's name and mine and expose whoever had set this up. I couldn't make it look like we'd returned the painting. It had to look like I'd found her in the museum. I had given up so much for this already. One last sacrifice would be nothing.

CHAPTER 29

I couldn't take credit for having found the painting. And that was fine. The problem was determining who to trust to find it and deliver it to Mr. Gibbons. And how to gather a crowd at that time so I could watch and see who was the most surprised it had been returned. I no longer just wanted to save our reputations. I wanted to destroy whoever had set us up. At least destroy the one who deserved it the most. Mr. Althorp at the Midas Society seemed to suspect Gibbons. I believed the culprit was Hugh.

Sybil had helped. As she always did. I had called to tell her what had happened but could barely get the words out over the phone. She insisted on coming over and had arrived just after lunch.

I made us tea, and we sat in my living room as I poured out the story of the last few days. She let her tea get cold listening to every word. I showed her the painting, and together, we marveled at having it here, this masterpiece, in my flat.

"I've not as much to tell you," she finally said over a fresh pot, which we both sipped. "But it's not for lack of effort."

"About Mr. Gibbons?"

"And a bit about Hugh, as well. First the director. It's all rather bland, nothing at all salacious or criminal, unfortunately. Basically, if it weren't for his impressive position at one of the most prestigious museums in the world, he would probably be running a B&B in Bristol. One small fact is that he writes poetry. A friend of mine at the publishing house John Murray knows him and said he's been writing since university. Historical ballads about long-dead artists that are tedious and laborious, though well researched. They've been published in small literary journals. I was able to find a few in the library. Nothing worth reading there. He did have one minor success, though, in his twenties, and had a dozen passionate love poems published in a slim volume that got some attention."

"Love poems?" I tried to picture Mr. Gibbons pouring out his heart with pen and ink on paper.

"Filled with lust and longing, which were very shocking at the time. It was the early 1900s. We were still a very moralistic Victorian society. I found a copy and read them. It appears he was very much in love with a woman who first encouraged him but then spurned him for a rival. There were a few items in the gossip columns since Mr. Gibbons had made a game out of her identity and told critics and friends he'd included hidden clues in the lines of his work as to her identity. People went on wild chases trying to decipher who she was."

"And who was she?" I was fascinated.

"No one ever figured it out, and there was talk that there never was a real woman at all. That he invented it all to get attention and make a name for himself as a literary talent."

"Quite crafty."

"I thought so, too. Suggesting aspects to his personality we should pay attention to."

I poured more tea for us both. "Maybe, maybe not. You said you found some information about Hugh?"

"I have."

I felt a flutter of excitement. Hopefully, she'd discovered

what we needed to tie the stolen painting to him.

"Well, as you know, he became engaged to Edith Wilson Brown during the war, and after he returned, she cut it off."

I nodded.

"It seems she'd been having an affair while he was at the front, got pregnant, and had the baby in secret to protect her reputation."

I was disappointed. That wasn't anything bad about Hugh and only slightly worth printing in the gossip columns on a slow news day.

"It made me feel sorry for him," Sybil said.

I arched my eyebrows. "Not you, too."

"What do you mean?"

"He's incorrigible, but no one but me seems to see it. Not my assistants. Not you. Certainly not Mr. Gibbons."

"Maybe because you're wrong about him. I know how much you loved and admired Clio, but is it possible she made a mistake?"

"Hugh made an advance on me the other night at work," I said.

"That doesn't make him incorrigible, Jeanine, just attracted to you. "

"Either way, it doesn't really matter now. I have a bigger problem to solve. I need to return the painting to the museum. His being jilted doesn't alter my plan to plant the Botticelli in Hugh's portfolio so everyone will see he has it when he presents his exhibit plans on Wednesday."

"Putting the blame on a possibly innocent man?" Sybil said, sounding a bit too much like a disciplinarian.

"Or a possibly guilty one. Either way, he'll deny it. He'll say someone put it there. Which will be the truth, after all. And knowing my colleagues and how they feel about him, he'll be believed. He'll come to no harm. But since Gibbons and I will be there when it happens, the director will have to take immediate action, clearing my father's name."

To her credit, Sybil tried to talk me out of my plan, but I wouldn't budge. We didn't exactly argue, but I could tell she was disappointed in me. Well, it was mutual. I was disappointed in her that she wasn't one hundred percent on my side.

When it was time for her to leave, she pulled me to her for a hug.

"Think this through before you carry it out and set up Hugh. I'm worried about you, Jeannine. I know you want to return to Ashe, but you're messing with things we don't understand."

"I love him, Sybil." I felt tears threaten.

"I know you do. Just don't leave again with talking to me first, all right? I have nightmares that you'll go back there and stay."

I couldn't tell her that was exactly what I was planning. Not yet, anyway.

On Monday, I snuck into the janitor's closet and got a copy of the key to Hugh's office from the wall of duplicates. On Tuesday night, I stayed late, and at eight p.m., entered his office. I found the portfolio I'd seen him carrying around that contained his plans for the exhibit.

When I opened it, I was surprised to see that the sketches and schematics had nothing to do with the proposal he'd spoken about—Shakespeare's greatest love stories—but was rather based on the theme of love and war on both the geopolitical stage and the personal. He had collected love letters from soldiers from wars throughout history and connected them to art and artifacts from the period.

Surprised and impressed, I read through his catalog copy, stopping when I got to a certain line.

It was during the war that I found my own heart returning to a girl with fiery curls. I'd never told her how I felt about her in my efforts to protect her, and found myself wanting to write her and confess all. I kept thinking that if I was killed in battle, she'd never know. It is that memory that inspired this collection. The art and literature we create out of loss and longing that has given civilization some of its masterpieces.

I stopped and reread it. Was he referencing me? He'd often talked about my *fiery curls*. I was distracted for a moment and felt my heart soften toward him. Perhaps I had misjudged him. Maybe Sybil and so many others were right, and Clio had been wrong.

I shook my head. It didn't matter now. Hugh, whether innocent or a deceitful cad, was a very convenient prop I intended to use. All I cared about was having the Botticelli found in Hugh's portfolio with everyone there to witness it. That was the only way I could clear my father's and my names.

I spent a half hour rearranging the order of the illustrations so the painting was in the first third but not too close to the front—in case he opened the portfolio to check on it before the meeting. I didn't want him to notice it.

The next morning, at nine o'clock, I was standing outside Mr. Gibbons' office with my show notes when Hugh arrived. I was nervous. So much was riding on what would occur in the next few minutes.

We were ushered inside. Two other senior Keepers were there. Mr. Gibbons asked me to go first, and I made my presentation. Not as smoothly as I wished. My voice sounded strained to me, and I stumbled a few times when reading my copy. Afterward, I handed Mr. Gibbons my signed and dated notes, indicating when my office had been gone through.

"That was a marvelous presentation," Hugh said when I sat down. "And a great idea. I have no doubt that people will be giving you high praise. And those lovers' eyes—that's inspired." He smiled at me. Was it genuine? Was he actually surprised by my ideas or just playing his part? *Once an actor…* I thought. Except what if he was innocent? I remembered Sybil's expression of disappointment in me when I told her what I had planned to do with the Botticelli and felt a stab of guilt.

Perhaps he had not been the one in my office that day. Or maybe he had only wanted to see what I was doing, hoping that if he knew, he could for sure outdo me. But it was too late for me to wonder. Hugh had already stood, opened his case, and had begun explaining the theme of love and war and how he intended to incorporate them. From inside the portfolio, he carefully pulled out one example after the next of what he was planning, the sketches that had so impressed me the night before. He went through the first four when he came to the Botticelli painting.

"My word," Gibbons said in a voice more expressive than his words. "Almost three months to the day since it went missing, and here it is."

"What the hell?" Hugh sounded astonished.

The other Keepers had crowded around, exclaiming their surprise, as well.

Hugh stared at the painting as if he'd never seen it before. I watched his face, looking for some kind of clue.

"This is impossible," Hugh whispered.

What did he mean? That he knew it couldn't be there because he knew where he'd hidden it to set me up? No, he looked truly shocked. How could he be? I was certain he had been behind the deception.

Mr. Gibbons was silent, looking from the Botticelli to his mentee. Hugh felt the stare, turned from the painting to his director.

"Mr. Gibbons," I said, "how this happened isn't any concern of mine. But I do expect you will contact the Midas Society immediately and let them know you've recovered the painting. And that neither my father nor I had anything to do with its disappearance. I'd also like you to issue my father a formal apology."

Mr. Gibbons didn't say anything, simply grunted an *all right.*

"I had nothing to do with this," Hugh sputtered.

"Jeannine, I do want your job, but I would never do anything underhanded to get it."

"Well, someone did something underhanded. And who but you would want to cast aspersions on my ability to do my job?"

He lifted his arms and let them drop, defeated. "Mr. Gibbons, you have to believe me. I didn't take the painting."

The director didn't answer.

"There has to be some other explanation," Hugh continued.

"We will discuss this further, Hugh. And yes, Mrs. Maycroft, I will contact the Society now."

I felt a wave of relief. And then something struck me. When Mr. Gibbons had first seen the painting, he'd said, *"Almost three months to the day since it went missing, and here it is."*

Hugh had not yet returned to the museum three months ago. He'd barely been back three weeks.

CHAPTER 30

It won't be long now before I can return to Ashe, I told myself as I entered my flat that night. I'd telegraphed my father from the office and received a telegram right back, expressing his relief and thanks. He was on his way home to Woodfern and would be there by the weekend.

Now, I just had to decide how much longer I was going to stay.

Mr. Gibbons had told Hugh and me that his first priority would be seeing to the Botticelli and continuing the search for whoever took it. For now, though, we should both carry on with our exhibit plans. I wanted to see my show through and visit with my father before I left the twentieth century for good. But how long could I stay here while Ashe was there waiting for me with all the promise of his love? *Am I insane?* I wondered. Sick with love for certain, but to step back in time possibly forever? I fell asleep that night thinking of my grandparents and how I would be able to spend time with them again.

In the morning, I gave the eye miniatures to the restorer, and he estimated it would take him about a week to repair and clean them. At least I wouldn't have to think about my decision for the next seven days.

I set up the final photo shoot for the following week, alerted the designer that I'd have the copy and photographs for him by the cutoff date , and then sat down to complete my essay for the catalog.

I opened my notebook to where I'd jotted down some ideas, and there in a hand that was not mine was a page of script I didn't recognize. I skipped to the end and looked at the signature.

With all my love,
Ashe

I felt my heart speed up.
When had he written this?
Why hadn't he told me?
I began to read.

My darling Jeannine,
So strange to think that you will be reading this ages from now. Sometime in the faraway future for me. While you are gone, I will be counting the days—nay the hours—nay the minutes—until you return to me. But as much as I paint fantasies and dreams, I live in reality, and am aware that you might not be able to return.

I know how much you love your work. How much your current position means to you. And if you are in fact unable to come back to me, I want to help ensure you keep your beloved job.

So I have done something that might work. I do hope it does.

Our family has a plot in Highgate. It has a statue of a winged angel standing on a plinth. And on the bottom of it is a code of sorts. It's a secret hiding place. You have to know what to touch and in which order to get the trapdoor to open. Over the years, family members have hidden things inside the plinth when political strife or financial trouble erupted.

I've hidden something there for you. It has your name on it. I know there is the possibility that someone might find it before you get to it, and even though I've clearly indicated it has been left for you, they could take it. But in case they don't, please go and attempt to retrieve it. The jewel has been passed down in my family, a gift from a queen to her lover to commemorate the hours they had together so he would never forget. She was quite famous. He less so—an ancestor of mine from Sweden, which is how I obtained it. Their love story inspired my art.

I know how much this memento will mean to you, and I want you to have it.

The history of the piece is that it was on loan to the South Kensington Museum for the last two years. The Keeper had asked if they could keep it on exhibit because it was so beloved, and I allowed it. But yesterday, I went to him and retrieved it so you can have it and return it to the V&A, as the museum is called in your time.

Either way, you will be a hero for being the one to bring it back to the museum.

I wish I could write as eloquently as others about love. About how I feel about you. About how you came into my life and made me remember what joy and happiness could feel like. My greatest wish is that you return to me and we can grow old together, basking in the understanding and love we have found.

But if it is not meant to be somehow, know that I looked into your eyes and saw your soul, and you looked into mine and saw me and we were forever altered. We became part of each other's hearts. Whatever god or fate or magick has allowed us this brief but life-altering love is to be thanked. Nothing will ever dim the light you have brought to me...Tennyson's words do my feelings better justice than I can.

> I hold it true, whate'er befall;
> I feel it when I sorrow most;
> 'Tis better to have loved and lost
> Than never to have loved at all.

With all my love,
Ashe

CHAPTER 31

I went to the cemetery the next morning and headed straight to Clio's plot. It was cold, and there had been frost overnight, so it was quite a trek. I slipped a few times and cursed my weak ankle. But I had a destination and a goal.

For so long, Clio and I had tried to decipher the designs on the bottom of the Angelos statue. Neither of us had any luck at all guessing, even with her detailed rubbings. But now, I had the answer. In my notebook. We had never guessed the solution to the puzzle. *If only I could tell her*, I thought. She'd be there with me, every step of the way, even rushing ahead.

Reaching the plot, I said a silent hello to Angelos and then, with my gloved hand, cleared the clinging frost at the plinth. I'd never really thought about the fact that the base was metal and not stone like the rest of the monument.

But now, I understood.

From my pocket, I pulled out the notebook, opened it, and studied the instructions.

Ashe had written them out very clearly.

Among all the vines of flowers and leaves and the ancient Egyptian symbols, there is one of the Eye of Horus.

I knew the meaning of the eye, the story of Set and Horus

and how the symbol was believed to have magical protective properties. I knew where the eye was on the base. Clio and I had discussed it often. Why were there Egyptian symbols on the bottom of the statue guarding her family's graves?

Soon, I would know.

Ashe had said to bring a regular household nail with me, and I'd retrieved one from the head of maintenance in the museum. Now, I took it out and, following his instructions, found the small hole in the pupil, a depression no one would notice if not told to search for it.

Pushing the nail in, I heard a loud creak as a section of the metal base opened. A drawer! Lined, I presumed, with lead to protect it from the elements.

Inside the space, I found an envelope which I withdrew, and underneath, a silver box, quite lovely on its own. Opening it, I saw it was lined in midnight-blue velvet, still fresh to the touch—astonishing considering how long it had been here. Nestled in it was a small leather pouch. I untied the string that held it tight and tipped its contents into my gloved hand.

I let out a small cry.

I was staring down at an eye miniature. One Clio had shown me a drawing of. Perhaps the most famous eye miniature that ever existed. Or rather, I should say, that *had* existed and was presumed lost. This was the portrait of Marie Antoinette's eye that she'd had painted by her trusted portraitist as a gift to her lover, the Swedish nobleman whom Ashe Lloyd Lewis was related to.

I sat back on my heels, holding the eye. Astonished by Ashe's kindness, his care, and his generosity. This would be the crowning glory to my show. The missing eye that I had left space for in the catalog.

Nothing that Hugh could come up with could compare to the piece that represented the tragic love story of the French queen who had been guillotined October 16, 1793—over one hundred and fifty years ago.

And now this treasure was mine to do with as I wished. And as Ashe guessed I would, my wish was to give it to the museum.

I rewrapped the stickpin in its pouch, placed it back in the silver box, and put that in my purse along with the envelope. Before I shut the now-empty drawer, I touched its sides. Possibly, the last time this had been opened was when Ashe had come here and left this gift for me. Almost eighty years ago.

I closed the drawer and, hearing the click, felt as if my heart was cleaving in two. I couldn't wait to return to him. I needed to finish what I had started. I couldn't wait. I had to wait.

Standing, I turned and looked over in the corner where Ashe was buried. The fox was sitting there. She'd arrived without making a sound. Or if she had, I had been so engrossed in my task that I hadn't heard her.

As I made my way over, having gotten my attention, she ran off. There were leaves covering the stone, and I brushed them away and then looked down at the now-familiar inscription. I read it aloud, hearing my voice crack a little.

That was when I noticed there was a change on the stone. Every time I'd been here it had read:

Ashe Lloyd Lewis. 1828-1868
"Eternity was in our lips and eyes." William Shakespeare

But it was different now. The year of his death was no longer 1868, it was *1900*.

Ashe had lived another thirty-two years!

My mind's eye was flooded with images of his artwork from the studio, masterpieces that had been destroyed in the fire. Then I corrected myself. Now that there had not been a fire, the artwork must have survived, as well. Where was it? What museums held it now? I couldn't wait to find out.

And then I thought of something else and was caught up in a wave of sadness.

The other stone beside his was for Ashe's wife and two children who had died in the train crash before I'd met him. Sarah Lewis, Thomas Lewis, and Eliza Lewis had been lain to rest in 1863. That was still there. But there was not a fourth stone.

Had Ashe not married again? What about me? Then I realized that, as of now, it had to be because I was still here in the present. Everything would change again when I went back to him once more. And the time was coming for me to do just that.

CHAPTER 32

Inside the envelope found with the silver box, Ashe had included two letters. One proving its provenance, and the other a receipt stating that the stickpin had been bought by Imogine Belcourt in 1867 from Ashe Lloyd Lewis.

This would protect me and clear the way for the stickpin to belong to me legally since I had inherited my grandmother's estate. I had plans to donate it to the museum, where it belonged, but first it would appear in my half of the Valentine's Day exhibit.

I had planned a photography session for Thursday, the day after the restorer returned the pieces that needed fixing. Luckily, the stickpin on the queen's eye miniature didn't need any restoration or cleaning, as it had been packed away for so many years.

The photographer worked all afternoon to make sure I was happy with the staging. After he'd finished and left, I placed all the miniatures back in their trays. When I got to Ashe's eye, I held it for a moment longer than necessary. It was my ticket to the past. The tool that would return me to my love.

I didn't feel the change at all. I didn't even notice it. I was lost in thought about returning to Ashe when the show was over and how all I had to do was prick myself with the pinpoint. I fingered the edge of the brooch, ran my finger over the opals, and then looked down.

What was different? Something, but what?

At first, I couldn't figure it out. I turned it to the right and left. The restoration had been perfect. So, what was it? I turned it around. The back of the brooch looked the same. Perhaps a bit shinier. I examined the markings. Intact and correct. But something was off—and then I realized what it was.

The pin bar itself wasn't the original, a slightly bent and blackened rough, pointed rod. Instead, it was a brand-new gold bar.

My heart quickened. What had happened?

I finished gathering all the pieces, and with the tray in hand, went to the restoration department.

Mr. Ellis was working on a small diamond tiara and looked up when I came in.

"Good afternoon, Mrs. Maycroft. Can I help you?

"Yes." I showed him the brooch. "Did you happen to change the pin?"

"I did. It wasn't gold like the rest of the piece but gold over silver, and it had been damaged. Silver is so soft, as you know. It fell apart even before I had a chance to clean it. I never like to replace any part of an item in our collection but the pin itself is not considered historically important."

"Did you keep it?"

"The pin?"

I nodded.

"No, it had crumbled."

It wouldn't matter, I thought. It couldn't. Certainly, the magick would work anyway. I had the brooch. That had to be all that was needed.

I thanked Mr. Ellis, returned to my office with the tray,

and sat down at my desk. Ignoring all the other pieces glinting up at me, I focused on Ashe's eye. I had to know if it still worked, except I wasn't ready to go back. I had never tried to send an object back without me, but maybe it would be a good test. I had an apple on my desk, so I scratched it with the pin. Nothing happened. But I was determined not to worry. I had no idea whether an inanimate object could travel through time. Only that I had been able to.

What to do?

Test the brooch now or stick to my plans—put on the show in three months, see it through, spend time with my father, and then when all was done, leave?

But how could I wait?

I had the layout of the catalog on my desk with indications of where each photo should go. The photographer had taken all the pictures. I had written my essay and descriptions of each eye. Could Alice, Andrew, and Jacob carry out the rest of my plans for the staging of the exhibit and work with Sybil on the publicity efforts? I could just visit my father and then return to 1867. He'd arrived home from Egypt two nights before, and we'd spoken by phone. I had plans to visit that weekend.

I dreaded the visit. How to say goodbye to him, possibly forever? I was the only family he had left. He would need me as he grew older. And yet, he'd had his life. His wife, his children, his career. He had a wide circle of devoted friends. Except, what kind of daughter was I to even contemplate leaving him?

I took the train out on Saturday. At sixty-eight, my father was as healthy as he'd ever been. When he opened the door to me, his tan skin and sparkling eyes allayed my fears that he was growing old. His active lifestyle, doing what he loved, kept him vibrant. The lines around his eyes and mouth had deepened, of course, but that had happened when my brother died.

My father took me into his arms and held me close.

"We spend too much time apart," he said, almost as if he'd had a premonition about what I wanted to talk to him about. And yet, he couldn't have. Only my mother's side of the family had a sixth sense about such things.

We sat in the library, his favorite room, and he regaled me with stories of his last months in Egypt. I listened raptly as I always had since childhood when he shared his adventures in the land of tombs and pyramids.

I wouldn't tell him yet, I determined. I had the whole weekend ahead of me. I wanted us to enjoy the time we had.

And we did. We ate well and drank fine wine from the cellar and good port after dinner. On Saturday, we went horseback riding on the estate, and that night he invited a few of his closest friends who had houses close by for a small dinner. It was an emotional evening for me as I greeted each guest as hostess to my father's host, playing the part my mother should have been playing.

Sitting at the dining room table, I couldn't help but look around at our friends and wonder if I'd ever see any of them again. This was like a prelude to death. But surely I would be able to come back again and visit. Nothing my cousin Opaline or my grandmother had told me suggested that my ability to time travel was a one-way street. Yes, it was a risk to keep returning to the same place, but not a certain problem. Perhaps I could vary the destinations, meet Ashe in other cities, even countries.

The conversation at dinner was a heady mix of politics, art, and gardening, and it was around the end of the main course that I noticed my father conversing with the woman on his left and putting his hand on her arm.

It was our dear friend Lady Barbara Silversmith. A widow now, I'd gone to her husband's memorial service three years before. Not only had she protected priceless artwork at her estate, as did we, she was an avid gardener and often helped my father with our grounds. What was new was a certain unmistakable intimacy between them that made me unquestionably happy.

When all the other guests left, Lady Silversmith stayed back, and my father invited me to join them in the sitting room for brandy.

"It's so wonderful to spend time with you again Jeannine, I've missed seeing you," she said.

"I've missed seeing you, as well." I turned to my father. "And you, too."

"Time apart is time lost. But now you are here, and we're both so glad. We wanted to talk to you," my father said to me as he handed me a crystal balloon, glasses that had belonged to my grandmother Ruth when this was her home.

I took the post-prandial drink, noting the use of the word *we.*

"Lady Silversmith—Barbara—and I have grown closer over the last three years," my father said. And then there it was again, the *we.* "Barbara has actually spent the last four months with me on the dig."

"I had no idea," I said, surprised and pleased. As he spoke, the burden of him being alone, of my leaving him without support, was floating off my shoulders.

"We felt it was important to tell to you in person, not in a letter," Barbara said, smiling brightly.

Father took her hand, and she smiled at him. It was heartfelt and quite lovely. I'd known Aunt Barbara, as I called her, my entire life, and had always admired her gardens and goodness. "We've decided to marry," my father continued. "And we wanted you to be the first to know."

I felt my eyes fill with tears. As did Aunt Barbara's. Even my father's eyes looked a bit wetter than usual.

"I'm so happy for you both," I said as I got up and first

kissed my father and then his bride-to-be. "Truly. It makes my news even easier to share."

"Your news?"

I nodded. Now was as good a time as any.

"I'm going to be traveling a bit and not sure when I'll be back."

My father looked confused.

"You are leaving your beloved job?"

"You've fallen in love haven't you?" Aunt Barbara asked before I could even answer my father's question.

"I have." I smiled. "There's just a little bit of a hitch."

"What is that, dear?" she asked.

"He lives quite a bit away."

"Can't he move to London? It's not such a terrible place to live."

"Well, he actually does live in London."

They both looked confused, as they had every right to be.

I took a deep breath. My father knew about our family's gifts, of course. And so did Aunt Barbara. She had been my mother's close friend since they were girls.

"How does he live both far away and in London?" my father asked.

"The distance is not in space, but in time," I said and told them the story.

CHAPTER 33

Once I returned to London on Sunday evening, I began to prepare. The goodbye with my father and Barbara had been tearful, but I was quite convinced that since I had made the trip twice without any trouble, I would be able to do it again. They didn't believe me at first—or at all, perhaps. But in the end, they didn't know what to say or do. Their plan was to marry in February, and I promised to return by then. The timing meant I would also make it back here for the opening of my show, not that I cared as much about that anymore. Hugh could take my job if he wanted it so badly. All I wanted was Ashe.

When it was my father's turn to say goodbye, he held me close and whispered, "Godspeed. I don't understand this at all, my darling girl. I'm frightened for you, but at the same time, I feel like you are on the cusp of a marvelous adventure, and I'm the last man on Earth to talk anyone out of adventures. Life really isn't worth living if you don't at least try for them."

I smiled through my tears. Yes, I was his daughter, and he'd taught me that lesson through all his actions and deeds. Now it was my turn for a fabulous adventure.

My plan as I outlined it for him was to spend December and all of January with Ashe. Then I would come back for the show, see the success I had worked so hard for, and return again to old London, mostly for good.

At eight o'clock on Monday morning, I arrived at the museum before anyone in the curatorial departments arrived.

With my door shut, I went through all my papers and plans, making sure everything was in perfect order. On top of everything, I left a note for my research team saying a family emergency had pulled me away. I included instructions for the completion of the catalog and the hanging of the show. I also wrote a note for Sybil that was much harder to compose.

I stared at the blank card with my initials embossed on the top. How could I explain? How could I say goodbye?

You are my dearest friend. You always have been and you always will be. Don't be mad at me for leaving. I don't have a choice. Collect all the gossip for me for when I come back.
With all my love, J.

I put it in an envelope, sealed it, and wrote her name on the top.

I had one more thing to do. I took the copy of *Winged Pharaoh* off my shelf, opened it and on the fly leaf wrote two words and two letters.

H - I'm sorry, J

I wrapped it in paper, affixed a label, and wrote out Hugh's full name.

There, I was done.

I looked around my office one last time and felt the tears come. I felt sure I would be able to come back, but there was always a chance I might get stuck in the past. I sighed. I couldn't know the future. I couldn't even be sure of the past. I was only certain that, in this moment in time, I longed for Ashe.

I'd left all the eye miniatures but one in the vault. Now, I withdrew that one from my locked desk drawer. I held the brooch that had been my ticket to the past since Halloween.

I poured a little rubbing alcohol on the tip as my grandmother had warned me to do since the wounds had become infected the other times I'd scratched or pricked myself.

Then quickly, because it was difficult to do, I pricked the fleshy part of my forefinger with the end of the pin.

I saw the blood pool. I intoned the spell.

"Make of the blood, a journey. Make of the journey, a passion. Make of the passion, life everlasting."

And then I closed my eyes and waited.

There was no dizziness. No change of atmosphere. Nothing at all like the other two times. I opened my eyes, hoping to see anything but my office in 1947, but that was all I saw.

I inspected my finger. There was a clear globule of blood. There were real tears on my cheek. I wiped one away and rubbed it over the pinprick.

Nothing.

I took the brooch and raked it over my forefinger, gashing a line in my flesh that sprouted more fresh blood and pain. I began to weep, in fear for what I did not want to believe.

I spoke the words again.

"Make of the blood, a journey. Make of the journey, a passion. Make of the passion, life everlasting."

Nothing happened.

I cut myself again on another finger, then shut my eyes and thought the spell this time.

Make of the blood, a journey. Make of the journey, a passion. Make of the passion, life everlasting.

Nothing. By now, there was quite a splatter of blood on my desk.

What was wrong? Why wasn't it working? I had to go back to Ashe. What was wrong?

And then I remembered. The repair. The restorer had replaced the old pinning mechanism. Was it possible that in doing so, they had destroyed my chances of getting back to the only man I had ever truly loved?

Sobbing, I cut myself again and again. And then again. Until finally, it happened. I felt the dizziness. And then blackness.

CHAPTER 34

I awoke in a room I didn't recognize. White, pristine, smelling of antiseptic. I lay on a hard surface, covered with a blanket, and looked around trying to figure out where I had landed.

I reached up and discovered my hands were bandaged when I heard a voice.

"Oh, good, you are awake. Let me get the doctor and the gentleman who has been pacing so anxiously."

She left before I could ask her anything.

The gentleman? So Ashe was here? I was so relieved.

The door opened, and a doctor came in accompanied by—no, not Ashe, but Hugh Kenward. And with him, Sybil.

"Where am I?" I blurted out, confused.

"The infirmary," the doctor said.

"I found you in your office, Jeannine. You had passed out and there was blood everywhere," Hugh said.

"You have given us such a terrible fright."

"What day is it, what year?" I cried, ignoring what all of them had said.

"Perhaps you should tell us," the doctor said.

I shook my head. "Tell me," I shouted.

Sybil took my unbandaged hand, but it was Hugh who spoke. He told me the exact day, date, and year that it had been that very morning. December 2, 1947.

The brooch had lost its magic.

I had lost Ashe.

CHAPTER 35

The Valentine's show opened on February 14, 1948 as scheduled, and was a huge hit. The press had caught wind of the competition, and people flocked to see how Hugh and I had approached our tasks. The contest, though, had been abandoned. My father had gone to the board of directors at the museum and told them about the games the director had been putting Hugh and I through. And why. And they'd come to a different decision about how to proceed.

His deceit had begun to unravel when Mr. Gibbons first saw the painting I'd brought back from 1867 and said, "Almost three months to the day since it went missing, and here it is."

When I realized Hugh had not yet returned to the museum three months before—that he'd barely been back three weeks—I went to Mr. Althorp at the Midas Society, who then investigated further. It didn't take a lot of detective work. Knowing that my father and Mr. Gibbons had gone to university together, Mr. Althorp started there. As it turned out, he ended there, as well.

The missing clue, the real reason it turned out—much to my surprise—for Mr. Gibbons' campaign, was my father. Both he and the director had been suitors of my mother's when they knew each other at Oxford. When she chose my father, it destroyed Gibbons. The poems he'd written were about her. His spurned love spilled onto the page and then poisoned him. Little had anyone suspected that he had continued to harbor his grudge. That my father had been knighted for his efforts during the war and Gibbons had not was the final straw.

Mr. Gibbons had been playing with me as far back as eight years ago when he saw that Hugh and I were having an illicit romance and tried to upend me. But it wasn't until Hugh's return that Mr. Gibbons launched his real revenge plot against my father—he would make my life as miserable as he could and then frame us, fire me, and embarrass the man he felt had stolen his love.

Knowing how ambitious I was, he made sure Hugh continued appearing suspicious to me. Having keys to all our offices, it was easy for Mr. Gibbons to break into mine and rifle through my notebooks. It was also easy for him to follow me through the vaults. He used my anger toward Hugh as a means of distraction, while he continued his long plan to ruin my father.

As director, Mr. Gibbons had no trouble taking the Botticelli, hiding it, and then claiming it had been stolen. When asked, he said he'd hidden it in a crawl space behind some shelves in the library that he insisted no one but him knew existed.

Mr. Gibbons was summarily fired. A new director was brought in, a contemporary of mine who had been at the British Museum for years. William Keane immediately abandoned the contest and created several new departments, allowing me to remain on as Keeper of the Metalworks and giving Hugh his own department as Keeper of Theater and Performance, covering the history of all areas of performing arts, including drama, dance, opera, circus, puppetry, comedy, musical theater, costume and set design, pantomime, and popular music. Given his first love, it was the perfect position for him. The museum department had been founded in the 1920s when a private collector, Gabrielle Enthoven, donated her collection of theatrical designs, memorabilia, books, and photographs. Being only a couple of decades old, there was much Hugh could do to improve and grow it.

I'd misjudged him all along. Sybil had been right about that. I'd given Clio's opinion of him too much weight. I'd never know why she'd felt the way she had about him. But I'd invited him to lunch and apologized. He'd been gracious in accepting.

Much to my surprise, Sybil had incorporated him into her social circle, and he was currently seeing a friend of hers whose husband had been killed in the war. From what I heard, it appeared to be a marvelous match.

Sybil also made sure the Valentine's show was the talk of the town. True to her word, she'd encouraged all her important acquaintances to come out. Including Thomas Randall, the man she had wanted me to sit next to at the anniversary party. He showed up escorting a glamourous American actress, which made all the gossip columns, putting my little show on the map and getting even larger crowds.

For me, though, the exhibit was a bittersweet success. It was a pure and perfect ode to love as I had meant it to be. A secret love song from me to Ashe Lloyd Lewis, but one which he would never hear.

I thought about him far too much and visited him at Highgate all through that cold December and January, fighting with the wind and often snow to make my way to his grave. I found solace in the later date on the stone and even more visiting his paintings at various museums around England, for he did, in fact, not only survive into his seventies, but also continued painting and creating marvelous works that were in many important collections.

It had taken me a few weeks to work up the courage to visit the room at the British Museum that housed seven of what were deemed his greatest works, all done after 1870.

I had gone alone early on a snowy Monday, the day and time I knew was always the least crowded at any museum—tourists having left London on Sundays, new ones arriving later that day.

As I had learned to do long ago, I walked through the galleries leading to number 16 without glancing at any other artwork on the walls. My father had taught me the first time we went to Paris and visited the Louvre that one must pick a small handful of works to see on each excursion. It was the George de la Tours that day. We sped through great hallways overflowing with masterpieces, not stopping to look at any of them until we'd reached our destination, our eyes still fresh when we devoured the magical canvases of the seventeenth-century master who painted religious chiaroscuro scenes lit by the most perfectly rendered candlelight. Looking at them, you could almost smell the beeswax.

So it was that I arrived at gallery 16, without having spent any time examining any other artwork in the museum. The room was empty, and my footsteps on the wooden floor were a paean to melancholy. A sound as lonely as I felt. The solitary steps of a woman entering the room devoted to the work of a man she had loved. And lost.

I let out a small "oh" as soon as I took in the first painting. And I think my mouth must have remained open for the rest of my time there.

From reading, I knew Ashe had become a popular portraitist after 1867, but not of formal portraiture. His patrons wanted their likenesses done in complicated, lush, allegorical paintings that fit within the movement that Ashe, along with Burne-Jones and Rossetti, had helped to make popular. These founders of the Aesthetic Movement believed the purpose of art was to create beauty, not serve a moral or didactic purpose. Ashe had infused his compositions with magickal elements, and the paintings all represented figures in history who had purportedly possessed special talents: Merlin, Greek gods and goddesses, the Fates, and the like. I couldn't help but think his encounter with me had influenced his interest in these realms of legend and lore.

But that was not why I elicited the exclamation upon walking into the room.

Ashe had captured my likeness and used it over and over in his paintings. Of the seven paintings, a woman with my face and coloring was in four. And always the object of affection.

The love and longing that I had first felt as a child looking at the single Ashe Lloyd Lewis, *La Bell Dame sans Merci*, was even more pronounced in these paintings. But there was something else, too.

In *La Belle Dame*, the woman is a temptress, a trickster; the man an innocent about to be ruined.

In these paintings, there was joy and exuberance mixed with the longing. A message of sorts that brought to mind the line Alfred, Lord Tennyson, had written in 1850 that Ashe had put in his last letter to me.

> *I hold it true, whate'er befall;*
> *I feel it when I sorrow most;*
> *'Tis better to have loved and lost*
> *Than never to have loved at all.*

I was glad I was alone in the gallery because I broke down. I missed Ashe so much. Every day, every cell in my body felt the loss. Every night, I endured complicated dreams where I made my way back to him through arduous landscapes of mountains, lakes, and ravines. I heard his voice in that time between sleep and waking, calling to me, asking me to come back. I would awaken with tears on my cheeks, my bedclothes soaked with my perspiration from working so hard to get back to him.

Slumping against the gallery wall, I slid to the floor and let myself cry in a way I had not since discovering I had no way of returning to him. I kept trying to convince myself that I had done a noble thing, saved a man so he could fulfill his promise, so he could live a long and happy life. But it was of little solace.

Had Ashe found happiness? Had I left him heartbroken the way his wife had? Was his sorrow greater than his joy for all his following days?

Since realizing I couldn't get back, I'd scoured books, old magazines, and newspapers, anything I could find in libraries searching for some mention of Ashe's personal life. I'd read that he'd gone on to become a respected member of the movement, remained friends with Rossetti, and was with him at the time of his death. He'd worked closely with William Morris and had been in high demand for portraits, including eye miniatures. But there was nothing about who he'd gone on to love—if he had. If he had married—and why wouldn't he have? He was only in his forties and was a passionate man with a sensitivity to beauty. It would have been a shame for him not to enjoy his life with a woman by his side.

I wished for him that he had. That he had not mourned losing me the way Fanny had said he'd mourned his wife. *He couldn't have,* I tried to convince myself. After all, we'd only spent a handful of days together. Even if we had felt that we belonged together, that our souls matched up in that way that happens so rarely, surely he could not have remained faithful to that memory for the next thirty years.

And yet, there was my face, in all these paintings.

Over the next months, I managed to visit all the museums that housed his work and found my face in five other paintings. And with each one, I felt the wound in my heart open and throb again. Ours had been but a moment in time, a fleeting passion, and yet it had seared my soul, and I did not quite know how to go on.

CHAPTER 36

Months passed, and I was still lost in missing Ashe. In wondering what his life had been like. In hoping he knew I'd tried to come back to him. Oh, how hard I had tried.

I was on my way to my office on a cool morning the second week of May when I passed some wisteria in bloom entwined on the wrought iron gate of one of the private parks in Kensington. Lingering by its heavy lilac and lavender blossoms, I inhaled the sweet peppery scent and decided that it was time for me to find something to set my heart on. I was not returning to the past. I could not know the future. The present was all, and I was a fool to waste it.

I broke off a sprig of the flower—it was just growing on a railing that belonged to the city, after all, and I was an inhabitant of that city.

As I continued on my way to work, I brought the blossom up to my nose often to breathe in the magnificent scent. Even though I knew its moment had passed, once I arrived at my office, I placed the wisteria in a tiny crystal vase of water.

Wisteria, unlike many other flowers, doesn't do well after it's off the vine. I'd read such in all my grandmother's books.

The best time to cut all flowers, but especially wisteria, is early morning or dusk when the plant's moisture content is highest and cutting won't stress the flowers as it would in the heat. It was also important to get them into water quickly, and a lot of it. You are supposed to slice off the stem at a node with a very sharp knife—which I didn't have on my walk—but I'd used the edge of my house key.

Once I was in the office, I recut it clean across and shredded the woody stem so the wisteria could absorb the most water.

At most, I anticipated I'd get a couple of days out of it, if that. For the next two days, each morning when I arrived, I cleaned the vase and changed the water. I expected it to last through Tuesday, but was surprised when it was still in wonderful form on Wednesday. The petals still looked fresh and full.

On Thursday, it was just as healthy. And on Friday. I couldn't understand how the wisteria was holding on for so long. Every day when I freshened the water, I thought of my grandmother Imogine and how she had taught me to take care of plants and had imbued me with the wonder of nature. I had thought of her often that winter and spring. So many things she'd told me growing up now resonated in a new way. Her lessons had meant one thing to me before going back in time, but ever since, I'd come to understand how much advice she'd given me about what would come to pass without alerting me or giving me too much information.

One particular lesson struck me as more important than all the others.

By eleven o'clock, I was bent over my wisteria, smelling the flower's magickal perfume, when Alice knocked on my door.

"Come in."

"There's a gentleman to see you. He doesn't have an appointment, but he said to tell you he has an eye miniature he'd like to show you."

I told her to bring him in.

"Charles DeLyon." He held out his hand.

He was about my age. Taller than average with soft, dark hair a bit longer than was the style. He had strong features—a bony nose, high cheekbones, and a chin that jutted out a bit too much. Not handsome, but striking. His eyes were his best feature and gave me a start. They were not exactly the color of Ashe Lloyd Lewis's, but if Ashe's were twilight, these were that very evening. Just an hour or two later when there's less blue in the sky and more gray.

I realized I was staring, and that Mr. DeLyon was staring back at me with a similar intensity.

"I'm sorry. Please, have a seat, Mr. DeLyon. How can I help you?" My voice was still uneven.

"I apologize as well for just arriving without an appointment, but I didn't know until today about your exhibit. I was out of town in Venice this winter and just returned. I found the catalog to your show in my sister's living room and had to come right over."

"It's not a problem, I have some time. How can I help?"

"Your photograph in the back of the catalog…"

He had brought it with him and opened it now. I'd certainly seen it often enough not to look. I'd included some photographs in the catalog that showed me, Alice, and Andrew putting the exhibition together—a sort of behind-the-scenes look at the restoration of the eyes and the gathering of the letters.

"When I saw you, I realized that I'd seen you before. And that I'd always thought you looked familiar, but it wasn't until I saw the catalog that I understood why."

His words put my brain in a twist. "I'm afraid I'm not quite following you, Mr. DeLyon."

He pulled a snowy white handkerchief out of his pocket and put it on the desk. Unwrapping it, he pulled out a small leather box. He pushed the box toward me.

"I found this at the house I share with my sister, niece, and nephew. It was many years ago. There had been an artist's studio in the garden that had gone to ruin."

I realized he was talking about Mrs. Whitfield, and that she was his sister.

"You see, I'm a jeweler," he continued. "And thought I'd build another workspace in the same spot. During the renovation, I found this buried in the dirt and debris. I cleaned it and saw how fine it was. Since it's my profession, I knew what it was right away. I made the frame…that isn't original. There's a sad story about it, or so I've been told. In the 1860s, a famous painter lived in our house. Dante Gabriel Rossetti. For a time, he had an assistant who lived there with him, a man who went on to be a famous artist in his own right."

"Ashe Lloyd Lewis," I whispered.

Mr. DeLyon nodded. "Yes."

He opened the box. I was looking at a beautiful inch-long painting of my eye. Exact and explicit. It was the portrait Ashe had done of me. So he could have a keepsake of me to match the one of his eye he had painted for me.

"The thing is, as soon as I found it, it felt familiar. In time, I did some research and came to recognize this eye as belonging to one of Lewis's models. She's in at least a dozen of his famous works. A woman you bear an uncanny and striking resemblance to."

I reached out and lifted the eye from its case. Yes, Ashe had painted this of me. Memories of me sitting for him flooded me. The afternoons in his studio followed by long sultry nights in his bed. The overwhelming love I'd felt for a man now lost to me.

Mr. DeLyon didn't say anything for a few moments, and I allowed the images of those days to occupy my mind.

"Living in Mr. Rossetti's house, I was naturally curious about him and his world and have done extensive research into him. I've read all his writings and books. I read all about his seances and his fascination with reincarnation."

I nodded. Not at all sure where the conversation was going, but I, too, had read all of those poems and writings.

"There is one story about an artist who falls in love with a woman and comes to believe that he and she were together in a previous life."

"I know the story," I said.

"I believe in past lives, in connections, in souls finding each other. I always have, though I've never had any proof. At least, until..."

He stopped speaking. We had not broken our gaze. I was transfixed.

"When I saw this eye, I recognized you. Even though I didn't know you. Do you think I'm mad saying all this?" He broke off.

"No, no, I don't. Please, tell me."

"When I saw the paintings that featured you, I had the feeling Rossetti spoke of. Being here with you now, looking at you now, it's so clear that Lewis saw you the way you needed to be seen. The way I see you."

I held my breath. The very words my grandmother had predicted. That Ashe had used. And then the next words out of his mouth were almost the same words I'd heard him say—months, no...decades before. "I would know you anywhere, our souls—yours and mine—are made of the same stuff. The stuff, as Shakespeare said, that dreams are made of."

"Is it possible?" I looked away from the brooch I held in my hand and into Mr. DeLyon's face.

"I don't know. I want to believe it because this feeling has to mean something."

"Perhaps it does," I said in another whisper, thinking about my grandmother again and what she had told me.

"Shall we spend the time to find out what it means?"

"Yes, I think I'd like to, very much," I said.

Perhaps it was a trick of the sunlight shining through the window illuminating his face just right, but I saw a familiar twinkle in his eyes, lightening them for a moment and changing them in color to twilight. Suddenly, I felt a surge of something wonderful that I had thought was lost to me—hope.

AUTHOR'S NOTE AND ACKNOWLEDGMENTS

I first saw my first lover's eye in Paris, in the 1990s, when I visited the atelier of the astonishing artist and jeweler JAR. I was entranced by a mesmerizing brooch that featured an antique eye miniature surrounded by a silver and gold frame of amethysts and white and colored diamonds.. But it was the single diamond briolette teardrop hanging from the edge of the piece, signifying all the glory and grief of love, that captured my heart.

I didn't know there was a rich history behind jewels that featured eyes until 2021 when, during the height of the Covid pandemic, my friend, the art historian and author Marion Fasel, sent me a book to review for her online publication, *The Adventurine*.

Lover's Eyes: Eye Miniatures from the Skier Collection, written by Elle Shushan immediately captured my imagination. As I pored over the volume, examined the photographs, and read the essays, the idea for this novel was born.

So, my first thanks are to Marion for giving me the assignment. Next to Nan Skier, who generously spoke to me about her pieces and their history. Whenever possible, I stuck to the history, customs, and descriptions of these jewels.

While we don't know if Marie Antoinette ever had her eye portrait done for the man we now know was her lover, Count von Fersen, it was entirely possible since the queen employed an artist in residence, Élisabeth Vigée Le Brun, who painted over thirty portraits of Her Majesty during her lifetime.

In London, Dante Gabriel Rossetti's house is indeed at

16 Cheyne Walk, and the exterior still looks very much as it did in 1867. Most of the facts about the residence, descriptions, and life of the great artist are true. Fanny Cornforth was, in fact, his model, muse, and mistress, and we know for a fact the dinner guests I included were visitors.

The Smeralda Bandinelli portrait done by Botticelli was bought as described, then sold by Rossetti and eventually donated to the Victoria and Albert Museum and is still there.

Although Rossetti had various artists and assistants in residence over the years, Ashe Lloyd Lewis is my fabrication, as is the Highgate family plot and the people who I have living in the house in 1947.

As often as possible, what I have written about the V&A is true; however, the names of the staff in my novel are fictitious.

The Green Room and the Pre-Raphaelite galleries are as described, but I'm not sure I've done them justice.

The heroic activity of employees hiding and protecting the museum treasures in during the war is also as described, but Woodfern Manor is not an actual house, and the Botticelli was never missing as far as we know.

Which brings me to thanking Victoria Henry for her invaluable research. She brought Victorian London and the art scene alive for me with her knowledge.

For continuing to be so supportive of my work and for helping elevate jewelry to an art, I'd like to thank Marion Fasel, Christine Cheng, Lin Jamison, Levi Higgs, and the rest of the core team at Gemx Club, as well as the hundreds of jewelers I follow on Instagram, who astound me every day with their wonders.

Especially one of them. To the exceptional jeweler, one half of David Michael Jewels, Michael Robinson, who so unexpectedly and generously created the lovers' eyes on the cover of this book—I appreciate it more than I can say. It is a dream come true.

To Alan Dingman, the finest cover designer who exceeds my expectations every single year.

Gratitude also to Chelle Olson, who goes over and beyond, improving my novels every single time.

To Dan Conaway, Kate Boggs, and everyone at Writers House, literary agency par excellence, thank you for your hard work on my behalf.

To all the authors who support me, our community is so important and crucial, and I for one never take any part of it for granted. If I started naming you all I know I'd leave too many of you out. But I thank each and every one of you for your spirit, your books, and your steadfast devotion to our art.

To the readers who read me, and librarians and booksellers who carry my books, thank you. You make it all possible.

To Natalie White, my right and left hand at AuthorBuzz.com. I always say this but it's true: Without you, I wouldn't have the sanity or the time to write.

As ever to my most wonderful friends, business partners, and sisters of my heart, Liz Berry and Jillian Stein. I am in awe of both of you and so grateful to have you in my life every single day.

To Alyson Richman, who shares my love of all things beautiful and is the very definition of a best friend.

To Richard Shapiro and Ellie, to Gigi, Jay & Jordan, and Mara Gleckle—your love means the world to me. We are all so lucky to have each other.

And most of all to Doug Scofield, who is my very heart and soul.

About M.J. Rose

New York Times bestseller M.J. Rose (www.mjrose.com) grew up in New York City mostly in the labyrinthine galleries of the Metropolitan Museum, the dark tunnels and lush gardens of Central Park and reading her mother's favorite books before she was allowed. She believes mystery and magic are all around us but we are too often too busy to notice... books that exaggerate mystery and magic draw attention to it and remind us to look for it and revel in it.

Rose's work has appeared in many magazines including *Oprah* magazine and she has been featured in the *New York Times, Newsweek, Wall Street Journal, Time, USA Today* and on the Today Show, and NPR radio. Rose graduated from Syracuse University, spent the '80s in advertising, has a commercial in the Museum of Modern Art in New York City and since 2005 has run the first marketing company for authors - Authorbuzz.com. She is also the co-founder of Evil Eye Corp.

Rose lives in Connecticut.

Made in the USA
Coppell, TX
23 April 2024

31603124R00163